# Short Change

## Also by Patricia Smiley

*False Profits*
*Cover Your Assets*

# Short Change

## Patricia Smiley

 New American Library

New American Library
Published by New American Library, a division of
Penguin Group (USA) Inc., 375 Hudson Street,
New York, New York 10014, USA
Penguin Group (Canada), 90 Eglinton Avenue East, Suite 700, Toronto,
Ontario M4P 2Y3, Canada (a division of Pearson Penguin Canada Inc.)
Penguin Books Ltd., 80 Strand, London WC2R 0RL, England
Penguin Ireland, 25 St. Stephen's Green, Dublin 2,
Ireland (a division of Penguin Books Ltd.)
Penguin Group (Australia), 250 Camberwell Road, Camberwell, Victoria 3124,
Australia (a division of Pearson Australia Group Pty. Ltd.)
Penguin Books India Pvt. Ltd., 11 Community Centre, Panchsheel Park,
New Delhi – 110 017, India
Penguin Group (NZ), 67 Apollo Drive, Rosedale, North Shore 0745,
Auckland, New Zealand (a division of Pearson New Zealand Ltd.)
Penguin Books (South Africa) (Pty.) Ltd., 24 Sturdee Avenue,
Rosebank, Johannesburg 2196, South Africa

Penguin Books Ltd., Registered Offices:
80 Strand, London WC2R 0RL, England

First published by New American Library,
a division of Penguin Group (USA) Inc.

First Printing, July 2007
10  9  8  7  6  5  4  3  2  1

LIBRARY OF CONGRESS CATALOGING-IN-PUBLICATION DATA:

Smiley, Patricia.
    Short change/Patricia Smiley.
      p. cm.
    ISBN: 978-0-451-22144-5
    I. Title
PS3619.M49S56 2007
813'.6—dc22          2006035119

*Set in Centaur MT*   •   *Designed by Elke Sigal*

Printed in the United States of America

To Elizabeth, for teaching me how to fly

# Acknowledgments

The most difficult part about finishing a novel is finding enough space on this page to thank all of the friends, family members, and readers that have encouraged me along the way. To all of you, please accept my heartfelt appreciation.

Several accomplished wordsmiths read and critiqued early drafts of my manuscript and by doing so saved me from the quicksand. They are Patricia Fogarty, Stephen and Cathy Long, and William Solberg. I am also indebted to the following writers who shared their viewpoints on various chapters: T. M. Raymond, Barbara Fryer, and Elaine Medosch.

A number of experts kindly answered my endless questions about DNA, private investigators, construction trailers, Spanish phrases, and the real estate industry. They are D. P. Lyle, M.D., Steven Wachtel of Brady Investigations, Ed Cox, Anne McCune, Paula Tebbe, Michael Grafft, and Matt Grainger.

Many thanks go to my friends at the Los Angeles Police Department Pacific Station for providing information and inspiration. Of particular help with this book were Sergeant Stan Schott, Sergeant Charles Worthen, Senior Lead Officer Anthony Vasquez, and Lieutenant Richard Mossler.

Kudos goes to my friend Captain Andy Svatek for coming up with the title for this novel.

Last but not least, I offer my enduring gratitude to my agent, Scott Miller of Trident Media Group, and to my editor, Kristen Weber of NAL/ Penguin, for continuing to believe in me and for navigating the perilous waters with skill and good humor.

# Chapter 1

I was conceived in the backseat of a Corvair Monza while my parents were listening to an NPR special about Sophie Tucker, last of the red-hot mamas. That was why my mother named me Tucker. My middle name is Bodhi because at the time of my birth she had just embarked on what turned out to be a lifelong journey to reach the higher level of her vibrations. Sinclair is my last name. That came from my father; at least that was what Pookie had always led me to believe.

It was early June, and for the past four days, I had been working in the most unlikely of places for the most unlikely of clients. Charley Tate is a retired Los Angeles Police Department bomb squad sergeant turned private investigator. He claims he became a PI because he had a young wife whose expensive tastes were outpacing his police pension. That may be true, but I suspected he also missed the good old days of catching bad guys and unraveling mysteries.

Tate Investigations was operating out of a small second floor office on a pie-shaped slice of land between Washington Boulevard and Washington Place in Culver City. It consisted of two rooms, a small but neat reception area and a back office. The reception area had enough square footage for a desk, a couple of guest chairs, and room to pace if your stride wasn't too long. Several framed posters of famous paintings hung on the walls, compliments of Charley's wife, no doubt. The posters shared wall space with a bulletin board that was covered mostly with jokes and cartoons thumbtacked to the cork. Charley didn't like lawyers, including his landlord, Manny Reygozo, who had an office just down the hall, so a lot of the jokes went like this. "Q: What do lawyers and sperm have in common? A: Only one in three million has a chance of becoming a human being." Near the door between the two offices was a potted plant that was so gray with dust it reminded me of a flocked Christmas tree.

I'd met Tate a couple of months back and not under the best of circumstances. We had parted on good terms, but I was nonetheless surprised when he called to tell me that Tate Investigations was in financial trouble and needed my help. Charley's business had a lot of potential. His solid credentials had earned him a number of high-profile clients, but he hadn't been able to translate that success into black ink on a spreadsheet. He wasn't exactly my dream client, but I'm a management consultant and rescuing companies is what I do for a living.

Besides, I needed the money. I had recently taken a huge pay

cut when I left my job in corporate America. I'd been one interview away from a partnership at Aames & Associates when somebody set me up as a suspect in a fraud case that quickly turned
into a homicide investigation. Eventually I cleared my name, but
I became disenchanted when the partners failed to rally around
me during the crisis. That was when I decided to start my own
firm, Tucker Sinclair and Associates, current employee population, one.

To make financial matters worse, I also had a mounting
pile of legal bills, the consequence of a probate battle with my
aunt, who was trying to take away the house I inherited from my
grandmother. So for the time being, I was stuck with Charley
Tate and vice versa, I guess.

Looking back, I can pinpoint the exact moment trouble began. It was Thursday. Three o'clock. I was sitting at the front
desk, writing copy for a Web site I was developing for Tate, when
his wife, Lorna, sashayed into the office carrying a sleek stainless steel thermos. She was in her late thirties with violet eyes
and chestnut hair that she had twisted and clipped haphazardly
on top of her head. Her getup consisted of a saffron skirt and
matching camisole that had rows of sequins crisscrossing her
chest like a bandoleer. If she hadn't been wearing a pair of gold
rhinestone slides with four-inch heels, the outfit could have dou-
bled as a uniform for a militant faction of the Hare Krishnas.

Over the past four days, I'd endured Lorna's numerous impromptu visits to the office. I hadn't observed much perfection
in her, but I had to admit, that outfit was the perfect paean to
summer. June is the time we Angelenos begin wearing flashy san-
dals instead of clunky sheepskin boots with our miniskirts, and

we paint our toenails summer pinks instead of autumn browns. We also buy the latest self-tanning products, because it's still too cold to go to the beach and because we would rather take our chances with chemicals than premature aging any day.

When Lorna noticed me sitting at the desk, her eyes opened wide in surprise. Her expression reminded me of a baby experiencing a particularly painful gas bubble. She set the thermos on the desk next to my briefcase.

"Tucker," she said, "you're still here."

"Yes, I am."

I tried not to sound annoyed by her interruption.

She frowned as she picked up the stack of unopened mail on the desk and began sorting through it. "I thought you'd be done by now."

"Done with what?"

She looked at me as if I was some kind of mental pygmy. "The résumé. I told Charley I wanted to turn it in today."

I had no idea what she was talking about. Charley might need a résumé to look for a job if my rescue plans for Tate Investigations didn't pan out, but he didn't need one now.

"I don't know anything about that," I said. "Is it for you?"

Lorna scowled. Her skirt billowed as she turned toward the back office, where I had just put her husband to work locating some missing billing records.

"Charley!" she called out, full volume. "I came to pick up your résumé for Pauly. I told you he needs it to make things official. Have you finished it yet?"

Lorna and Charley had a mysterious alchemy that I didn't totally understand. She wasn't exactly Albert Einstein and her butt was too flat to be considered sexy, but she had some kind of mojo that left Charley weak in the knees. It was obvious from the twinkle in his eye whenever Lorna entered the room that he loved her. Maybe the attraction wasn't so difficult to understand after all.

Charley Tate appeared at the door dressed in a green-and-beige Hawaiian shirt, Bermuda shorts, and huaraches. He's about two inches taller than I am, five eleven or so, and has sandy hair that's turning to gray. He's in his late fifties but still in good shape with a flat stomach and ramrod straight posture.

He ran a freckled hand over his crew cut, as if stalling for time. "The résumé isn't done yet, but we're working on it."

Lorna crossed her arms over her chest. "We? Tucker says you never even mentioned it. You were supposed to ask her to help you. What's the deal? I canceled a very important nail appointment so I could pick it up today."

Charley looked to me for backup, but I still had no idea what they were talking about. Maybe I was missing some obvious clue. Just to be thorough, I glanced at the nails on Lorna's fingers and toes. No jagged edges. No chips in the polish. They looked fine to me, but admittedly, my knowledge of life-and-death manicures was slim to none.

"We've been sort of busy, Lorna," he said. "We'll get to it later."

As if heading off defeat, Lorna changed tactics. She smiled seductively and pointed to the thermos on the desk. "I have raspberry vodka martinis for when you finish."

Charley rolled his eyes, clearly embarrassed. "Lorna, what part of 'later' don't you understand?"

Lorna's unspoken promise of a boozy afternooner had been summarily rejected. Apparently, that didn't set well with her. Her jaw muscles clenched as she crossed her arms over the rhinestone bandoleer as if preparing for a showdown.

Getting sucked into their domestic dispute was not my idea of fun. I could generate enough of those problems on my own. It was better to leave them alone until things cooled down, so I decided to walk down the street to Tito's Tacos for churros and coffee. I turned toward the door leading to the outside hallway and saw the knob slowly turning. A moment later, it swung open.

A woman with shoulder-length brown hair stood on the threshold. She was about five three with a svelte body, round brown eyes, and rosebud lips. She was probably somewhere in her early forties but her petite figure made her seem younger. Her dress was well made with high quality fabric, but it looked rumpled and oddly out of fashion as if she had just emerged from some 1980s time capsule. The brown Louis Vuitton handbag she was clutching to her chest looked worthy of carbon dating. Overall she reminded me of an abandoned puppy, adrift and vigilant.

"Mr. Tate?" Her voice was high-pitched without being shrill.

"That's me. What can I do for you?"

Her gaze darted from Lorna to me to Charley as if she was logging our positions into an unseen database. "My name is Eve Lawson. I want to speak with you about a problem I'm having."

"Sure. Come on in. This is my business associate, Tucker Sinclair," he said, gesturing toward me. "And my wife, Lorna."

Eve studied each of us for a moment and nodded.

No one said anything. To fill the conversation gap, I decided to collect some client data for my marketing plan. "Do you mind if I ask who referred you to Mr. Tate?"

Eve Lawson closed her eyes. Her eyeballs roved as if she was reading text printed on the back of her lids. "I saw his ad in the Yellow Pages."

I made a mental note to factor that feedback into Charley's marketing budget. Most private investigators don't advertise in the telephone book, preferring to get business by referrals, but Charley was relatively new to the game, and it was an inexpensive way to get his name out there.

"Let's talk in my office," Charley said.

Eve followed him into the back room. I found myself hoping she wouldn't notice that the place looked like a refuge for Clutterers Anonymous. I suggested that Tate make the room more presentable but he'd resisted my efforts, countering that he knew where everything was. I didn't see how. His oversized oak desk was buried under piles of paper, yellow number-two pencils, and gummy eraser crumbs. Manila folders lay in stacks all over the gray industrial carpet. It wasn't as if he didn't have a place to store things. There was a row of metal cabinets lining one wall that had plenty of empty drawers to accommodate his files. I prefer to choose my battles, so for the moment I had given up trying to persuade him. A moment later I heard Charley grinding a pencil to a fine point in his electric sharpener. The thing reminded me of a sci-fi fire truck—red with all sorts of chrome and flashing lights.

I returned to my desk and resumed working on the Web site

copy. Lorna slouched in the chair across from me, looking frustrated and annoyed. Aside from my paperwork, the desk was bare except for a telephone and an old-fashioned dome-shaped bell that looked like it belonged on a schoolmarm's desk. There were no personal gewgaws in sight because the front office position was currently vacant due to an employee retention problem that needed to be addressed in the near future.

The next thing I heard was Charley's voice behind me. His tone was low but urgent. "I need you two back here. Pronto!"

I hurried to the back office and found Eve Lawson slumped over in a chair in front of Charley's desk. Her body was trembling. Charley made no attempt to touch her. Instead, he sat down and waited.

I mouthed the words, *"What happened?"*

He threw up his hands as if to say, *Beats me.*

I grabbed a tissue from a box on the desk and laid it on her lap. When she reached for it, I noticed that the cuticle on her thumb looked as if it had been chewed raw. Her shoulders seemed bony and frail beneath the fabric of her dress. I wanted to comfort her, but I took my cue from Charley and didn't try to touch her, knowing it wasn't always a welcomed gesture. I squatted down next to her and called her name. She didn't respond. I kept talking in low soothing tones for what seemed like a long time. Finally she stopped shaking, but her face remained buried in her hands as if she was embarrassed to look at me.

"I'm sorry," she said in a measured voice. "I'm just so scared."

Charley looked uncomfortable. He cleared his throat. "Can I get you something? Water?"

Eve glanced up. The lashes framing her round brown eyes made two languid sweeps before her rosebud lips blossomed into an appreciative smile. "No, thank you. I feel better just being here."

I studied Eve Lawson's face. Her eyes weren't red. Her make-up wasn't streaked. Her nose wasn't stuffed up or running. It was almost as if she hadn't been crying at all. Maybe she had a tear duct malfunction or perhaps she was one of those women who thought that even fake tears softened men's hearts.

My legs were starting to cramp, so I stood in preparation to leave. Charley shook his head, obviously wanting me to stay. I didn't have time to play nursemaid to his clients, so I glanced around the room, looking for help from Lorna. I found her standing in the doorway with what looked like a chamois from an eyeglass case and a bottle of correction fluid thinner. She was using them to dust the leaves of the plant. There was nothing about her expression that read Florence Nightingale, so I took the chair next to Eve, hoping the interview would soon be over.

Charley folded his hands and placed them on top of a legal tablet. "Feel like talking?"

Eve tucked a strand of hair behind her right ear, exposing a dimple in her lobe from some long ago piercing.

"Los Angeles is my home," she said. "I've been away for a while, but I came back to do research for a nonfiction book I'm writing." She paused as if to judge the reaction before moving on. "For the past several days, I've had the feeling that I'm being watched."

*Not surprising*, I thought. A wannabe nonfiction writer? The paparazzi must be all over that story.

Charley leaned forward in his chair. "Tell me what happened."

Eve was still clutching the purse to her chest as if somebody might try to snatch it from her. If she weren't careful she'd have a permanent LV embossed on her liver.

"Two nights ago I was at my computer, transcribing interview notes," she said. "I heard a noise outside the window. I thought it was my neighbor's cat. The next morning I went outside to get the paper. I found clumps of dried clay on the landing in front of my door, as if somebody had been standing there."

"I hate to tell you but dirt happens, especially outside." There was Lorna, holding a branch of the plant. The leaves looked a little greener as a result of her dusting efforts but not for long. You didn't need a degree in botany to know that toxic chemicals and photosynthesis do not mix.

Eve turned toward Lorna, appraising her with hard-edged intensity. Charley glared at his wife. Lorna opened her mouth to protest but was stopped by a second, more withering gaze. Eve watched the two of them with interest, as if she, too, was trying to understand the attraction.

"Sorry for the interruption," he said to Eve. "Please continue."

Eve returned her gaze to Charley as if he was the center of her universe. "Sometimes I hear clicking sounds on the telephone like my line is tapped. And yesterday morning I looked out the window and saw a man wearing a hooded sweatshirt and sunglasses. He was hiding in the bushes across the street, watching."

"How do you know he was watching *you?*"

"He was looking right at me. It gave me the chills. I ran to get the telephone to call for help, but when I went back to the window, he was gone."

That wasn't exactly ironclad evidence but it didn't seem to bother Charley, because he moved on to the next question. "Who do you think it was?"

From Eve Lawson's lengthy pause, I gathered she had more than one candidate to consider.

"I don't know," she said.

"You live alone?"

"Yes. I never married. It isn't easy finding Mr. Right."

Eve leaned back and crossed her legs, allowing her skirt to creep up and expose six inches of a well-toned thigh. Charley remained poker-faced, but out of the corner of my eye, I saw Lorna's violet eyes narrow into slits.

"You have a boyfriend?" he said.

She flashed a demure smile just for him. "Not at the moment."

Charley nodded and wrote something on the tablet. Then he asked Eve if she'd had any financial disputes or recent altercations at a grocery store or parking lot, on the Internet, or in a bar. To all these questions, she answered no.

"You have family in the area?"

She hesitated. "My father lives in Bel Air. He's old. I hear he's also sick."

Charley wrote "Bel Air" on the page and underlined it. "You don't sound very close to your family."

"We're estranged. Is that a problem?" There was a self-protective tone to her voice.

"I don't know," Charley said. "At this point, I'm just collecting information."

Tate sat back in his chair, apparently digesting what Eve had just told him. I was doing a little processing myself. In the span of a few minutes, her demeanor had gone from distraught to flirtatious to defensive. That seemed odd. She had come to Charley for help. She should be answering all of his questions as well as volunteering information on her own. Then again, people don't always react to stress in the same way. Maybe her judgment was impaired by fear or maybe there was a syndrome in some psychology book that had her name written all over it.

"Who knows you're back in town?" Charley said.

"No one. I haven't been out socializing. I spend most of my time at the library, researching."

"For your book?" I said.

"Yes."

"What's it about?" I continued.

Eve hesitated so long that I began to think she wasn't going to respond at all. "The real estate boom in Los Angeles after World War Two. Why do you ask?"

I shrugged. "I just wondered if anybody would object to what you're writing about."

"A story about houses? I don't think so." Her response was curt as if she was eager to change the subject.

She was probably right. I sometimes have an overly active imagination. On the other hand, post–World War II LA wasn't just about houses. What if she had inadvertently uncovered some juicy old scandal? The city was a boomtown back then. Take a notoriously corrupt city government and add a little creativity and you have a conspiracy theorist's petri dish. At least my hypothesis made as much sense as Eve's loopy idea that her clicking telephone foreshadowed something sinister. Hadn't she ever heard of call waiting?

"So what do you want me to do?" Charley said.

"You're the expert, Mr. Tate. What do you suggest?"

"I could stake out your house for a few days and see what happens. On the other hand, twenty-four-hour surveillance costs money, and there's no guarantee it will produce results."

Eve leaned forward in her chair, clearly agitated. "How much money are you talking about?"

Charley shrugged. "I think a thousand-dollar retainer should do it."

She frowned. "I didn't think it would be so much."

"Of course, I'll refund any money I don't use."

Eve gnawed on her inflamed thumb for a moment, and then started rummaging around in her purse, conducting some sort of secret transaction in there. She pulled out a stack of one hundred dollar bills and placed the Ben Franklins on Charley's desk. Her hand lingered on the money, as if she was reluctant to part with it. Given her appearance—those old clothes and ancient purse—I was surprised she had that much discretionary cash. I wondered where she'd gotten it. Maybe it was part of her book advance.

"You'll give the extra back," she said. "Right? Because I'm running a little short right now."

Charley stared at the cash for a moment as if assessing something important. He reassured her once again, and then slipped the thousand dollars into the top drawer of his desk.

"I'll start by setting up cameras around your place. We should know pretty quick if you have a problem. If necessary, I can camp outside your door for a few days. Where do you live?"

"I'm renting a cottage near the beach in Playa del Rey." Eve recited the street address. Charley jotted it down on his tablet.

"It'll take a few minutes to get my equipment together," he said. "Either you can meet me at your place, or if you don't feel comfortable going home alone you can wait for me."

"You won't be long?" Her tone was brittle and edgy.

"No."

"Then I'll go on ahead."

I heard a loud snap. I looked up to see Lorna holding something in her hand, a branch that was no longer connected to the plant.

"Charley!" She managed to stretch two syllables into three. "Can I talk to you a minute? Outside."

Tate turned toward his wife. His spine was rigid, his jaw muscles tight. He glared at her for a moment before excusing himself to join her in the reception area. At the last minute, he gestured for me to tag along.

Lorna closed the door between the two offices and turned toward her husband. The blowback from her dusting efforts had left a brown smudge on the front of her saffron tank top and grime on her hands.

"What are you doing?" she said. "I thought we agreed. You're taking the job with Pauly."

"Pauly isn't for sure. A thousand bucks is. Besides, Eve only lives fifteen minutes away. I'll set the cameras and be back in an hour or so."

Lorna shook her head in a gesture of disbelief. "Clicking telephone lines? Dirt on the porch? So what?"

He shrugged. "So it could be nothing. That's what I'm going to find out."

"Nobody's watching her, Charley. She's making it up."

"If there's one thing I learned as a copper it's never jump to conclusions. Half the time you're wrong. The woman may be a liar, but in my book, she deserves a chance to prove it."

"You're making a mistake."

"Look, Lorna, I've seen a lot of victims in my day, and they don't all act alike. I think the woman's freaked out about something. Is she freaked out because somebody's watching her house? That I don't know—yet."

"Don't do it," Lorna pleaded. "It's a measly thousand dollars. Pauly's job pays a hundred and fifty thousand. You think you're the only one who wants that kind of money? You're going to ruin everything, and for what? For some loony tune."

Lorna had a point. There *was* something slightly off-kilter about Eve Lawson, which could make working with her a little risky. On the other hand, maybe the woman was really in danger. If so, I admired Charley for giving a damn.

"If it makes you happy," he said, "I'll take Tucker with me. We can work on the résumé on the way over."

Lorna threw up her arms in frustration. "And how much extra is that going to cost? You told me this was her last day."

That was news to me. I was sensitive to Charley's financial troubles, because I had a few of my own. That was why I had lowered my fees to accommodate him. I wouldn't have done that if I thought he was planning to give up so early in the game.

Either Charley had lied to his wife about his plans to resuscitate Tate Investigations or he was lying to me. I couldn't afford to waste my time playing games. One way or another, he had to decide what he was going to do, and he had to do it soon.

"Look," I said. "You two duke it out. Just call me in the morning and let me know who won." I walked toward the reception desk to get my things.

A dangerous flush was creeping up Charley's neck. "Hold on. You're not going anywhere."

"Wrong," I said, stuffing papers into my briefcase. "I'm out of here."

Charley shot me an awkward glance. He caught Lorna's gaze and held it. "Here's what's going to happen. I'm taking this case. Lorna is staying here to answer the phones. Tucker is coming with me to work on the résumé, because we have a contract and because I'm asking her pretty please. Is everybody on the same page here?"

It was clear from the way Lorna was glaring at me that she wasn't on the same page at all. In fact, she wasn't even in the same book. She wanted Charley's PI business to disappear, and she wanted me to disappear along with it. If I managed to save Tate Investigations from bankruptcy, it would put a serious crimp in her plans. And if there was one thing I wanted to avoid, it was getting on the bad side of a woman who owned a pair of rhinestone slides. You never knew when one of those four-inch heels might end up in the middle of your back.

A few minutes later Eve Lawson drifted out of the office through a sea of tension. As soon as she was gone, Charley began loading his camera equipment into boxes. It didn't take long.

Given Lorna's piss-poor attitude, he seemed highly motivated to distance himself from her. He finished and we headed downstairs, leaving Lorna sulking at the front desk.

I probably should have parted company with Charley in the parking lot, but I didn't for a couple of reasons. It was already after four o'clock so the day was shot anyway, but mostly I was curious to know what Eve Lawson was up to.

I slid into the passenger seat of Charley's van, transferring a stack of receipts and envelopes from the seat to the ledge between the windshield and the dashboard. Charley slid open the side door and set the boxes inside on the floor.

As soon as he got behind the wheel, he turned to me and grinned. "You're not going to hit me, are you?"

"Don't tempt me."

"I had to get us out of there or Lorna was going to be all over this résumé thing like ants at a picnic."

I was losing my patience. "What résumé are you talking about? And who is Pauly?"

Charley started the engine and pulled into traffic. "Believe me, you don't want to know."

# Chapter 2

Charley was wrong. I did want to know who Pauly was. So on the drive to Eve Lawson's house I pestered him until he finally confessed. Pauly was Pauly Ridge, Lorna's brother-in-law. Until two years ago, Pauly's biggest achievement had been winning a trophy for eating forty-five corn dogs in eleven minutes in a contest at the Barstow Fourth of July celebration. Shortly after accepting his trophy, he gratefully retired to a public restroom to give something back to the community. While Pauly was hanging his head over the porcelain toilet bowl, something happened to him that changed his life forever. He found religion. Shortly afterward he found TV. The combo turned out to be pure mojo. Now he was a successful televangelist who could cry on a dime, on lots of dimes, all sent by faithful followers from around the world.

As a result of Pauly's success, Lorna's sister now had more diamonds than a De Beers delivery truck. Obviously that amount of bling-bling required protection. Pauly wanted to make sure that the great unwashed masses got close enough to put money in the offering plate but not close enough to crowd the jewelry. As a result, his organization was in the process of hiring a new director of security.

Seeing her sister's success had made Lorna crave a little bling of her own, so she was lobbying her brother-in-law to hire Charley for the position. At least she would be rubbing elbows with the money. And a girl has to start somewhere.

Charley's background with the LAPD certainly qualified him for the job, but I sensed that he was tired of being somebody's employee, especially if it meant working for a teary-eyed evangelist with a weakness for corn dogs.

"Why don't you just tell Lorna you don't want to work for Pauly?" I said.

"Pauly's okay."

"That's not the point, Charley. You're splitting your focus. It's a recipe for failure. You have to decide what you want to do, and then put everything you've got into it. And you have to tell Lorna how you feel."

"Obviously you're not married."

"I was . . . once."

He nodded in sympathy. "Didn't work out, I guess. How long did it take you to figure it out?"

"Four years."

"Took me seventeen the first time around. With Lorna it's two and counting. You ever think of doing it again?"

"Not really."

"You don't want kids?"

I hesitated. "I don't know. I haven't thought about it much."

"You ask me, parenthood is overrated. I haven't had a meaningful conversation with my kid since the day he discovered girls. He's twenty-seven now and still discovering one or two a week. Some days I wonder if he'll ever settle down. Maybe it's my fault for calling him dickhead once too often in his formative years."

I looked at Charley and wondered what it would have been like to have him as a father—certainly better than growing up with no father at all, like me, and probably a whole lot better than that.

I smiled. "It could have been worse."

"Yeah. He could have been twins."

A few minutes later, we arrived in Playa del Rey, an off-the-beaten-track community on Santa Monica Bay that's squeezed between what is left of the Ballona Wetlands and the runways of the Los Angeles International Airport. The modest houses and narrow streets near the ocean still have that old beach-town look about them, leaving the impression that the place has escaped the sort of gentrification that can destroy the soul of a community.

The sun was low but still bright, typical for a June afternoon. The morning sky is usually shrouded by an oppressive gray marine layer caused by the collision of warm land air moving out over the cool water of the Pacific Ocean. We Angelenos fondly call this foggy phenomenon June Gloom. The haze generally burns off at around midday and the temperature may warm by a whopping five degrees. That's when we're apt to say to the grocery checker at Vons, "Turned out to be a great day, huh?" Because it *did* turn out to be a great day, and what else do you say to a guy scanning the price on your tomatillos?

Eve Lawson's address wasn't difficult to find, but the odds of scoring a parking place along the narrow street were about as good as meeting Prince Charming at a kegger. Charley tried to slip the van in behind a chalky red Nissan parked in the carport, but the back end jutted too far into the street to safely leave it there. After circling the block a few times, we were forced to leave the van at a strip mall a few blocks away.

"Why didn't you drop off the camera equipment first?" I said.

"You got a thing against walking?"

"No, but I do have a thing against wasting time."

"I'm not hauling all this crap up the stairs if I don't have to," he said. "I want to scope out the place first, then I'll decide what I need. Until then, the equipment stays in the van."

The house was a slim Cape Cod design built above a carport. Paint was peeling from the trim and several blue shingles were missing from the facade. Near the bottom of a staircase that led to the front door was a squat wooden barrel filled with the parched carcasses of some unidentifiable plants that were draped in their death throes across the dry soil.

The weathered planks creaked under our weight as we walked up the steps to the landing. I looked for the clumps of dirt that Eve had mentioned. If they had ever been there, they were gone now. Charley tapped on the door with the knuckle of his index finger but got no response.

"Maybe she's in the bathroom," I said.

Charley knocked again, louder this time. I hung over the railing that enclosed the landing and peered into a window. The miniblinds were slanted so that I could see the back of a computer screen and a stack of paper on the mottled gray vinyl surface of a kitchen table. I wondered if they were research notes for the book Eve was writing.

"Her car is in the carport," I said. "She must be here."

"Did you see her driving it?"

"No."

"Then don't assume it's hers."

Charley walked down the stairs and made his way to the Nissan. He shielded his eyes from the sun as he looked through the car's window. A moment later, he touched the hood.

"Still warm," he said.

"So I was right. It is Eve's car."

"If it is, she couldn't have beat us here by more than a few minutes."

"Maybe she's visiting a neighbor," I said.

"I'm going to look around."

He pulled a small black notebook from the back pocket of his Bermuda shorts and began jotting down license plate numbers, first the red Nissan's and then those of other cars parked along the street.

I knocked again. Nobody answered. The doorknob was pockmarked with rust. I stared at it for a moment before my curiosity got the better of me. I turned the knob. To my surprise, the door opened.

"Hey, Charley, come here a second."

His voice came from somewhere near the side of the house. "What's up?"

"I found something."

He bounded around the corner and took the steps two at a time, stopping on the top riser just as I put my foot over the threshold.

"What the hell! You can't go in there."

"Why not? The door was open."

"The door wasn't open. It was unlocked. There's a difference. In case you don't know, breaking and entering is a felony."

"Look, Charley, Eve Lawson just paid you a thousand bucks to protect her from a stalker. Okay, so I was skeptical at first, but she's not here. That changes everything. What if she came home and found the guy waiting for her? What if she's inside bleeding to death while we stand out here discussing the California penal code? Did you bring a gun?"

"Shit, no. Who do you think I am? Sam Spade?"

"Obviously not." I opened the door a bit farther and poked my head inside. "Eve? It's Tucker Sinclair. Are you in there?"

The house smelled of dust, mildew, and cat urine. From somewhere inside I heard the ticking of a wind-up clock. There were no other sounds. No faint whimpering. No death rattle.

"Oh, for crissakes, move over." Charley nudged me aside and cautiously stepped into the room. "Jeez. It stinks in here."

The kitchen included a small refrigerator, a three-burner stove, a sink, and a cat box overflowing with buried treasure. The living room decor was serviceable but uninspiring and included a white fabric couch, Mexican pottery arranged on a Parsons table, a few paperback books stacked on a chair, and travel posters hanging on white walls.

It was obvious that Eve wasn't there. From all appearances,

neither was her cat. Charley moved toward a narrow hallway. I followed. As I passed the bathroom, I fought the urge to shout, "Yoo-hoo, Eve, you in there?" The bathroom was empty, too. At the end of the hall was a door. It was closed, but I assumed it led to the bedroom.

Charley put out his hand to stop me. "You better go back to the van."

"Why?"

"Just do what I say."

"Charley, there's something you should know about me."

"Oh, jeez, spare me."

"I don't respond to that macho protecting thing."

"Suit yourself. Just don't puke if you see something ugly."

"I can handle myself."

"Yeah," he said. "I bet you can."

Charley pressed his body against the wall. I followed suit. Despite my bravado, my heart raced as I watched him turn the knob and ease the door open. I took a deep breath and peeked over his shoulder.

A king-sized bed dwarfed the rest of the room. The closet door was open, revealing a mound of clothes jumbled together in a haphazard pile on the floor. Either tidiness was a low priority for Eve or somebody had been in a hurry to find something. The perfect 1980s ensemble, perhaps? The room was too small for both of us, so Charley searched the space but found no trace of Eve Lawson.

"Let's jam out of here before somebody calls the cops," he said.

"What about the cat?"

"What about it?" He began walking toward the front door.

I hurried to catch up. "Shouldn't we try to find it? What if Eve doesn't come back right away? Who's going to feed it?"

"Shit happens to cats. That's why they have nine lives."

"I don't know, Charley—"

"Look," he said. "I'm allergic. In about two minutes my nose is going to start dripping like a damn faucet."

Maybe he was right. I didn't know much about cats. I had a dog, a Westie named Muldoon. As I passed the kitchen table I made a detour to take a peek at the papers lying there.

"These must be the notes for Eve's book."

Charley grabbed my elbow. "Forget it, Sherlock. Time to go back to Baker Street."

"Aren't you even curious?"

"No."

"What about the cameras? Aren't you going to put them up?"

"Not till I find out what's going on."

"Seems to me you'd find out sooner if you monitored who's coming and going."

"You're starting to irritate me, Sinclair. Come on. Let's move it."

I followed Tate down the creaky stairs. A flinty-looking gee-zer was standing across the street watching us. He was wearing a pair of chinos and a T-shirt that read GO NAVY. He looked to be in his early seventies, balding, and hopelessly out of shape. Hanging over his belt was fifty pounds of stomach that looked like bread dough left to rise in a too small pan. He was lean-ing on an old two-tone Studebaker station wagon that sported a bumper sticker, which read SUBMARINERS GO DEEPER. Somehow I found that to be a deeply disturbing thought. He watched for a moment longer before walking toward us.

"Aw, shit," Charley said. "My all-time favorite thing. A nosy neighbor. Listen, if he starts asking questions, tell him you're Eve's friend and you're here to give her a permanent or something."

"That's the corniest lie I've ever heard."

"It's not a lie. It's called a pretext."

"Whatever you call it, it's bullshit. Why don't I just tell him the truth?"

"The truth makes people curious. Look, tell him whatever you want, just make it not the truth and make it convincing."

"You looking for somebody in particular?" the man said.

I smiled. "Yes. Eve Lawson. Her car is here, but she doesn't answer the door."

"You friends of hers?" he said.

"I am. This is my cousin . . . uh, Dan. Eve thought she saw some termite damage in the eaves, so Dan offered to take a look. He's very handy with wood. I call him Dr. Dan the Fix-it Man. Don't I, coz?" I felt a blunt object poking my back, probably Charley's finger.

"Where's your ladder?" he said. "Can't check for termites without a ladder."

"I think Eve has one."

"Nope."

"I have a ladder in my van," Charley said. "It's parked down the street."

The man nodded in sympathy. "Parking around here is a bitch all right." As an afterthought he added, "Pardon my French."

I still thought it was possible that Eve had dropped in to visit a neighbor, so I asked the guy if there was anybody close by that she socialized with.

"You should know that better than me. Thought you said she was your friend."

I chuckled to let him know that I accepted his comment as a classic example of brilliant wit, not as a challenge to my integrity. The man assessed us for a moment longer before pointing toward a lavender house with white shutters that was located one house down from Eve's place.

"Check with Neeva Moore. She's head honcho of the neighborhood grin-and-grip crowd. She works, though. Doesn't get home till five thirty or so. And if you plan to stop by, don't stay long. It's Thursday. We have an AA meeting at seven, and I don't like to be late. Now, about that ladder, if you can't get to yours you can borrow mine. When you're done, just put it back in the garage where you found it."

"Thanks," I said, "but I think we'll wait for Eve."

"You'll be waiting a long time, then. She left in a taxi not five minutes before you got here. She was in a big hurry, too. I thought she was going to break her neck running down those stairs."

## Chapter 3

Moments later, Charley and I left the submariner leaning on his two-tone Studebaker and headed toward the strip mall where we had left the van.

"How in the hell did Eve Lawson get a cab so fast?" he said.

I shrugged. "Maybe it was a timed pickup and she forgot, or maybe she's a flake and her whole story is a product of an overworked imagination."

"Jeez! You mean Lorna was right? I hate it when that happens."

"Too bad the submariner didn't remember the name of the cab company. What are you going to do now?"

"I don't know," he said. "Maybe I'll cruise the neighborhood until Neeva Moore gets off work."

"Afraid to go home?"

"To Lorna? Hell, yes. Wouldn't you be?"

"Yep."

"Wanna wait around with me?" he said. "We can work on the résumé."

"I have plans for the evening."

"When?"

"Seven."

"Not a problem," he said. "We'll be done way before then."

"Charley, I can't hang around with you all night. I have things to do."

"Neeva Moore might be more talkative if you're with me. Don't forget I hired you to save my ass. This is part of it. If you make me take you back to the office it's just going to waste time, and I know how much that irritates you."

I glanced at my watch. It was almost five o'clock, a little over half an hour before Neeva Moore was due home from work. I guessed thirty minutes for the interview and twenty minutes to get back to my car in Culver City. It would be cutting it close, but I thought I could still make it to San Pedro by seven. Charley was right. If I made him take me back to Culver City, he might not connect with Neeva before she left for her AA meeting. The day was over for any meaningful work, and I was curious to find out if Eve's neighbor had any clues to her whereabouts.

"Okay," I said. "I'm in."

Charley's van was parked in front of a small neighborhood hangout called Le Tastevin, so he decided to duck in and have an early dinner. The place didn't exactly look like the hub of haute cuisine, but there was a big blue "A" hanging in the window, which meant that the health department hadn't found any cockroaches floating belly up in the ratatouille. Charley opened the wooden screen door and gestured for me to go in first.

"You don't have to do that," I said.

He rolled his eyes. "Don't bust my chops for being a gentleman. Lorna just got me trained."

It wasn't worth fighting about, so I walked in ahead of him. The place was cozy inside. Framed headshots of actors I didn't recognize lined a ledge just below the ceiling. Original art covered the walls, all of it for sale, not all of it good. There were only five tables. We took the only one that wasn't occupied. At the counter taking food orders was a lanky teenage boy with a concave stomach and an easy smile who could have easily been a cover boy for GQ magazine. Charley requested a meatball grinder, which seemed more Hoboken than Paris. I was having dinner later, so I had an iced tea. While we waited at the table for the sandwich to arrive, I jotted down notes for the résumé.

"So where did you go after Internal Affairs?" I said.

"Club Dev."

I have friends who work for the police department, so I knew he was referring to Devonshire Division, which was one of the northern outposts of the LAPD's 468-square-mile jurisdiction. It was considered light duty compared to high crime areas like 77th or Southwest.

"What did you do there?"

"I parked my ass in Community Relations for three months while I recovered from a gunshot wound."

"How am I supposed to quantify that?"

"Easy. The bullet was a forty-five. The shooter was a fifty-one fifty. The guy is on death row for a one-eighty-seven he committed six days later. Does that help?"

"No, it doesn't," I said, annoyed. "A résumé is a sales tool. Pauly isn't going to be impressed by your bullshit police jargon. He wants to know how you changed things for the better. For example, did you cut crime? Increase morale? And by how much?"

"The morale in CRO definitely improved after they kicked me back to patrol."

"You're fighting me on this."

"Now you're talking like Lorna."

I gave him what I hoped was a warning glance. "Let's move on. You said you worked on the summer employee picnic. Did you create it or organize it?"

"What's the difference?"

"Create means you thought it up. Organize means you ordered the weenies and buns."

"I'd say it was more like managed. As in I managed to be off on the day the picnic went down."

I stared at him for a moment. Then I put the notepad back in my briefcase.

He grinned. "You give up easy."

"Look, Charley, writing your résumé was not part of our bargain. I was supposed to save your career, not help you find another one. But since you asked me to help—"

"Okay, okay. Man, you get cranky when you haven't eaten."

The *GQ* waiter delivered Charley's grinder, which was the size of Mount Shasta. After that, we avoided any discussion of résumés or Pauly Ridge. At five thirty we were standing on Neeva Moore's front porch, introducing ourselves using the Dr. Dan termite pretext.

Neeva was as sturdy as an old-growth sequoia. She had two oversized front teeth that could have qualified her for a run in the Kentucky Derby and a mass of brown hair that had been twisted into a French braid as thick as a jungle vine. Her getup consisted of a funky peasant skirt, Birkenstocks, and a faded tank top. She wasn't wearing a bra and her breasts looked as though they had grown weary of standing at attention and had collapsed onto her rib cage for a long siesta. She definitely looked like the health food type. She probably churned her own butter for kicks. I wondered if she attended AA meetings because of an alcohol problem or an addiction to granola.

When Neeva heard that we were friends of Eve's, she ushered us into the living room and gestured for us to sit on the couch. She went into the kitchen and returned a few minutes later with two glasses of green tea over ice and a bowl of Japanese rice crackers wrapped in seaweed. Charley picked one up, sniffed it, and lobbed it back into the bowl.

I glanced down the hall and saw an orange tabby slinking into the room. When Charley noticed the cat, his body tensed. The cat seemed to sense his discomfort and predictably made a beeline for him, threading his sleek body through Charley's hairy legs. Tate shuffled his feet to discourage the assault, but the cat was undeterred. Without warning, he jumped into Charley's lap and lifted his tail to provide Tate with a choice view of his butt. With formal introductions out of the way, the cat nestled into Charley's lap for a snooze.

"As I mentioned earlier," I said, "we were supposed to meet

Eve this afternoon, but she didn't show. We were hoping you might have an idea where she went."

"I don't know. I try to make friends with all the neighbors, but Eve was a challenge. I don't think she trusts many people."

"Did she tell you she was estranged from her family?" I said.

"No. Mostly we talked about her travels. I guess you know she was sent away to boarding school in Switzerland when she was thirteen. She's lived in other places, too. Australia. England. Spain. I never left the state of Oregon until I was twenty-one, so I loved hearing her stories."

It was hard to imagine Eve Lawson hunched over a bowl of seaweed crackers and green tea, baring her soul to this earthy Oregonian, but Neeva had learned a lot about her neighbor in a short amount of time. I wondered what her secret was. Eve had not been that forthcoming with Charley. She'd failed to mention anything about her international jet-setting days. If she was being stalked, presumably everybody she had ever known was a suspect.

"I'm wondering if Eve decided to patch things up with her father," I said. "Maybe she went to stay with him for a few days."

Neeva shrugged. "Why don't you just call him and find out if she's there?"

I looked at Charley for direction, but he was too distracted trying to shoo the cat off of his lap. Charley's eyes were beginning to water. The cat's tail twitched in annoyance. I was on my own.

"I'd call," I said, "but the number's at home. And it's unlisted. You don't have it by chance?"

"No." She frowned. "I wonder if Eve is having boyfriend

problems again. That's why she came back to LA in the first place, to get away from him, but I guess you know more about that than I do."

I paused to collect my thoughts. I wanted to ask her where Eve had been living prior to her return but I couldn't. That was the kind of information a friend would already know. This lying business had its limitations.

"Um . . . yeah," I said. "She mentioned him but I never met him, and she didn't say they were having problems. Probably didn't want to worry me. You think he followed her here?"

"It's possible, I guess."

"Have you seen any strangers hanging around her house?" I said.

"People cruise down our street all the time looking for parking close to the beach, but I never noticed anybody who fit his description."

I glanced at Charley to see if he was going to jump on this latest development. Not likely. The cat was the only one that looked poised to pounce, but only after he finished kneading the section of Charley's thigh not covered by his Bermuda shorts. Tate squinted in pain. He tried to lift the cat off his lap, but it hissed, and Charley let go. Neeva didn't seem to notice.

"You know what the guy looks like?" I said.

"Not exactly. She showed me a picture once. It was of the two of them standing on a beach somewhere. He was wearing sunglasses, so I couldn't see his face very well. His hair was blond but from a bottle because the roots looked dark, and he was thin like her and tall. I'd say over six feet."

"Did Eve ever mention his name?"

"Rocky, but I assumed that was his nickname. She told me they fought a lot. He was the jealous type and was always accusing her of cheating on him. He also didn't like that she was writing that book."

"The book on World War Two?"

"No. Some kind of memoir. I got the impression Eve was using it as an excuse to flame everybody who had ever hurt her."

"Like the boyfriend?"

"Like everybody."

So the book was not about houses as Eve had claimed. I wondered why she had lied to us. If she was planning to trash people in print, she might have inadvertently broadened the pool of suspects who wanted to harm her. Why would she hire a private investigator and not tell him an important fact like that?

I asked a few more questions, but Neeva had little more to offer.

"If you see Eve," I said, "could you give me a call? I'm worried about her." I took a business card from my purse, and at the last moment, I jotted Charley's office number on the back of it. "If you can't reach me at the main number, use the one on the back. It belongs to a client of mine. I'll be working there for the next few days."

Neeva studied the card. "What's a management consultant?"

"I diagnose and treat sick companies, sort of like a business doctor."

"Like a vet for corporate jackals?"

"That's it. Just me and the animals."

Neeva got up to usher us out. "By the way, our Neighborhood Watch group is having a block party on Saturday. Why don't you two come? There'll be lots of food. Our city council-person is coming. Eve promised to show up. I sure hope she's back by then."

"What do you think, Dan?" I said to Charley. "Sound like fun?"

"Yeah, sounds like a real blast."

Apparently Neeva had finally noticed that Charley's voice seemed gravelly and raw. She walked over and peeled the cat off his lap.

"Tyrone loves everybody," she said to Charley, "but not everybody loves Tyrone." She addressed her last remark to the cat and followed it up with a noisy kiss on top of his furry head.

"By the way," I said, "who takes care of Eve's cat when she's gone?"

"Fergie? I don't know. She'll be okay until Eve gets back as long as she has food."

"What if she gets out?"

"She's an inside cat. Eve never lets her out."

Fergie might have been at the house when Charley and I were there, but the place was small, and I couldn't imagine where she would have been hiding. On top of that, the door was still unlocked. Everybody and his uncle could have been traipsing in and out of the house since we left, creating numerous opportunities for the cat to escape.

"Maybe you could keep an eye out for Fergie, too. Just in case Eve doesn't come back right away."

Neeva looked puzzled by my request, but agreed nonetheless.

As soon as we were out on the street, I turned to Charley, annoyed. "Thanks for all the help back there. Why did you make me do all the talking?"

"Gimme a break. My throat felt like sandpaper. Damn cat. Besides, you did fine without me."

It was getting late, so Charley and I made our way to the van. Before heading back to Culver City, we cruised past Eve's house again. It was dark inside. No Eve. No boyfriend. No cat.

"Maybe we should take another peek inside," I said.

"No way."

"What we need is Eve's telephone records. If you were a real PI you'd be sleeping with somebody at Verizon."

"You watch too much TV, Sinclair."

"Maybe this is a job for Dickhead."

Charley smiled. "Did I tell you the kid's on a first-name basis with every bartender in Boise? Makes a father proud. Tell you what. Since he's not here, how about we go back to the office and I let you call all the cab companies in town? Tell them you left your edible underwear in the backseat of the taxi. That might get us the name of the driver."

"That would work if I was your partner, which I'm not, and if I didn't have plans for the evening, which I do."

"What kind of plans?"

"That's for me to know and you to find out."

"I *can* find out, you know."

He probably could. I just didn't like talking about my personal life with clients, even though Charley was more than just that. Our history was complicated. We'd met a few months back after somebody hired him to follow me. We worked through that issue and settled into a quirky kind of friendship. I found him to be smart, funny, and a bit of a challenge. I think he felt the same way about me.

If I'd been sure that Charley wouldn't have teased me about my dating habits, I would have told him that a man I'd been seeing for the past couple of months had invited me for dinner at his house. Joe Deegan was an LAPD homicide detective working out of the Pacific Station. There were challenges to dating a cop, even one from a division with a relatively low murder rate—calls in the middle of the night and canceled plans. He was also geographically undesirable, a term we Angelenos use when it takes over an hour to get from your place to his even on a good traffic day.

I had known Deegan for a total of seven months and had been dating him for two. That didn't mean I'd learned much about his personal life. I knew he could be charming and funny. He was also eye candy. Six foot two with the lean, muscular body of a swimmer, hair the color of toasted wheat, blue-gray eyes, and a confident smile. In fact, he was every woman's sperm donor fantasy. From all appearances he didn't have a clue how good-looking he was, which was definitely part of his charm.

I didn't know where things were headed with us. For the past couple of months, we'd just been messing around. Romantic dinners. Walks on the beach. Steamy sex. It had been fun. In fact, it had been more fun than I'd ever imagined messing around could be. The trouble was, I could get used to that kind of messing around and might never want it to end. That concerned me, because I'd been hurt before and didn't much like the feeling.

Tonight was different. I had never been to Deegan's house before, much less been a guest for dinner. I didn't take the invitation lightly, because I had the impression that Deegan didn't let many people get close to him. It made me feel a little tense wondering if his move signaled some kind of change in our relationship. The last thing I wanted was to get blindsided by decisions I wasn't prepared to make.

On the other hand, I was probably obsessing too much about the whole dinner thing. Deegan had likely entertained throngs of women at his house before, and I was just another at the bottom of a long list. Besides, where we got together didn't matter. I was looking forward to seeing him.

Charley dropped me off in the parking lot. "I'm going upstairs to check out a few things," he said. "Then I gotta go home, or Lorna will have me sleeping in the garage tonight."

I slid into the front seat of my Porsche Boxster. The roadster had been a parting gift from my ex-husband, Eric Bergstrom. I'd been upset when I learned how much he paid for it, but my attitude changed when I discovered that a pizza box fit perfectly in the rear trunk, and the heat from the engine kept the pie warm all the way home.

Since I was seeing Deegan anyway, I decided to ask his opinion about Eve Lawson's odd behavior. He wouldn't discuss the subject if it involved his job, but this wasn't a police matter. As a topic for discussion, it seemed safe enough.

# Chapter 4

San Pedro is a medium-sized harbor town located twenty-plus miles south of downtown Los Angeles. It hosts one of the busiest deepwater ports on the West Coast. It's also the most southerly outpost of the Los Angeles Police Department's nineteen area police stations. The residents are a cultural soup comprising Britons, Greeks, Italians, Scandinavians, Slavs, Portuguese, Russians, and Latinos.

Joe Deegan grew up in San P, which he pronounces "San Peedro." His father died some years back, but his mother still lives in the family home with the youngest of his three sisters. Apparently none of the siblings had ever felt compelled to leave the hood. All of them lived within a mile of their mom's place.

Deegan lived on a quiet street in a small 1960s-style ranch

house. The architecture wasn't anything special, but the taupe paint job was accented with charcoal and white on the sash and trim, which made the place look complex and appealing. His black Ford Explorer was parked in the driveway. As I walked past it, I recalled Charley's trick and put my hand on the hood. Cold. He must have been home for a while. I rang the buzzer.

Deegan appeared at the door looking as if he had just stepped out of the shower. Delicate ringlets of wet hair curled softly on his neck. The collar of his white polo shirt was sticking up as if he had dressed in a hurry. A holstered cell phone was clipped to the waistband of his Levi's.

Soft music played in the background. I stepped over the threshold and saw a room cloaked in dim light from at least a dozen flickering candles.

"Nice touch," I said. "Where's the rest of the coven?"

He leaned over and kissed me so lightly that I felt only softness and warmth. "Tonight it's just you and me and maybe a ritual or two. Champagne?"

He knew the answer was yes. Champagne was my drink of choice. Without waiting for my reply, he walked toward what I assumed was the kitchen. When my eyes adjusted to the light, I scanned the room. I saw bleached oak hardwood floors, a black leather sectional, two sleek accent chairs placed around a chrome and glass coffee table. Beneath the table was a white sheepskin area rug. An ebony baby grand piano stood off in a corner by itself. The room was modern and sophisticated. That surprised me.

"You play the piano?" I said.

"No. You?"

"Pookie never had the money for stuff like piano lessons."

I followed Deegan into the kitchen and was confronted by a retro aluminum-trimmed diner table and matching chairs. Near the stainless steel sink was a bottle of liquid soap that matched the muted yellow of the chairs' seat cushions. An oval plate had been left to dry in the dish rack. The plate featured a blue cow and matching blue text that read JE DEMANDE DU BOEUF. That cinched it. No guy bought French plates of his own free will. Deegan had help with the decor. The only question was designer or ex? Ex-girlfriend or ex-wife? If our relationship was ever to move forward, I had to know which. Now seemed like a good time to find out.

He popped the cork on the champagne bottle, filled a flute to the brim, and handed it to me.

"The place looks great," I said. "Did you decorate it your-self?"

Deegan walked into the living room, ignoring my question.

"How's the music?" he said. "Too loud?"

Luther Ingram was singing "(If Loving You Is Wrong) I Don't Want to Be Right." The volume was loud enough for me to hear that he didn't care about it being wrong if it meant he was going to get laid.

"No, the volume's good," I said. "Did you use a designer?"

Even though I had already approved the volume, Deegan fiddled with the knobs on the stereo, lowering the sound a notch.

"You know, Deegan, sometimes you drive me crazy."

"Good crazy or bad crazy?"

"Every kind of crazy."

He looked over his shoulder and smiled. "Thanks, ma'am. I aim to please."

For a moment I considered making an issue of the unanswered question, but I decided to let it go. Champagne. Music. Dinner. He was definitely aiming to please.

"I've never been to your house before," I said.

"I know."

"Why not?"

"I don't invite just anybody here."

"Ah. So I'm special."

Deegan's smile was noncommittal. He took a chef's apron that was draped over a chair and slipped it over my head. I didn't bother to tie the strings. I wasn't planning to have it on that long.

On the counter next to the champagne bucket was a wooden tray that held chives, a cucumber, a couple of tomatoes, and a swordfish steak the size of Moby-Dick.

"Here," he said, handing me a knife and pointing to the vegetables. "Make yourself useful."

"Aren't you going to take me on a tour of the house?"

"Later."

I began chopping and sorting the vegetables into neat little piles.

Deegan opened the oven door using a mitt that matched the blue on the cow plates. He pulled out a pan of something that looked both crispy and oozy and transferred it to a serving dish. He placed some crackers around the perimeter and set the tray down near me.

I stared at it in awe. "Baked Brie."

He smiled and scooped the chopped vegetables into a glass bowl filled with brown liquid. Then he began mixing everything together with a tiny whisk.

"So how's work?" he said.

The Brie was making me feel domestically challenged, so I was happy to move on to another topic of conversation. His question gave me the perfect opportunity to tell him about Eve Lawson. For the next few minutes, I filled him in on her visit to Charley Tate's office. I glossed over details of my trip to Playa del Rey, because I didn't want to admit that Charley and I had been in Eve's house without her permission. I hadn't even gotten to our interview with Neeva Moore when he interrupted.

"Why the hell is Tate getting you involved in this?"

Deegan was only being protective, but hearing that familiar authoritarian tone in his voice always made me edgy.

"He isn't. I tagged along because he wanted to get me out of the office. His wife was mad at him and—"

"Ah, I get it now. Tate's playing you off his woman for sport."

"Come on, Deegan. You don't even know the guy. He wouldn't pull that kind of shit. Besides, he's an ex-cop. I think I'm safe."

Deegan spread the marinade on the fish with a wood-handled pastry brush and gave me his *Yeah, sure* look. "When's this job over?"

"A couple of weeks or so. Why?"

He glanced at me and noticed that the apron strings weren't tied. He turned me around, crisscrossed the ties behind my back, and then reached around my waist to tie them in front. As he did, I leaned my head back and rested it against his chest.

"Why do you want to know how long I'll be working for Charley Tate?" I said.

Once the apron strings were tied, Deegan began massaging

my shoulders. His hands were strong. As my muscles loosened, my need for an immediate answer to that question evaporated like bubbles in bathwater.

"Feel good?" he said.

"Mmm."

His hands moved slowly down my back, kneading the muscles until all tension was gone. I felt so relaxed that I was barely aware of his arms slipping around my waist. His lips pressed against my earlobe and began a slow descent toward my shoulder.

"What about this?" he said.

"Uh-huh."

"And this?"

I whipped around to face him. "Deegan!"

He smiled. "What? That didn't feel good, too?"

"Well, yes, but . . ."

"So do you want to see the rest of the house now?"

"That's a sneaky way to keep from answering my questions. Why did you ask how long I'd be working for Charley? And why do you think he's using me to make his wife jealous?"

He pulled me toward him. "I could answer that, but wouldn't you rather go on the tour first?"

Well, duh, of course I wanted to go on the "tour," but Deegan had a bad habit of only answering questions he wanted to answer. I assumed his training as a cop had taught him to hold his cards close to his chest, but I hated not knowing things. I decided it was time to take a stand.

I playfully pushed him away. "Answer me first."

He rolled his eyes. "Okay, maybe you don't know everything there is to know about men."

"I never claimed to be an expert. So educate me. Let's start with you. Tell me something about you that I don't know."

He turned toward the counter, loaded the fish on a tray, and headed for the back door. "Like what?"

I followed him outside to a patio that abutted a small backyard. "Oh, I don't know. . . . Have you ever written any alimony checks?"

He opened the lid of a stainless steel barbecue grill that was already preheated and slid the fish onto the rack. "I pay my bills online."

"Stop playing games, Deegan. Why won't you tell me if you've ever been married?"

He prodded the fish with a fork and closed the lid. "You really want to know?"

"Yes."

"No."

"Ever come close?"

He didn't answer for a moment. "Once."

"Only once? You're lying."

He headed back toward the kitchen. "I never lie to women. That's why I'm still single."

"So what happened?"

He picked up a kitchen timer from the counter and set it for ten minutes. "It didn't work out."

"I assumed it didn't work out or I wouldn't be in your house inhaling secondhand candle smoke. *Why* didn't it work out?"

He turned and locked his gaze on mine. "Your timing's off, Stretch. Why are you pressing me about this now?"

It was a legitimate question. Why did I want to spoil a beautiful evening by torturing myself with the details of Deegan's love life? Maybe because I'd had my share of botched relationships, including one failed marriage. Deegan knew how difficult it had been for me to end that chapter in my life, because he'd been my date for my ex-husband's marriage to a little red-haired girl named Becky Quinn. Maybe I just needed to reassure myself that Deegan had failed at love, too, and that his past relationships were truly in the past.

I shrugged. "It's just that you know everything about me—"

"Not everything—"

"Almost everything. But I don't know anything about you."

"You know enough to be here tonight."

"I don't like secrets," I said. "They feel like lies."

For what seemed like a long time, he stood with his arms crossed, staring into the living room, watching the candles throw eerie shadows across the wall.

"It's pretty simple," he said finally. "She cheated. I found out."

The only thought in my head was *Holy shit!* If she wasn't satisfied with a guy like Joe Deegan, there was no hope for any of us.

"Is she a cop?"

"No. Look, it's been over for a long time. That's all you need to know."

"I see."

But I didn't see, not at all. Maybe he was still recovering from a painful breakup, but why not just say so? Obviously he didn't trust me. And if there wasn't trust between two people, there wasn't anything.

Percy Sledge was singing "When a Man Loves a Woman." Deegan didn't seem to notice the irony.

"We've been here before, haven't we?" he said.

"Once or twice."

The timer went off. Deegan went out to the patio and returned a few moments later with the swordfish on a tray.

"Yum," I said, trying to diffuse the tension.

He set the tray on the counter. "Somehow I don't feel like eating anymore."

I took off the apron and laid it on the table. "Look, I'm sorry I ruined your appetite. What you did tonight—dinner, champagne, candles—it was really impressive. I guess I'm not very good at this relationship thing. I've only had two important men in my life. One dumped me for my best friend. The other left me for a lawyer. That should tell you everything."

Deegan's expression was opaque. I had no idea what he was thinking.

"You know something?" he said finally. "Sometimes you talk too much."

"Like when?"

"Like now." He put his hand behind my neck and pulled me close. "I think you should stop before one of us says something we'll regret."

"Talking is how people communicate."

"There are other ways," he said.

"Are they included on the tour?"

"Yup."

"Can we talk on the way?"

"Anything you want."

"Really? Anything?"

A hint of a smile lifted the corners of his mouth. "Yeah, anything."

I felt a tingling sensation shoot through my body. Deegan was sexy but not that sexy. It was the cell phone on his waistband vibrating on the silent mode.

"Your phone's ringing," I said.

He read the number on the display panel and frowned. He answered the call with a tone that sounded unusually gruff. He listened quietly for a moment, then disappeared into the living room, returning a few minutes later with a somber expression on his face.

"Who was that?" I said.

"The watch commander."

"I assume he wasn't calling to get your baked Brie recipe."

"I have to go. I'm not sure when I'll be back. You're welcome to stay and have dinner."

"If you're going to work, then obviously somebody is dead. That doesn't make me feel much like eating. What happened?"

Deegan must have been distracted by the call, because he actually answered my question. "The desk clerk at a motel on Lincoln heard what he thought was gunfire around six p.m. He's in the country illegally, so he didn't call it in. Instead, he waited a couple of hours for the night manager to come to work. When they went to investigate, they found a body in one of the rooms, dead from a gunshot wound, probably with a thirty-eight. The victim was carrying two sets of ID, a Mexican tourist card in the name of Brian Smith, and a California driver's license issued to Rocky Kincaid. The guys at the scene ran both names. Noth-

ing on Smith. Kincaid has an outstanding warrant for embezzlement."

I felt light-headed and off balance and not because that was
the most information Joe Deegan had ever given me about his
work. It was because the room was spinning. I closed my eyes and
pressed my palms to my temples.

"What's wrong?" he said. "You okay?"

I shook my head, because I wasn't okay, not by a long shot.
"What did the guy look like?"

Deegan's tone was wary. "White male, six one, blue eyes,
bleached blond hair. Why are you asking?"

"Eve Lawson's boyfriend," I said. "His name is Rocky. He
was tall and he had blond hair but from a bottle."

Deegan's eyes narrowed. "Who told you that?"

"Neeva Moore."

"Who the hell is Neeva Moore?"

I told him, but it didn't improve his mood. A moment later
he said, "Get your things. You're coming with me."

# Chapter 5

Deegan went into the bedroom to get his service revolver. I wrapped Moby-Dick in foil and slipped it into his refrigerator. Then I snuffed all the candles, which despite producing clouds of smoke didn't trigger any alarms. Deegan might be at the crime scene for hours. I didn't want to get stuck somewhere without a car, nor did I want to share a ride with a man packing a 9 mm Beretta who didn't seem too pleased with me at the moment. We agreed to meet at the police station.

The LAPD's Pacific area encompasses just over twenty-four square miles of land and two hundred thousand people in Westside neighborhoods that include Playa del Rey, Venice, Palms, Westchester, and parts of Marina del Rey. The police station is located approximately three miles inland from the beach in a nondescript, two-story brick building, which used to operate as a mental institution. Amazing how things change and yet how they stay the same.

The detective squad room had been remodeled since I'd last visited. While nobody was looking, some space planner had transformed it from a ragtag thrift shop into the corporate offices of IBM. The old metal desks had been replaced with a series of modern workstations with low gray walls and computer terminals. The funky wooden signs that had once hung above the desks labeling the various tables—AUTOS, BURGLARY, HOMICIDE— had been traded for plastic placards with computer-generated lettering.

Deegan led me to his cubicle and pointed to a chair.

"Sit tight while I get a car."

"Where are we going?"

He raised one eyebrow. "*You* are not going anywhere."

I searched his expression for any remnants of the sensual smile that had held so much promise just a short time before but found only a mask of grim determination.

"But if you're there and I'm here, how are you going to take my statement?"

He leaned in close and lowered his voice. "I'm going to the crime scene. My partner will take your statement. Then he'll join me and you'll go home." He raked his hand through his hair. "Look, Stretch. I'm in kind of a bind here. If the lieutenant finds out I'm dating somebody involved in this investigation, he's going to pull me off the case so fast it'll make your head swim."

"So what? This is LA. There'll be more murders for you to solve. What's so special about this one?"

"Nothing. Let's just say the lieutenant and I haven't always seen eye to eye. He'd welcome any excuse to cause me grief."

"Oh yeah?" I tapped my chest with both thumbs. "Tell him if he wants a piece of you, he'll have to get past me first."

Deegan smiled. "That'll do the trick, all right." He lifted his hand as if to touch my cheek but pulled it away at the last minute. "Try to distance yourself from Tate. It doesn't look good that you're working for a PI."

"I can't lie. I was with Charley when I learned about Rocky."

He took a deep breath and blew it out in one long, soft stream of air. The look on his face said, *What have I gotten myself into?*

"Of course I don't want you to lie, but right now PIs are at the top of the department's shit list. I just don't want anybody to connect the dots between you and me and Tate and come up with the wrong impression. And whatever you do, try not to mention that we're sleeping together."

"Don't worry. My mother doesn't even know."

"Fine. Just so we're clear."

He turned and walked toward a door that led to the hall.

I knew that Deegan had a new partner, but we hadn't met. I wondered if *he* knew that Deegan and I were sleeping together. Probably not. While I waited for him to show, I tried to open the desk drawer to see what was inside. It was locked. There was nothing on top of the desk that revealed anything about the person who worked there. By contrast, the next cubicle over had a bust of Beethoven and a grouping of photographs featuring a chubby-cheeked toddler. I tried to imagine Deegan proudly displaying pictures of his pudgy offspring, but the image didn't compute. He didn't seem like the type to share details of his personal life in such an obvious manner.

"Excuse me. Are you Tucker Sinclair?"

I hadn't heard anyone approach, so the voice startled me. I whipped around to see a man in his midthirties. He had curly black hair and eyes the color of fine Cuban cigars. He was around six feet tall and wore an olive green tank top and a pair of baggy shorts that just covered his knees. A very large gun was holstered and hanging from a belt fastened around his waist. He looked like the type of guy who could do it ten times a night and not break a sweat. The type of guy whose foreplay consisted of one word: *Strip*. Nonetheless, I imagined a block-long line of women waiting to sign on.

He flashed an intoxicating smile. "Detective Tony Mendoza."

I shook his hand, hoping mine wouldn't end up crushed in the exchange. His palm was rough but his touch was surprisingly gentle. Mendoza grabbed a chair from the neighboring workstation and rolled it toward me. He set a tape recorder on the desk and after a few preliminary comments, he pressed RECORD. Considering that his fingers were proportionally as large as the rest of him, it was amazing that they found the button. I told him about Eve Lawson and what little I had learned from Neeva Moore about Rocky Kincaid. I soon ran out of information to tell, and he turned off the recorder.

A moment later I heard the sound of voices coming from somewhere nearby. I turned to look. A half dozen people had spilled into the hall from the second floor stairway. Deegan stood near the kit room talking to a woman in her late twenties.

She was five three or so with lustrous honey hair that sported at least three shades of chunky, salon-induced blond highlights that must have cost a bundle. The skirt of her navy pin-striped suit was hemmed at midthigh, exposing the toned legs of a gym rat.

The woman reached up to smooth the collar of Deegan's polo shirt, allowing her hand to linger near his neck just a beat too long. It seemed inappropriately flirtatious given the setting and the circumstances. I wondered if beneath all those pinstripes was the soul of a woman who had a charge account at Trashy Lingerie.

What happened next took place in present time but its genesis seemed rooted in the past. In rapid succession, Deegan said something to the woman. She pointed her finger in his face as if lecturing him. He grabbed her wrist and forced her hand away. She flipped him the bird and stormed down the hall with her high-heeled shoes pounding the floor with a staccato beat. As she neared the squad room, I could see that her face was flushed with undisguised anger. Our eyes met briefly before she turned the corner and walked out the back door. A moment later Deegan followed her.

Mendoza whistled softly.

"What was that all about?" I said.

He shook his head and chuckled. "Who knows?"

"Who is she?"

"Tracy Fields."

"She a cop?"

"Deputy DA."

"She seems to have a problem with Detective Deegan."

Mendoza gazed pensively toward the hall, where Tracy Fields had been standing only a moment before as if he wanted to linger in the afterglow of that sexually charged moment.

"Tracy has a problem with a lot of men."

"What's she doing here so late?"

"Task force meeting," he said, almost to himself.

"What kind of task force?"

Mendoza glanced at me and frowned as if he knew he'd been caught in a candid moment and wondered if he should regret it. Suddenly he was all business.

"I'm going to cut you loose now," he said. "If I need anything else, I'll call."

"Those two looked like they were leaving together."

"It's possible."

"Does that mean Rocky Kincaid's death has something to do with the task force investigation?"

Mendoza stood. "Sorry. I can't talk about that."

The parking lot was quiet when I got back to my car, but my head buzzed with competing thoughts. Tracy. Homicide. Tracy. Task force. Tracy. Deegan. Tracy. I had no idea what connection Deegan had to Tracy Fields, but I was sure they had a history.

I didn't have Charley Tate's home number, so I called his cell but didn't get an answer. I left an urgent message for him to contact me as soon as possible. Fifty minutes later I pulled into the driveway of my cottage in Zuma Beach.

In recent years the neighborhood has become decidedly upscale. My house has not. It's still the same little brown shoebox on the sand that my grandmother built back in the 1940s as a summer retreat from the Pasadena heat. Even if I could afford to tear it down and build a starter castle, I wouldn't. I love its history, its weather-beaten appeal, the sand on the deck, and the Pacific Ocean at my front door. From what I'd been told by my mother, my father spent his summers here, surfing. He died before I was born, but I sometimes sense his presence when the waves get gnarly. Aside from my friends, my mother, my grandma and grandpa Felder, and my dog, the cottage is the thing I love most in the world.

The floor plan consists of two small bedrooms and a bathroom on the street side. The front part of the house has a breakfast bar that separates the kitchen from the living room, which faces the beach. Two French doors lead to the deck. For now, a small alcove off the main room doubles as my home office. It has just enough space for a desk, a chair, and a two-drawer file cabinet.

I retrieved the mail from the box and headed inside. The moment I cracked the side door I saw a black nose poking through the opening. It belonged to a West Highland white terrier named Muldoon. Muldoon is a used dog. He was two and a half when his previous owners discovered that their new baby was allergic to animal dander and put the pup up for sale. My mother saw the ad and the rest is history. Since my mother adopted him, she's moved on to other things, like marriage. We still share custody, but mostly he belongs to me now. The little Westie seemed happy to see me but even happier to be out in the fresh air exploring the beach for a while.

While I waited for Muldoon to come back inside, I sorted through the mail and found a couple of client checks for work I'd completed. There was also an ominous-looking letter from my lawyer, Sheldon Greenblatt. For the past two years, he's represented me in a legal battle with my aunt Sylvia, who has used every trick in the book to reopen probate on my grandmother's estate so she can repossess my house.

In the pyramid of dysfunctional families, mine is right up there near the pinnacle. After my father died, the Sinclair clan abandoned Pookie and me. My mother was twenty-one years old with a new baby to support. She claims that the Sinclairs never approved of the marriage or her acting career. Maybe that's true or perhaps there's more to the story than my mother chooses to admit. Regardless of the reasons for the estrangement, the Sinclairs were never part of my life. So you can imagine how stunned I was when I learned that my grandmother had left me the house. Maybe she'd had a moment of moral clarity or perhaps the bequest was some horrible mistake, as my aunt believes.

Shortly after the will was read, Sylvia claimed that one of the witnesses was under age, rendering the document invalid. Next, she floated the theory that my father had borrowed money from the estate but never paid it back. The loan principal plus interest was—surprise—about what the house was worth. Both of those theories were shot down. Recently she'd produced a new will that she maintains was handwritten just days before my grandmother died. That will leaves the house to her, of course.

My aunt is loaded, so greed probably isn't her motive. Revenge? Jealousy? All I know is that she wants to permanently cut off our branch of the family tree. Things had been quiet for a while, but I always understood that the calm wouldn't last.

The letter from Shelly Greenblatt was a one-pager. The news was not completely bad. He had found a handwriting expert who would testify that the signature on the new will did not match my grandmother's, although he warned that my aunt's attorney would find her own experts who would disagree. More troubling was the paragraph stating that my aunt had lodged new allegations. Shelly called them "sensitive" and requested that I call his office at my earliest convenience to discuss the details. The cryptic tone of his letter was unsettling, but it was too late to call now. I would have to wait until morning.

I left the letter on the kitchen counter and checked the message machine, hoping for more cheery news. There were three increasingly strident messages from my friend and former administrative assistant, Eugene Barstok.

When I left Aames & Associates to start my own firm, it was under less than cordial circumstances. Eugene took sides. Mine. Once I was gone, he was demoted to receptionist and marooned at a busy front desk, answering telephones and signing for packages. The pressure was getting to him. Not a good thing. Eugene was already in therapy for an anxiety problem. For a while he found that knitting calmed his nerves, but he had to stop when he developed carpal tunnel syndrome. Lately he's been taking antianxiety medication, which seems to take the edge off of his panic attacks. I had to call him back, or he would be awake all night worrying.

Eugene picked up on the first ring. "They hate me. I should just resign and avoid the humiliation of being fired."

"Eugene, we've been through this before. The partners can't fire you without cause."

"Exactly. That's why they've hired an undercover operative to manufacture charges against me."

"Perhaps a small exaggeration?"

"Hardly. Harriet in HR just hired a new assistant for one of the partners. His name is Hershel Bernstein. The guy is forever lurking around my desk, staring at me like he's a NASA nerd waiting for the Mars rover to malfunction. And if that weren't enough, he includes me unnecessarily. Solicits my opinion on issues completely out of my control. Wants me to proofread his memos. And yesterday he actually asked me to call him Hershy. I mean . . . puhleeze."

"None of that sounds very clandestine."

"No? Listen to this. This morning he asked what I was doing for lunch. I didn't want to get into it, so I told him I had to drop off a couple of sweaters at the dry cleaners down the street. Then—get this—he asked if I could pick up his boss's cleaning while I was there."

"Did you do it?"

"Of course not. What does he think I am? His Goy Friday? Besides, pressuring me to perform personal favors for a partner is totally against company policy. I'm telling you the guy is setting me up."

"Hershy is new. Maybe he just wants to be your friend."

"Fat chance. I have to get out of this gulag, Tucker. Hire me. Please. Just say the word. I'll give my notice first thing in the morning."

"I can't, Eugene. You'd lose your health insurance, your pension, everything."

He sighed. "How much longer do I have to wait?"

I wanted to sound hopeful. Business *was* picking up. I just needed a couple of big contracts. Then I could rent office space, hire Eugene and possibly another consultant. I didn't want to tell him my worst fears, that if Shelly's news was bad—really bad—I might not have a home to call my own, much less an office.

"Soon," I said, hoping that it was the truth.

For the rest of the evening, I tried to remain upbeat and positive. It wasn't easy. Every passing minute brought to mind a new worst-case scenario until I no longer believed that reality could possibly be worse than my imaginings. As it turned out, I was wrong.

## Chapter 6

The following morning the marine layer had brought an unwelcome chill to the house. I turned on the heat and waited for the law offices of Heller, Greenblatt, and Hayes to open for business. At two minutes after eight, I dialed Shelly's number.

Sheldon Greenblatt was everything you would want in an attorney: smart, tough, and not good-looking enough to be a distraction in court. He belonged to the same tennis club as my ex-husband, but in all the times I had been there, I'd rarely seen him with a racket in his hand. Mostly he held court in the clubhouse dining room, nattily dressed and oozing success.

I went through several layers of administrative staff before I heard Shelly's gravelly voice on the line.

"Are you sitting down?" His tone was somber.

"Just give it to me straight. What's my aunt up to now?"

He cleared his throat. "She says Jackson Sinclair is not your father and therefore you're not in line to inherit from his mother's estate."

At first I was stunned, then angry. I remembered a conversation I had with my aunt on the steps of her house some months back. She had accused me of being a Sinclair by accident only, a fluke. At the time I thought she was just being spiteful, but maybe she was already cooking up this latest harebrained idea.

"That's ridiculous. Of course I'm a Sinclair. Ask Pookie."

"I'm afraid your mother's word will not be enough to convince Sylvia Branch. I've told you before, reopening a probate case is not easy unless fraud is involved and even so, the evidence has to be compelling. Your aunt obviously thinks she has that kind of evidence."

"Did she say what it is?"

"She's alleging that your mother had an affair with another man and that you are the product of that union. She also claims that you and your mother conspired to withhold this information, thereby perpetrating a fraud on the court."

My aunt had pulled some vile stunts before, but this one took the prize.

"That's insane."

"I doubt that she'll get anywhere with the allegation, but from all appearances, she intends to try."

"Fine," I said. "I'll have a DNA test. That should settle the issue once and for all."

"That can be arranged, but it's expensive and it takes time. There is also a problem of comparisons. I understand that your father died many years ago and that his body was never recovered. I'm not an expert on DNA, but I believe you need samples from both the mother and father to prove conclusively that he was your biological father."

"What should we do?"

"Find the man your aunt claims is your father. His name is Hugh Canham. Ask Pookie if she knows where he is. If he will give us a DNA sample and there's no match, at least we can eliminate him from your gene pool."

I felt a headache coming on.

"Fine. I'll talk to her."

"Make it sooner rather than later."

After we hung up, I paced for a while until the movement made Muldoon nervous and he took cover under my bed. Several times I picked up the telephone to call my mother, but each time I chickened out. Perhaps I wasn't ready to hear what she had to say.

I coaxed Muldoon out from under the bed and took him for a stroll on the beach, thinking that exercise might ameliorate my concerns. The walk made me tired but not tranquil. When I got back to the house I forced myself to return to my computer and resume working on a situation audit I was writing for Lesco Industries. The CEO had hired me to analyze the company's current business plan and make recommendations on how to increase market share. I had been working on the project for several weeks and was in the process of summarizing my findings. The report was due on Monday. I checked my research notes and began to type, willing myself to concentrate.

*Lesco is a family-owned, vertically integrated, and product-driven company with a successful history of innovation. Agricultural drainage pipe contributes fifty percent to total sales with twenty-four percent market share. The agricultural drainage market is driven by increasingly sophisticated farming techniques and economic pressures to increase productivity and return, per acre of land. The market has been stagnant but growth is expected. The market for residential leach field piping has declined thirty-eight percent in the past year and is expected to stabilize at its current level. Competition is mainly from regional manufacturers. Currently, the company seeks to increase market share in agricultural drainage with a successful marketing and pricing strategy for a new product called Easy-Flo.*

In the middle of composing all that brilliant prose, the telephone rang. Muldoon was sleeping under my desk with his head on my foot. When I reached for the receiver he voiced a muffled *grrrr* to indicate that he didn't appreciate being disturbed.

It was Charley calling. His voice sounded raspy and faraway.

"Sounds like you slept in the garage last night after all," I said.

"Not exactly."

Mendoza hadn't told me to keep quiet about Rocky Kincaid's murder or the task force meeting, and Deegan's only caveat was that I shouldn't tell anybody we were sleeping together. Not a problem. I wasn't about to tell Charley Tate the intimate details of my love life. I would never hear the end of his teasing.

"I was at the police station last night," I said.

"Some date. Who is this guy anyway?"

I ignored his attempt at humor. I told him about Rocky's

death, the fake Mexican tourist card, and Kincaid's outstanding warrant for embezzlement.

"Nobody's saying for sure," I said, "but Neeva Moore's description of Eve's boyfriend matches the one for the dead guy. It's just too coincidental. It has to be the same person."

"How do you know all this?"

"My hot date is a homicide detective."

"What's his name?"

I told him.

Charley's tone was cross. "How much did you tell him about my case?"

"Everything. I had to."

"Do they have anybody in custody?" he said.

"If they do, they didn't tell me."

"Did they say how long the vic had been dead?"

"Not officially," I said, "but you're thinking about the time line, aren't you? Eve Lawson disappeared at around four thirty. The hotel clerk heard gunshots at six. The body was found at eight. At this point nobody can account for Eve's time. Do you think she's a suspect?"

"Of course she's a suspect. Neeva Moore said Eve had boyfriend problems. Happens all the time. Maybe the guy roughs her up once too often. She moves back to LA to get away from him. He follows her. Threatens her. She gets a gun and kaboom. The guy becomes a statistic on somebody's COMPSTAT report."

"Or she could be the killer's next victim."

He paused. "Like I said before, I try to keep an open mind. Anything's possible."

"There's something else," I said. "There was a meeting at

the station tonight, some kind of task force. It looked like six or seven people were there, including a woman from the DA's office. I couldn't tell for sure, but I think she went to the crime scene. What do you think that means?"

"The department can put together a task force for anything from clearing up backlogged paperwork to investigating a serial killer. Usually if it's something major, they send it downtown for the big dogs to handle. Even if they kept this one in-house, it seems too coincidental that the Kincaid homicide happened the same night the task force was meeting *and* it fit their profile."

That news didn't make me feel better because it meant that Tracy Fields was following Deegan to the crime scene for reasons other than business.

"Maybe they're investigating drug-related crimes in the area," he said. "If Lawson's boyfriend just rolled into town from Mexico, they may have decided to check out the scene to eliminate it from some profile they've developed."

"At least I know Eve Lawson isn't a drug kingpin. She would have been wearing better clothes."

"Look, Sinclair, I called because I need your help."

The serious tone of his request was so unlike him that for a moment I thought he'd found some new way to give me a bad time.

"What's up?" I said.

"I'm in the hospital."

I held my breath waiting for the rest. Heart attack? Stroke? Maybe he'd developed a life-threatening hernia from carrying Lorna up the stairs Rhett Butler style.

"What happened?" I said.

"Somebody ran me off the road last night."

For a moment I couldn't make sense of the news. "On purpose?"

"Looks that way."

"Are you okay?"

"Yeah, but the van is totaled and my back is screwed up."

Eve's appearance at Tate Investigations with her tale of being stalked and Charley's subsequent accident seemed odd to me. Cops didn't believe in coincidences, that much I had learned from Deegan. I doubted that ex-cops like Charley Tate believed in them, either.

"Do you think the incident had something to do with Eve Lawson?"

"I don't know," he said, "but I intend to find out. In the meantime, I filed a police report. Let's see who finds the asshole first."

"Has Eve called?"

"No, but after you left last night, I found out the name of her old man. His name is Frank Lawson. He's a real estate developer. I've never heard of him, but I guess he was a mover and shaker in the seventies and eighties."

"How did you find him?"

"I contacted Eve's landlord. She rented the Playa del Rey house about six weeks ago and listed her father's name as a reference on the rental agreement. The telephone number she put down was wrong, so it took me a while to find him. I called Lawson's house last night. They live in Bel Air, just like Eve said. The old man was sick and couldn't come to the phone, but I talked to his wife. Meredith Lawson confirmed that Eve is her stepdaughter."

"How did a rich girl from Bel Air hook up with an embez-zler like Rocky Kincaid?" I said.

"Good question."

"Does the stepmother know where Eve is?"

"No. The family hasn't had any contact with her for a year. They didn't even know she was back in town. Mrs. Lawson seemed concerned and agreed to help in any way she could. I arranged to meet her at ten, but the doc ordered an MRI for sometime this morning, so I'm stuck here for a while. I need you to go to Bel Air and question her."

"Can't you just call her?"

"You can't read expressions over the phone. Somebody has to look her in the eye. Make sure she's playing fair with the truth."

"Why not wait until you get out of the hospital?"

"That's too late. Until Eve tells me otherwise, she's still my client. She may be in trouble. I need to find her, and the only lead I have at the moment is her stepmother."

"I don't know, Charley. . . ."

"I wouldn't ask if it wasn't important."

In my head I began to calculate how I could rearrange my schedule. The Lesco report could wait until the weekend, but I was supposed to meet a client named Marvin Geyer at the LA Mart at noon to help select merchandise for his mail order catalog. I was also pitching my services to a prospective client in Newport Beach at three. I could interview Mrs. Lawson before making the drive south but only if I postponed my meeting at the Mart or found somebody to go in my place. That was begin-ning to feel like an insurmountable problem until I remembered Eugene.

Several months back he had helped me organize a focus group for Geyer and had actually pitched an idea for a promising line of clothing for the catalog. The two had established a good working relationship. I didn't think Geyer would mind if he subbed for me this one time. I just hoped Eugene could get away from work.

"Okay, Charley. If it's that important, I'll talk to Mrs. Lawson."

"Thanks. I owe you one."

Charley gave me directions to the Lawsons' place and a list of questions to ask. I hung up and dialed Eugene's number at work.

"I have an assignment for you," I said, "but you'll have to sacrifice your lunch hour."

"What do you mean by sacrifice? This assignment isn't dangerous, is it?"

"Eugene, you know I wouldn't put you in danger, at least not intentionally."

"Why am I not convinced?"

"All you have to do is meet Marvin Geyer at the LA Mart."

He groaned. "The Mart? I hate that horrible underground garage. It's like spiraling into inner earth. Last time I was there I got so dizzy I almost passed out."

"At least you'll get a break from playing receptionist."

"You know I would do anything to help you, Tucker, but—"

"Look, life doesn't come with guarantees. Maybe it's better to go out dizzy than have your creative genius die a little bit every time you put on that telephone headset."

He sighed dramatically. "Oh, all right."

"Thanks, Eugene. You're a trouper."

"What do I have to do?"

"Help Geyer evaluate merchandise for his new catalog. Look at the stuff he's picked out and tell him what you think of it."

"You mean the truth? What if I hate it?"

"He can take it. Besides, he respects your opinion. He loved your skinny muumuu idea. Maybe the Hula Bitch line is a little too edgy for his customers right now, but I think he'll go for it eventually."

I gave Eugene the particulars and told him to call me if he had any questions. With that problem solved, I had one more. Muldoon. I try not to leave him alone if I can avoid it, because he has abandonment issues from his puppyhood.

I called my next-door neighbor Mrs. Domanski to ask if she would pup sit. Of course, she said yes. Mrs. D loves Muldoon and spoils him with toys and filet mignon. Her largess is responsible for his favorite gift, a yellow cashmere sweater that he likes draped over his shoulders for warmth on cool evenings on the beach.

The Domanskis live in a McMansion. Their house makes mine look like a swimming pool cabana. Mr. D is a movie producer, although I don't think he has actually made a film in more than twenty years. Even so, he still goes into town about three times a week for "meetings" at the bar of Musso & Frank Grill, surrounded by the ghosts of Humphrey Bogart and Orson Welles.

Mrs. D never talks about her age. If I had to guess I would say midseventies. She's pencil thin because that's what happens when you drink most of your meals. Martinis are her beverage of choice, and in a blind taste test, she can tell if the gin is

Beefeater, Bombay, or Boodles. She's also fussy about the way her martinis are made. She fills the glass to the brim with gin. Then she spritzes a fine mist of vermouth into the glass from a height of twelve inches and stirs gently so she won't bruise the booze. Mostly, it doesn't seem to bother her that more vermouth lands on the countertop than in the glass. That's just part of the art.

Most days Mrs. D practices her art late into the day. Eventually she collapses on the bed for a nap. I never know if her body will sag next to Muldoon's or on top of it. Sometimes I worry about leaving the leg-lifter in her care, but he's used to her quirky routine. Whatever happens, I'm sure he'll land butter side up.

My neighbor was present and still sober when I dropped Muldoon off. When the pup was settled, I headed for Bel Air.

## Chapter 7

The Lawsons' house was located north of Sunset Boulevard in Bel Air Estates, an exclusive residential area located in the chaparral-covered Santa Monica Mountains just west of Beverly Hills. Finding your way around up there is not for the direction-ally impaired. Walls. Serpentine roads. Dead ends. Hidden addresses. I kept Charley's directions close at hand.

I entered Bel Air at the east gate, and after a couple of false turns, I finally arrived at the entrance to the Lawsons' walled compound. I used an intercom to announce my arrival. When the gate opened, a man with a handheld radio was waiting for me in a golf cart. He wore what looked like some sort of uniform, khaki slacks and a navy polo shirt with a tree motif embroidered on the left chest area above the words *Wildwood Properties*.

I abandoned my car at the gate and joined the man on the golf cart. We drove along a winding road past a large house and an adjacent multicar garage. Three of the garage doors were open. Behind one of them was a fleet of golf carts. Behind another was the ass-end of a Ferrari. The third held a Bentley. I assumed the house was used as an office or perhaps it was where the chauffeur lived. In the distance I saw a small lake, terraced gardens, and another residence that was about the size of the employee house. Eventually we stopped in front of a third place, a colonial mansion that looked like a grander version of Tara. A female security guard met me at the door and escorted me inside to a private elevator, which took us on a slow journey up one or two floors before stopping with a jolt.

The guard led me down a domed hallway that was adorned with oil paintings to a large room where a petite woman sat at a gilded partner desk. Hanging on the wall in back of her was a tapestry in muted autumnal colors, depicting scenes of hunters killing a variety of forest creatures. To her left was a panel of floor-to-ceiling windows. Sunlight filtered through the glass, causing the silver highlights in her white hair to shimmer.

Meredith Lawson looked to be somewhere in her late sixties. She had the porcelain complexion of a Dresden figurine and eyes as blue as glacial ice. She was the vision I conjured up whenever I thought of women with old California money: slightly made, patrician, and as tough as a steel poppy. When she motioned for me to sit, I could see that her hands were deformed by arthritis.

"Mr. Tate said he would be sending an associate named Tucker," she said, "but I didn't expect someone like you. A private detective! What an unusual profession for a young woman. I imagine there's an interesting story behind that."

"Actually I'm not a PI. I'm a business consultant. Tate Investigations is one of my clients."

Her smile was pleasant but wary. "Well, that makes more sense. Could I get you something to drink? Tea perhaps? It's Fleur de Geisha. I think you'll like it."

Without waiting for my reply, she reached for an ornate silver teapot on a wooden cart next to her desk and poured amber liquid into two porcelain cups. The security guard delivered my cup and left the room, closing the door behind her.

"I'm sorry to hear that your husband is ill," I said. "I hope Eve will be able to see him." I stopped myself from adding, *Before he dies.*

Meredith Lawson's sigh was weary. "It's been a year since we've heard from her. At first, Frank was sick with worry. Now his Alzheimer's has progressed to the point that he doesn't even remember that she left. I was beginning to lose hope we would ever see her again. That's why I was relieved when Mr. Tate told me she'd been in contact with him."

"I'm sure he also told you that Eve didn't show up for a second meeting they'd set up. In fact, she seems to have disappeared. Do you have any idea where she might be?"

Meredith gazed into her teacup. "No. Eve has always been"—she paused as if searching for the right word—"unpredictable."

"Is her mother still living?"

"No," Meredith said. "She committed suicide when Eve was five. Eve has been in and out of therapy ever since."

"How old was she when you and Frank Lawson married?"

My question had forced her to go back in time. From the troubled expression on her face, the journey wasn't a pleasant one.

"My son was fifteen, so Eve had to be around twelve."

"And a year later you sent Eve to boarding school in Switzerland."

Meredith inhaled a deep breath through her patrician nose. "Yes. I'm afraid it was our only option."

I nodded. "I'm sure it was. It's just that thirteen seems like a vulnerable age to be starting a new school with your family living halfway around the world."

"Adolescence is difficult no matter what the circumstances. For Eve it was impossible. Her behavior became intolerable. We did everything we could to help her, but nothing worked. We were forced to find a school that specialized in dealing with problem children."

I wanted to ask if she had looked for a school like that in LA, but I wasn't there to tackle hot-button issues. I'd been sent to collect information for Charley.

"You said you hadn't heard from Eve in a year. Was that normal?"

"She didn't always keep in touch on a regular basis, but this was different."

"In what way?"

"When Eve got out of college, she began traveling around the world, living in so many places it was difficult to keep track of her. She came home to visit occasionally but didn't stay long. The last time she was here she lived in our guesthouse for about three months. It was the longest she'd stayed with us since before she went away to school. Frank was thrilled. He thought she had finally conquered her demons. One day the maid went into her bedroom to clean and saw that all her things were gone. We eventually got a letter from her postmarked Phoenix, but she made it clear it wasn't her final destination. She said she didn't want any further contact with us. It broke Frank's heart. He tried so hard."

"Why did she leave?"

"I have no idea."

"Does she have any friends or relatives in the area?"

"No relatives. I doubt she has any friends here, either. She hasn't lived in Los Angeles for a long time. Even in her younger years, she was a loner. She preferred socializing with the household staff more than playing with children her own age. She pestered our cook to the point where it became a nuisance. I had to put a stop to it."

I asked Meredith if Eve had any former employers that Charley could interview. She told me that her stepdaughter lived off a trust that her father had set up for her years ago. The only work she had ever done was as a volunteer for a place called the Sanctuary, a suicide prevention center in Venice. She added that Eve hadn't been able to handle the pressure and had quit before completing the training.

"Mrs. Lawson, have you ever heard the name Rocky Kincaid?"

Meredith stared into midspace as if she was searching her memory data bank. "Was he that boxer?"

I didn't know if Charley wanted me to tell her that Rocky Kincaid was Eve's dead boyfriend and that her stepdaughter might be a suspect in his murder, so I said no and changed the subject.

"Did you know Eve was writing a memoir?"

Meredith frowned and placed her teacup on the desk in front of her. "How interesting." Her tone lacked sincerity.

A tap on the door interrupted our conversation. A tanned and fit man in his midforties hurried into the room. He wore khaki trousers with knifelike creases and a white shirt with a button-down collar. A white cable-knit sweater was draped around his neck. His delicate features looked familiar, but when I saw his blue eyes I knew that he was related to Meredith Lawson, perhaps the son she had mentioned earlier.

"Kip, dear," Meredith said. "This is Tucker Sinclair. She works for that private detective who called last night."

He walked over to me and stuck out his hand. "Kip Moreland. How long have you been a PI?"

His manner was abrupt. Where I had seen a hint of kindness in his mother's blue eyes, in his I saw only arrogance.

"I'm not a PI. I'm a business consultant working for Mr. Tate."

If he was surprised by that news, I saw no indication of it.

"Do you have a card?"

I found a Sinclair and Associates business card in my purse and handed it to him.

"I've never heard of Tate. How long has he been doing this kind of work?"

"About a year. Before that he was with the Los Angeles Police Department for twenty-five."

Since I had just worked on Charley's résumé, I was able to provide a quick rundown of his experience. I couldn't blame Moreland for wanting to know who was collecting information on his stepsister, but I was surprised when he continued to pepper me with questions about Charley. What kind of cases had he handled in his career, what percentage of them had he closed, how well did he work under pressure. I answered everything to the best of my ability until I grew uncomfortable.

"I understand your concern, Mr. Moreland, but I assure you that Charley Tate is not only good at what he does, but he's completely trustworthy. That's why people like your stepsister hire him."

Moreland glanced at his mother. I saw her nod slightly.

"If you're wondering why I'm asking all these questions about Tate, it's because my mother and I might have a job for him."

That took me by complete surprise. The Lawsons obviously had a major security effort going on at their estate and probably an even larger one for their real estate development business. Getting on their payroll could be a golden opportunity for Tate Investigations. It might mean no Pauly Ridge, no unhappy Lorna, and no more worries about money. It could be a win-win situation. What I didn't understand was why Moreland thought Charley fit into their operation based on one telephone call.

"What sort of job?" I said.

Moreland didn't answer right away. Instead, he pulled up a chair next to his mother so that both of them were staring at me from across the desk like a couple of fifteenth-century Spanish Inquisitors.

"We're worried about Eve," he said. "We want Mr. Tate to find her."

I thought about Eve's claim that somebody was following her and about Charley's car accident the night before.

"You think she's in some kind of danger?"

"Yes," he said, "from herself. I'm telling you this in strict confidence, but over the years, Eve's mental state has become more and more unstable. The fact that she contacted a private investigator concerns us. She has a family history of suicide. We think she might be on the verge of a complete breakdown, especially now that she's disappeared again."

"Perhaps you should contact the police," I said.

Kip made a huffing sound to let me know that I was being ridiculous. "Eve is a forty-four-year-old woman who's run away before. The police won't be interested but the press will be, and that's bad for business. We want to hire Tate because he was a police officer. He'll know what to do and how to keep the investigation discreet."

"Perhaps you should give this some serious thought—"

"Don't insult me, Ms. Sinclair," Kip said. "I've examined the situation in every possible light. I will not risk Eve's life waiting for the authorities to react. When Mr. Tate called, my mother and I discussed the issues at length. We both agreed. We want him to find Eve before she harms herself. We're willing to pay Tate's fees and expenses and a bonus of one hundred thousand dollars when he finds her. If he can't handle it, we'll find somebody who can."

"It's not that he can't handle it—"

"What then? Not enough money?"

"Money isn't the issue."

There was a fixed stare in Moreland's winter blue eyes. "On the contrary, Ms. Sinclair, money is always the issue."

The room went silent as though all of us were holding our

collective breaths. I focused on the strands of radiant silver hair on Meredith's head while I fashioned an appropriate response.

"I can't answer for Charley Tate," I said. "I'll have to discuss your offer with him first."

"An hour, Ms. Sinclair," he said. "That's all you have. I think that's more than enough time to decide if he's going to save a woman's life. Whatever Tate does, this conversation remains inside this room or there will be consequences for everybody."

## Chapter 8

As soon as the security guard escorted me off of the Law-sons' property, I dialed the number for the hospital and asked for Charley's room. Three times I was connected to the wrong patient. On the fourth try, I reached a nurse who informed me that he was out of the room for tests, probably his scheduled MRI. She told me to call back in thirty minutes. Forget that. In fifteen minutes I could be at his bedside, talking to him face-to-face.

Traffic was heavy, so it was closer to twenty minutes by the time I arrived at Santa Monica–UCLA Medical Center. Charley was in his room watching CNN and looking aggrieved. If he was surprised to see me it didn't show.

There was a printout of a radiological diagnostic report on the bedside table. I wondered if it disclosed the results of his

MRI test. If so, it had been completed in record time. I glanced at the last paragraph labeled "Impression."

*At L5-S1 there is a right paracentral disc protrusion with superior prolapse of disc material into the right lateral recess. This appears to impinge the exiting right L5 nerve root as it joins the thecal sac. Disc material also abuts the right traversing S1 nerve root—*

Charley saw me gawking and turned the report over before I got to the conclusions, but what I had managed to read didn't sound good.

"How did it go with Mrs. Lawson?" Charley said. "Has she heard from Eve?"

"Not exactly."

His eyes narrowed. "What do you mean by not exactly? Where is she?"

I told Charley everything that I'd learned from Meredith and Kip, including their belief that Eve was on the verge of a mental meltdown. The room was silent except for the almost audible whirring of Charley's brain cells as they processed the information.

"Tough break, but if she's a missing person, they'll probably want the police to handle it from here."

"There won't be any police. Kip Moreland wants to hire you to find her."

"Me? Why?"

"Because you're a former police officer. Kip thinks you can find Eve before she kills herself and at the same time keep her troubles out of the press."

"Forget it. Too many things could go wrong. What if she went off the deep end and popped her ex-boyfriend? That means she has a gun and she's willing to use it. I could get killed and that would really piss Lorna off."

"Kip says if you don't respond in the next hour, he'll get somebody who will."

"Good luck finding some yo-yo who's dumb enough to take the job."

I paused, waiting for the right moment. "He offered to pay you a hundred-thousand-dollar bonus when you find her."

Charley's silence told me he was thinking about the money. A hundred thousand dollars was almost as much as he could make in a year working for Pauly Ridge and a lot more than he was making from Tate Investigations.

"That's a lot of dough," he said.

"Saving Eve is a lot of responsibility."

"This deal could go bad fast."

"You don't have to take the job, Charley. I'm just the messenger."

"Yeah. Right." He stared at the window as though he was watching something on the street, but the shades were drawn, so I knew he was looking at something only he could see. He was quiet for a long time before he called to accept the job.

Kip Moreland took the call in his guesthouse as he was supervising the installation of strobe lights above the dance floor. Charley asked him a lot of questions and even floated the theory that Eve might be orchestrating her disappearance as a means to punish her father or to extort money from the family. That obviously didn't set well with Moreland, because a moment later, Charley said, "No offense intended. I had to ask."

He also explained that Eve might be a suspect in a homicide. That information only made Moreland more adamant that Charley should begin an immediate search for his stepsister. Charley then asked if the family had any recent pictures of Eve. Moreland told him no. For security reasons Frank Lawson didn't like his family photographed.

After Charley ended the call, he was quiet for a while. Finally he said, "Tell me everything Meredith Lawson said in that interview."

I told him what I could recall but added, "She didn't seem to know much. The only possible lead she gave me was the place where Eve volunteered. The Sanctuary. She didn't work there long, but somebody may still remember her."

"It's worth checking out," he said. "Get my clothes, will you? They're hanging in the closet by the john."

"What are you going to do?"

"I'm checking out of here."

"What about your back? You can't leave until the doctor releases you."

"Says who?"

I groped for an answer. "Says Lorna."

"You know your problem, Sinclair? You think I'm afraid of my wife. Get my clothes or I'll get them myself."

I went to the closet and pulled on the door handle. It wouldn't open. I held up my hands in a gesture of defeat. "It's locked."

"Check on top of the cabinet over there. The key has to be somewhere."

There was no key. Charley wasn't pleased.

"Lorna took my wallet home," he said. "She must have taken the key, too. Give me your credit card."

"Why do you need that?"

"Because I don't have a paper clip—that's why."

"What are you going to do with it?"

"Pick the lock."

"You'll break my card."

"Relax. The lock is a piece of crap. I could charm it open."

I seriously doubted that, but I dug out my Visa card and handed it to him. Charley rolled onto his right side, wincing in pain. He pushed himself into a sitting position, which caused his hospital gown to gape open in the back. I didn't want to see any more of him than I had to, so I found a bathrobe draped across a nearby chair and helped him into it.

Charley shuffled to the closet and slipped the card into a gap between the jamb and the door just below the lock. He slid the card upward. The door popped open.

"Impressive," I said. "Will you teach me how to do that?"

"Give me a ride to Venice and I'll consider it."

"I have an appointment with a client in Newport at three."

"Don't worry. This won't take long."

Charley ducked into the bathroom to change clothes. I called information to get the telephone number and address for the Sanctuary. A few minutes later, he emerged wearing the same Bermuda shorts and Hawaiian shirt that he'd had on the previous day. His face was clammy with perspiration from the effort.

"I'll get a wheelchair," I said.

"Forget it. Just see if Nurse Ratched is still standing guard outside."

I checked the hallway. There was no nurse in sight. Charley laced his arm through mine for support as we made our way toward the elevator. No one seemed to notice his muffled groans or the trickles of nervous sweat in my cleavage.

By the time we got to the parking lot, Charley's right calf was numb. He took one look at the Boxster and rolled his eyes.

"I forgot about your damn car. The thing was made for con-tortionists."

"Wrong. It was made for people who want to go zero to sixty in five-point-two seconds. Stop complaining and get in."

Despite Charley's stoicism, I could see that he was in pain. Squeezing him into the Boxster was going to be a challenge. The butt-in-first method would cause too much stress on his back when he tried to lift his legs into the car. The left-leg-in-first approach required some pushing, pulling, and prodding, but he finally managed a successful entry.

"I think you should go home and rest," I said.

"Step on it, Sinclair. I'm getting claustrophobic in here."

On the way to Venice, we reviewed everything we knew about Eve Lawson's stint at the Sanctuary. It wasn't much, and we soon ran out of things to say. After that, I quizzed Charley about in-formation I needed to complete the Tate Investigations brochure. He detailed his role as a member of the bomb squad, one of fourteen sworn officers, two reserves, two bomb-sniffing dogs, and an array of robots, and told me about his training at the FBI Hazardous Devices School at Redstone Army Arsenal in Hunts-ville, Alabama. He confessed that his hearing was impaired from years of working around explosives.

Charley also talked about an old case he'd helped solve: a car bomb that killed a young woman and her daughter. I wanted to use his success with that investigation as a hook for his client brochure and Web site, but he wasn't too keen on the idea. His reluctance gave me the impression that he'd been a maverick back then and may have bent some rules to catch the killer. I also sensed that the deaths had been particularly wrenching for him.

"Are you sure I can't mention any of your cases in the brochure?" I said.

"Nah, but you can use the official Charles J. Tate safety rules. One, if anybody tells you he's an explosives expert, run. Two, if you can see the bomb, the bomb can see you."

I was used to hearing police aphorisms from Joe Deegan, but that last one was sort of catchy. I made a mental note to work it into the text if I could.

"How did you learn to pick locks?" I said.

"My brother-in-law was a locksmith."

"Pauly Ridge?"

"Nope. My first wife's brother."

"Not that it's any of my business, but you two made it for seventeen years. Why did you divorce?"

"Because the marriage turned to shit, just like they all do."

"Come on, Charley. You and Lorna have only been together a couple of years. The marriage can't be that bad already."

I glanced at him and saw a good-humored smile on his lips.

"Lighten up, Sinclair. I was only joking."

Once again I was reminded that what seemed like open warfare between Charley and Lorna was probably a complicated mating dance that kept their relationship novel and exciting.

The executive director of the Sanctuary was expecting us. As it turned out, Meredith Lawson was a benefactor and had called to alert him that we might be stopping by.

Nick Young's no-frills office was serviceable but it lacked verve, sort of like Young himself. He was probably somewhere in his fifties but he looked older because of his careworn expression and hangdog posture. According to the diplomas on his wall, he held a master's degree in social work and an MBA. According to the framed photograph on his desk, he had a wife and two teen-age daughters.

Young gestured for us to sit down, but before we had a chance, he said, "Meredith told me you wanted to know if Eve made any friends here. The answer is no. She only stayed a week. She didn't even finish the training."

Not surprisingly, the information was delivered in a service-able but abrupt manner.

"Did she have a bad experience with somebody on the phone?" I said.

"No. Only trained volunteers are allowed to answer calls."

Charley's face was flushed. A trickle of sweat was moving down his temple. His pain seemed to be interfering with his concentration, so I took over questioning Young.

"When did she leave the Sanctuary?" I said.

"About a year ago."

"Did you have any contact with her after she left?"

Young shook his head. "It was a mistake for her to come here. If she hadn't been Frank Lawson's daughter, I wouldn't have allowed it. Sometimes people who lose loved ones to suicide think it will bring closure if they save somebody else. Mostly the experience just brings up bad memories."

"So you knew about her mother's suicide?"

"Of course. It's the first question I ask people. I had to find out where Eve was coming from emotionally before I could let her work the phones. She seemed to be intellectualizing rather than feeling the pain of her mother's death. She was very young when it happened. I assumed that most of her memories were filtered through the experiences of others."

"Did you see any sign that Eve Lawson was headed for a mental breakdown?" I said. "Or that she may have been suicidal herself?"

He paused as if weighing his response. "I don't feel comfortable answering those questions, but certainly one of the risk factors for anybody is a family history of suicide."

"What are some of the other factors?" Charley said.

"Mental illness, especially depression, alcohol and drug abuse, child abuse, impulsive or aggressive behavior, loss of any kind, physical illness. The truth is that men are four times more likely to die from suicide than women even though women try it twice as often as men. The most important thing to know is that a suicide attempt is not a bid for attention. People who talk about killing themselves need immediate treatment from a mental health professional."

"Is there anyone else who may have come in contact with Eve in those few days she was here?" Charley said.

Nick Young tapped his fingertips on the desktop until it became annoying. "There was only one other person in her training group, a young woman named Christie Swink. She graduated from the program, but we had to terminate her shortly afterward. I have no idea where she is now."

Young checked his watch, signaling that it was time for us to leave. When Charley stood, he flinched in pain.

"What did Christie Swink do to get kicked out of a volunteer program?" I said.

Young frowned as though he thought my question was impertinent. If he had known me better he would have realized that I wasn't being cheeky. I just had a heightened sense of curiosity about arcane information.

"That's confidential," he said. "I'm not at liberty to discuss it."

After we left the Sanctuary, I asked Charley what he thought about Nick Young.

"He seemed sort of matter-of-fact, but I guess you can't afford to get too emotional when you're in the kind of business he's in."

"Eve left town shortly after she quit the Sanctuary," I said. "Do you think those two incidents were related? And if they were, shouldn't Nick Young have known that Eve had a bad experience under his watch?"

"Not necessarily. He may not be involved with the day-to-day issues of the volunteers."

"Or maybe he's withholding information to protect a wealthy donor."

"You're a cynic, Sinclair. It's one of the things I like about you."

We were quiet for a while after that. On the way to Charley's house, I pressed him for information about picking locks. After fifteen minutes my head was crammed with information about padlocks, pin tumblers, raking, and ways to pick locks with bobby pins and small screwdrivers. He told me to picture the inside of a lock as a series of pins that align when a key is inserted. Without the key, you had to artificially create that shear line in order to defeat the lock. He told me that most pin tumbler locks had either four or seven pins. The more pins, the harder it was to pick.

"Picking locks can be time consuming," he said. "The thing to ask yourself is if there's an easier way, a smarter way. If there isn't, then have confidence in yourself that you can do what needs to be done."

"I'll never learn all that," I said.

He chuckled. "Probably not."

Charley lived in Manhattan Beach, a medium-sized town about twelve miles south of Venice. He directed me to a modest house about eight blocks inland from the beach. The place was painted beige with white trim. It looked like Hansel and Gretel's gingerbread house. A flag with a smiling cartoon sun hung near the front door, signaling that summer had arrived. I walked Charley to the front door past a hand-painted birdhouse that read WELCOME TO OUR HOME. Flanking the front porch was a wooden cutout of Winnie-the-Pooh holding a pot of honey. Pooh had been glued to a stick and planted in a flower bed near several ceramic garden gnomes. Lorna had obviously decompensated in a craft store.

Charley frowned. "What are you looking at?"

"A bear on a stick."

"Don't pull that shit with Lorna. She'll make you pay."

"Right," I said. "What are you going to do now?"

"Look for Eve Lawson in the obvious places. Hospitals. Jails. County morgue. I'll also see if I can get a line on Christie Swink."

"Be careful, Charley. Call me if there's anything I can do."

"There is one thing. What do you know about real estate development?"

"Not much, but I can probably find out more. Why?"

"I'm just working all the angles. Eve Lawson may be crazy like her family thinks, or somebody from her past may be out to get her for what she's writing in that book of hers. It's also possible that somebody wants to get back at Frank Lawson for a business deal gone bad, and his daughter makes an easy target."

"Are you thinking somebody kidnapped her?"

He shrugged. "Sometimes you have to eliminate the lies to find the truth. Call me if you learn anything."

On the drive to my meeting in Newport Beach, I called my friend Venus Corday. She and I worked together as consultants at Aames & Associates. Her specialty is manufacturing, but she's consulted for companies in a variety of industries. I was hoping that she could give me an overview of the real estate development field and perhaps tell me some of its major players.

When I got her on the line, she explained that she wasn't an expert by any means but she had a former boyfriend who worked for a title insurance company. He was well connected and knew everything there was to know about buying, selling, and developing property. She said if I'd help her look for a new cycling outfit, she would invite him to join us afterward for dinner. We agreed to meet at six o'clock at Wheelz in Santa Monica.

In Friday rush hour traffic, it took two hours to make it to Newport Beach for my meeting with Gary Evers. Evers was president and founder of Evers Software Engineering, a start-up business that made medical billing software. He had quit a sales job with a rival company after a tiff with his former employer.

Then he sought revenge by forming a competing company in partnership with a programmer whom he had convinced to leave with him. Payback is a questionable motive for market entry. The programmer's enthusiasm had cooled, and Evers was now buried in debt. He was considering hiring me to do a strategic plan, which was a day late and a dollar short as my grandpa Felder always says.

Evers was a typical entrepreneur, brash and full of grandiose plans. I listened respectfully and methodically laid out my ideas. He abruptly discounted the need for market research and ranted about my fees. Thirty minutes into the conversation, I knew I had made the trip for nothing. When we parted company, he said he would get back to me the following day, but I knew that I would never hear from him again. That was fine with me. I'd worked with clients like Evers before. He was the type that would downplay my efforts and refuse to pay my fees. Right now he was more of a challenge than I wanted to face.

I headed back to Los Angeles, hoping that my meeting with Venus would be more productive.

## Chapter 9

Venus was already at the bike shop when I rushed through the door. She's in her late thirties with creamy caramel skin and eyes the color of French-roast coffee. Her crimped hair cascaded over her shoulder like a lava flow as she stared at her butt in a full-length mirror, assessing the fit of a pair of tight bicycle shorts in a nauseating shade of green. It was wise of her to take a second look. Venus's figure is not compatible with tight or green. The shorts made her look like an unripe Bartlett pear.

"You think these shorts make me look fat?" she said.

I collapsed in a nearby chair, hoping to unwind from what had been a stressful day. "Yup."

"Would they look more slenderizing in red?"

"Nope."

Venus put her hands on her hips and gave me her *Pay attention or pay the consequences* look. "We've been friends a long time, Tucker, but that could end at any time. I'm way too cranky for the truth tonight."

"What's going on?"

"For one thing, I'm so sore I can hardly move."

"Max?" I said.

"Yeah, Max."

Max was Max Huffman, Venus's new beau. He was just one in a long line of men who were wrong for her. I had to admit that he was appealing in many ways—sweet, playful, and eager to please—but there was something about his silky chestnut hair and his earnest expression that made me want to scratch behind his ears.

I raised my hands in surrender. "Please, no details."

Her glossy lips pursed in disapproval. "This isn't about sex. It's about cycling. The guy thinks he's some kind of Lance friggin' Armstrong training for the Tour de France. Last Sunday he took me to the bike trail along the beach to try out my new Bianchi. Fifteen minutes into the ride, I started to feel like I had a Doberman's head up my ass. Two hours later I was in a world of hurt."

"You could buy a wider seat, but considering your record with men, in another week you'll have a new guy and a new hobby."

"I don't know," she said. "Max could be my *maillot jaune*."

"Isn't that French for next ex?"

"Get with the program, Tucker. That's Tour de France talk. It's the yellow jersey, the winner. What I'm saying is Max could be the one. When he puts the hammer down? Oh baby!"

"Venus, you've said that about every man you've ever dated."

"I know, but he's different. Max is loyal and you should see how he looks at me—like I'm some kind of goddess."

"A golden retriever would do the same thing and the best part is when you break up with a dog you get to keep the Frisbee."

"Joke all you want, but I may just surprise you by riding into Happily Ever After with him."

"I hope so, but if you catch him having rough sex with your slipper, take him to the pound."

Venus rolled her eyes. She slid the hangers along the rack, looking through the merchandise. Finding nothing that pleased her, she motioned for the clerk to come over.

"Can you find me these shorts in black? And while you're at it, find me a bike seat that's made for a woman's derrière."

The guy disappeared into the back room. While we waited, I asked Venus if she had ever heard of Frank Lawson.

"I know who he is," she said. "He was the keynote speaker at a seminar I went to several years ago. He was old then. He must be dead by now."

"No. He's still alive. What did he talk about?"

"How to make money tearing down orange groves to build little houses made of ticky-tacky."

"Ever hear anything bad about him?"

"Isn't that bad enough? Truth is I've never heard anything about him personally. The guy is a recluse. The day of the seminar he came and went by a back door with a couple of guys who both looked like Conan the Barbarian. No cameras were allowed at the event. It was like he thought we were going to sell his picture to the tabloids. Made my blood boil."

At least that jibed with what Kip Moreland had told Charley. Frank Lawson was paranoid about anyone taking photographs of his family.

"Ever hear anything about his daughter?" I said.

"No. I didn't know guys like that were allowed to reproduce."

"I guess one slips through the net occasionally."

I told Venus about Eve Lawson, the death of her mother, her father's remarriage, and her banishment to boarding school in Switzerland.

"Sounds like the girl got shortchanged in the perfect-childhood department," she said. "Her daddy should have stood up for her."

Venus was probably right, but I suspected that Meredith could be a formidable obstacle, even for a powerful businessman like Frank Lawson.

"Yeah," I said. "Makes you wonder what really happened in that household."

"Why don't you ask Eve? Better yet, ask a nosy neighbor. If the Lawsons don't have one, I'll lend them one of mine."

The clerk came back a few minutes later with a pair of black spandex bike shorts with a chamois crotch, a lime green jersey, and a bike seat that looked as if it belonged on a John Deere tractor. Venus held up the shorts and jersey, eyeing them with distaste.

"I can't believe people actually wear this shit." She handed the clothes back to the clerk. "This isn't working for me. Show me something in a sweat suit."

"A sweat suit is not aerodynamic," I said.

"If it makes any difference," the clerk offered, "your boy-friend just bought an outfit exactly like this one."

The poor guy was trying to be persuasive but he'd picked the wrong sales pitch.

"That's it," Venus said. "I draw the line when it comes to dressing alike. That's for old people on bus tours."

"I think it's sweet," I said.

She gave me her version of the evil eye. "I don't do matching outfits. Period."

She ended up buying a gold warm-up suit that harmonized with her skin tone.

Sam Herndon was already seated at the table when we arrived at the restaurant. Venus's ex-boyfriend was a black man in his midforties with an engaging smile and the smooth patter of a natural raconteur. My first impression of him was that he had the confident demeanor of a man who was accustomed to winning, but from the look of desire on his face when Venus walked through the door, he seemed to be acknowledging at least one failure.

Venus and Sam both ordered filet mignon. I ordered a Cobb salad. Over dinner Herndon regaled us with his knowledge of the current Los Angeles real estate scene, explaining that the latest building trend was "mixed use" developments where condos and lofts were built above commercial businesses.

"So how are these deals put together?" I said.

"You would probably start with a limited liability company. Acquire the land. Get financing for the mortgage and construction costs. Big development companies are enormously sophisticated these days. Financing is multifaceted and done through

Wall Street investment firms or big banks. Labor unions may even take a position in the deal, especially if jobs are at stake and especially in towns where they control related businesses like lumber, cement, and trash haul away."

"I've heard that the Mafia controls some of those labor unions," I said. "Do they get involved in development projects?"

Herndon grinned as he raised his hands in a gesture of surrender. "Hey, everybody has to make a buck."

I acknowledged the joke with a smile and moved on. "So what happens when the financing is set?"

"When everything is in place, the plans have to be approved by the city council. The good thing is that mixed-use development satisfies everybody, so it's fairly easy to get the backing, but it always helps if the councilperson in the district is in your pocket."

"What do you mean?" I said. "You have to bribe him?"

He chuckled. "These days it's not called bribery. It's called making a campaign contribution. Let's say you're a developer and you're building two hundred and fifty apartment units above commercial businesses. That brings jobs and new services to the community. Sounds good to business-friendly constituents. In some parts of LA, fifteen percent of those units have to be for low-to-moderate-income tenants. That appeals to social liberals. If the project has across-the-board support among the councilman's constituents, it can get him reelected. For that, he owes you big-time. So when your environmental impact report is due to come before the city council, you give the guy a heads up. He lobbies his political cronies, and the plan passes. Then it's sent off to the planning commission.

Sometimes he can even convince the city to chip in a few million tax dollars to help you out, especially if the development is in a blighted area."

"So once I get the plan past the city council, I'm ready to cut the ribbon and start digging?"

"No. Before that happens the public can raise objections. Sometimes hearings are held. That's when things can get dicey."

"What sort of things could they object to?"

"Noise, drainage, environmental issues, traffic congestion, cleanup of toxic chemicals that may exist at the site. For example, before you can pound a nail, the groundwater has to be clear of benzene."

"Can homeowners actually stop these big developments?"

"Absolutely. A couple of years ago, neighbors killed a major construction site out in the San Fernando Valley with a class-action suit that alleged faulty environmental studies. But the project can be derailed by other types of problems as well like forged notary signatures in title transactions or a defective chain of ownership on a piece of property."

"Sounds like the stakes are high," I said.

"Extremely high."

"High enough to kill for?" I said.

Herndon raised his eyebrows as though he thought my question was intriguing but odd. "I suppose so. People have killed for less."

I thought about Eve Lawson's disappearance and Charley's speculation that her troubles may have had something to do with her family's business dealings. Realistically, I wondered how Eve would be the target of revenge against Frank Lawson.

She had been away from Los Angeles for a long time. I didn't see how her father's enemies would even know she was back in town.

"Are you familiar with Wildwood Properties?" I said.

Herndon took a sip of his wine. He let it slosh against his palette for a long time. "Of course."

"What can you tell me about the company?"

"It was founded by Frank Lawson in the early seventies. He turned the daily operations over to his stepson when his Alzheimer's started interfering with his decision making. Toward the end, I heard he had notes plastered all over the office to remind him of the simplest things."

"Lawson is seventy-eight now, so he must have been in his forties when he started Wildwood Properties. Sounds like a second career. What did he do before that?"

Herndon frowned. "Interesting question, but I don't know the answer."

"Does Frank Lawson have any enemies?" I said.

"Everybody in business has enemies. I never heard that Lawson had more than his share."

"What about his stepson? Kip Moreland."

He hesitated. "Why do you want to know?"

"I can't tell you. Client confidentiality. You understand."

Venus sensed Herndon's reluctance. "Sam, you'd be doing me a big favor if you told my friend what she needs to know."

He gazed into Venus's eyes before he answered. "It's just hearsay."

"Hearsay is good," Venus said. "Tucker always checks her facts before she leaks stories to the *Times*."

Herndon smiled. "Look, I have a friend who has worked on several projects with Wildwood. He could answer your questions better than I can, but I don't think he'd be willing to talk to you unless you gave him more information, like the name of your client."

I paused to consider the consequences of doing that, but decided that the information trade-off could be vital to Charley's case.

I dug out a business card from my purse and gave it to him. "The client's name is Eve Lawson. Make sure your friend knows it's important that I talk to him."

After dinner, Venus handed me a doggie bag with her leftover steak. "For Muldoon," she said.

"The pup will remember you in his will for this."

As soon as the words were out, I realized that I hadn't told Venus the latest news about my grandmother's will and my aunt's allegations. After thinking it over, I decided against saying anything. It would only upset her. Besides, the fewer people who knew, the better.

Venus was still lingering near the valet stand, chatting with Herndon, when I drove away. When I arrived home, I discovered Eugene's elderly Volvo parked in my driveway. I felt uneasy because it was unusual for him to drive all the way to the beach without calling first. I found him huddled on the deck in front of the house. His expression seemed woebegone as he watched the waves lap against the shore.

Eugene is in his midtwenties, five-feet-five or so, with blue eyes and sandy brown hair that he keeps short to control a cowlick that refuses to be tamed. He's thin, so he overdresses to stay warm. His outfit consisted of pleated pants, a long-sleeved shirt, and a wool scarf that he'd knitted himself.

"What happened," I said. "How long have you been here?"

He took a deep breath. "An hour or so. I wanted you to be the first to know. I'm unemployed."

My mouth gaped open in surprise. "Harriet fired you?"

A huge smile spread across his face. "No, I quit! Can you believe it? It was so scary, but I finally did it. I've been agonizing over the decision for eons. Should I? Shouldn't I? Liza thought I should, but cats are always sanguine. Anyway, today I got back late from my meeting with Mr. Geyer at the LA Mart. Hershy was covering for me at the front desk, answering phones and cutting everybody off. Harriet was fit to be tied. She started screaming at me about punctuality and responsibility. My heart was racing. I thought I was going to pass out. Then I started thinking about what you said on the phone this morning. Remember? About going out in a blaze of glory? That's what *you* always do. You never worry about anything. You just plunge ahead. But nothing really bad ever happens. I kept thinking about that and all of a sudden I had this incredible flash of clarity. Everything finally made sense. What's the worst that could happen? I would have to find another job, that's all. So I took a deep breath and said, 'I quit.' It was so liberating, Tucker, and you should have seen the look on Harriet's face. Total shock. It was priceless. I almost offered her one of my Lorazepam, but she finally pulled herself together. Of course, she gave me the usual corporate party line, 'We're so sorry to see you go.' Blah, blah, blah. The translation, of course, was 'Don't let the door hit you on the way out.'"

Eugene finally ran out of breath.

"How much notice did you give?" I said.

"Two weeks." In a gesture of faux drama, he slapped the back of his hand on his forehead. "But all the stress is creating flu-like symptoms. I may have to take the next couple of weeks off to recuperate."

"And look for another job."

A look of uncertainty appeared on his face. "Do you think that's going to be a problem?"

Eugene was certainly employable. He had excellent skills, and he was a hard worker. On the downside, he had a tendency to melt under stress. He was making improvements in therapy but he needed an employer who understood his unique sensibilities. Finding the right match could take a while. In the meantime what was he going to do for money? What if he got sick and needed insurance? I felt horrible that I had been the inspiration for his impulsive and potentially self-destructive behavior. Business was improving, but I couldn't afford a full-time employee.

"Let me ask around," I said. "I may be able to find you a job with one of my clients."

He smiled faintly. "It wouldn't be anything dangerous, would it?"

"Eugene—"

"I know, I know. No guarantees."

I put the leftover steak in the refrigerator and persuaded him to accompany me to Mrs. Domanski's to pick up Muldoon.

My neighbor looked a little droopy-eyed when she answered the door. Her ruby pageboy was disheveled as if she had been sleeping in an awkward position. The low-cut spandex shirt she had on emphasized her bony chest, and her black capri pants hung loose in the back where her butt should have been.

While Eugene and I waited in the foyer, she called Muldoon with her campy faux-English accent. When the little Westie finally appeared, Eugene and I took the pup and walked back to my place.

"My god," Eugene said. "The alcohol fumes in there could fuel every Prius in America. Please tell me she doesn't drive in that condition."

"Don't worry. If she runs out of booze, the store delivers."

Eugene gave me a short lecture on enabling people with addictions, but I wasn't sure what he wanted me to do. Mrs. D was a peach, and I would do whatever I could to help her. The problem was she hadn't asked for my help. In fact, she didn't seem to think she had a problem.

Eugene turned down my offer of hot chocolate, because he hadn't checked on his cat since he left for work that morning. His apartment lights weren't on, and he had convinced himself that Liza was afraid of the dark.

I watched until his Volvo disappeared into the night and then headed toward the house. As I reached for the doorknob to go inside, I noticed an envelope propped against the window near my side door. The paper was soggy from the moist air as if it had been sitting there for a while. Inside the envelope was a note from Joe Deegan. He'd been in the neighborhood. Was sorry to have missed me. He was working late on Saturday night, but he invited me to be waiting for him when he got home, around eight he thought.

At the bottom of the envelope was a key to his house. Again,

I wondered if it represented another step forward in our relationship or if it was a mere convenience. With Deegan it was hard to tell. I decided to be prepared for anything, which meant that I had only twenty-four hours to buy a travel toothbrush and a pair of edible underwear.

## Chapter 10

As soon as Muldoon and I got back inside the house, I called Charley Tate's cell phone number. He answered on the first ring.

"How's your back?" I said.

"It's killing me. I'm living on anti-inflammatories."

"Have you found Eve Lawson yet?"

"No." His tone was curt. "Look, I don't want to talk on the cell. It's not secure. Call me back on a hard line."

Charley gave me his home number, and a short time later, we resumed our conversation. He told me that he had checked all of the hospitals in the area, plus the jails and the county morgue. None of them had any record of admitting Eve Lawson or anybody who fit her description.

"Meredith Lawson called," he said. "She forgot to tell me

that Eve has a distant relative on her mother's side who lives in Scottsdale. I'm trying to locate her now. I may have to go there to interview her."

"You're in no shape to travel."

"I'll manage."

"Did you install the cameras at Eve's house?"

"I don't think that's a good idea. If the police suspect she knows something about Rocky's death, they might get a warrant to search her place. They could take my equipment."

I told him what I'd learned from Sam Herndon about the real estate development business and that I might have a lead on somebody who had worked with Wildwood Properties.

"Did Herndon say who it was?"

"No, and I got the impression that this person may not want to talk about his experiences."

Charley made a noise that sounded like harrumph.

"Have the police identified your hit-and-run driver?" I said.

"No. A witness called in a partial license plate number, but without a make or model, there are too many possibilities for them to connect the vehicle to an owner."

"But they'll keep trying. Right?"

"Maybe but not very hard. They'd have to interview hundreds of people. There weren't any fatalities, so it's not a high priority. Look, Sinclair. I hate to keep asking you for favors, so here's a proposition. Moreland is paying me a hundred grand to find his stepsister. Usually the job would be a routine skip trace, but I'm not myself right now. What I'm asking is if you could work with me full time for the next few days. I'll pay full price. No discounts. All you have to do is talk to people. Make some phone calls. Stuff like that."

"I have other clients, Charley."

"I know, but it won't be for long. It's just until I get back up to speed. I'm going to check out some leads from home, but I was thinking you could follow up on what Herndon told you. Maybe you could drop by my office in the morning and check out my databases. I'll give you the passwords and a list of sites to search. Just see what you can find out about Wildwood Properties. Okay?"

I paused to collect my thoughts. Time was slipping away from me. The Lesco report still wasn't finished, and I should have been out cultivating other clients. On the other hand, Charley was out of commission and Eve Lawson's life could be at stake. I couldn't live with myself if something happened to her because I was too busy to help.

"I can't do full time," I said, "but I'll give you as many hours as I can squeeze out of my schedule. Meanwhile, I have a proposition for you."

He chuckled. "Thanks for the offer, Sinclair, but I have my hands full with my wife right now."

"Don't flatter yourself. It's not *that* kind of proposition. I've found you a new front office person."

"She better be ugly or Lorna will never go for it."

"It's not a she. It's a he, my former administrative assistant."

"A male secretary? You gotta be joking. No way."

"He's not a secretary. He's an administrative assistant."

"Don't give me that PC crap."

"Eugene is really smart and creative."

"What do you mean by creative?" His tone was skeptical.

I had a feeling that now wasn't a good time to bring up Eugene's knitting hobby.

"He thinks outside the box, Charley. He could really help you run the office, especially while you're laid up with this back injury."

"Will he work for minimum wage?"

"No, but here's the other part of the deal. I could use some help, too. We could split his time and his salary fifty-fifty. He has to give notice at his current job, so he's not available for two weeks. You have time to think about it, but you have nothing to lose by saying yes now. If it doesn't work out, I'll find him another job."

"If I say no, will you still check out Frank Lawson for me?"

"Of course I will. I gave my word."

There was a long pause. "Jeez, Sinclair, why do you have to be so damn reasonable?"

"Just give him a chance, Charley. That's all I'm asking. You won't be sorry."

In the silence that followed, I imagined him rubbing his hand over his bristly crew cut and muttering under his breath.

"Okay," he said, "as long as he doesn't touch anything on my desk. I don't want anybody messing up my system."

Charley's decision both relieved and worried me. I was used to bantering with people like Tate but Eugene had a fragile psyche, compliments of a perfectionist father who belittled his children for sport. I just hoped he was strong enough to hold his own against Charley.

I hung up and dialed Eugene's number. I told him about his new job, explaining that it was only temporary, that Charley might give up the PI business and go to work for his brother-in-law. I briefly filled him in on my mission to search Tate's databases for information related to a missing client. Eugene didn't seem worried by any of that. He was just happy to be working with me again. He even offered to come in the next day to help me search for information about Frank Lawson's development company.

Saturday morning, before I left for Charley's office in Culver City, I called my mother. I was spending the night with Joe Deegan, and I needed a place for Muldoon to camp out while I was away. I didn't want him to wear out his welcome at Mrs. D's, so I asked if she could watch the pup for the weekend. She agreed.

I packed an overnight bag for Muldoon and one for me. I also brought along my laptop computer, hoping to find a quiet place during the day to finish the Lesco report.

When I arrived at Kismet Yoga Studio to drop off Muldoon, there were only three cars parked in the twelve-space lot. I walked inside and found the überserene Petal sitting at the front desk. Petal is the long, lithe yoga teacher wannabe that Pookie hired to greet students and sell merchandise like CDs, Nag Champa incense, and a small selection of yoga wear. Muldoon went on a sniffing frenzy. I kept an eye on him to make sure he didn't lift his leg on the meditation cushions.

My mother is a newlywed. Her husband, Bruce Lindsay, is living on money from a trust left to him by a grandfather who made a fortune in the cement business. The trustees had recently approved the purchase of the small two-story building in Santa Monica that they currently occupied. The lovebirds lived in an upstairs apartment, and Bruce taught classes in the ground floor studio.

I could see Bruce in the next room. He was teaching a class in a formfitting black leotard that made him look like a geriatric member of the Bolshoi Ballet. My mother was in the office hunched in front of a computer screen. She's five feet three inches tall, a hundred and five pounds, with blond hair that's razor cut around a pixie face. She used to be an actor and still uses her professional name, Pookie Kravitz, because she thinks it has more sizzle than her real name, Mary Jo Sinclair. She's never cared much for "Mom," either, so I call her Pookie. I suspect that she doesn't want to be reminded that she's fifty-one and has a thirty-year-old daughter. Bruce calls her Goldie, because after all those years of sex, drugs, and rock and roll in Haight-Ashbury, his memory has gone the way of flower power.

Pookie and Bruce's marriage surprised everybody, including Pookie and Bruce. They had bonded in the sweat lodge of a shaman boot camp in British Columbia the previous fall. After discovering that they shared a groovy kind of love, they decided to further explore their feelings at a kahuna workshop in Maui. They made a few other stops on their spiritual junket, and then returned to LA to move in with me temporarily, or so they claimed. They had been living in my spare bedroom for a few months when they decided to take an impromptu kiss-and-make-up trip to Las Vegas after an argument about gossip. While there, they got drunk and then they got naked. The next thing they remembered was a boom box pounding out DUM-DUM-TAH-DUM and rice crunching under their feet.

"This is so screwed up," Pookie said.

"What?"

"This accounting program. I've told Bruce over and over again not to use the computer. He always says, 'Sure, Goldie. No problem.' The next thing I know, he's erased stuff from the hard drive. Now I have no idea how much money we've taken in this month." She took a deep breath and blew it out. "I give up. There's a tea shop down the street. Why don't we take a break and go over some ideas for the studio? I'll treat."

She was referring to a marketing plan I'd promised to write for Kismet Yoga Studio. It was a freebie, so I hadn't devoted much time to it.

"I have a full schedule today," I said. "Maybe we can meet next week."

Her expression was a mixture of frustration and disappointment. "Sure, sweetie. No problem."

I understood her concern. She was under a lot of pressure to make a success of the business due to a living-a-productive-life clause in the trust Bruce's grandfather had set up for him. Kismet was required to at least break even or the trustees would pull the plug on Bruce's yoga dreams. The problem was that Bruce had no head for business. My mother wasn't exactly a financial wizard. Not because she's incapable but because she's inexperienced. She's never had much money to handle.

Bruce is nice enough but he's serene to the point of being vacuous. He's also technologically challenged and not just at the computer. He has trouble working the remote control on the television set, too. Then there's his feng shui obsession. He's constantly rearranging furniture to redirect the chi, which causes countless hazards to pedestrian navigation. I should have been more tolerant, but Pookie could have done better in the husband department. At the moment, I didn't have time to reflect on her poor choice in men. I had to meet Eugene in Culver City.

I left Muldoon sitting on Petal's lap, enjoying a full body massage, and headed to Charley's office. Eugene was waiting for me in the parking lot. He was tranquil all the way up the stairs and only somewhat nonplussed as he scanned the reception area and spotted the dying leaves of the ficus plant, thanks to Lorna and her correction fluid. Once inside Charley's office, I saw his gaze travel from the dog-eared manila folders stacked on the floor to the wood chips from the sci-fi pencil sharpener that were scattered across the desk like sawdust in a cow barn at the county fair.

His lips paled. "Please tell me we're in the wrong office."

"Nope. This is it."

I walked over to get him a chair, but he stopped me with his hand.

"Don't touch anything unless your tetanus shot is up to date. There's an antibiotic-resistant *Staphylococcus aureus* bacteria going around, and this place is a breeding ground."

"I guess it wouldn't hurt to tidy up your desk a bit before you start working."

"A bit?" Eugene turned and headed for the door.

"Where are you going?"

He turned to face me. "To find industrial cleaners. I'll be back in half an hour."

Charley's computer was set up on a metal typewriter stand that had been relegated to a corner of his office. While Eugene was gone, I pulled up a chair and logged on. I soon confirmed Frank Lawson's age (78), the square footage of his house

(17,000), when he bought it (1979) and for how much (five million dollars), but little else of interest.

When Eugene returned twenty minutes later, he handed me a piece of paper.

"What's this?" I said.

"A receipt for supplies."

I checked the totals. "Fifty bucks? That's a lot of money."

"Does a heart-transplant patient quibble with the cardiologist about the cost of the needle and thread?"

"I see your point."

"I thought you would."

Eugene unpacked a bottle of cleanser, rubber gloves, sterile masks, and a few miscellaneous items I didn't bother to inspect and began wiping the reception desk clean with the help of a pine-scented spray. When it was sterilized to his specifications, I wheeled Charley's computer out to the reception area and gave Eugene a quick introduction to navigating the databases plus a list of names to research—Eve, Frank, and Meredith Lawson; Rocky Kincaid; Kip Moreland; and Wildwood Properties. Eugene nodded and began scrolling down a long list of options that had popped up on the screen.

I was looking over his shoulder at the information when my cell phone rang. I had it programmed to play "Sempre libera" from the opera *La Traviata*. Loosely translated, *sempre libera* means, "Ever free shall I hasten madly from pleasure to pleasure," which seemed like a sentiment worth remembering. *La Traviata* is about two lovers who just can't seem to get it together. Poor Violetta. Poor Alfredo. Their story makes me weep. I flipped open the phone and was greeted by a deep baritone voice.

"Ms. Sinclair? This is Nathan Boles, president of N.B. Construction."

It took a few seconds but the name finally registered. N.B. Construction was plastered on nearly every high profile building site in LA County.

"Sam Herndon told me you were looking for information for Eve Lawson about real estate developers," he went on.

"Yes, I'm helping her research a book about the post–World War Two housing boom. I was wondering if I could ask you a few questions."

"I'm in Northern California on business."

"This won't take long. If you could just give me a minute—"

"I think we should talk in person. My pilot is flying the jet up here on Monday morning. You can catch a ride with her. There's a restaurant adjacent to the tarmac at Santa Monica Airport called Typhoon. She'll be waiting for you there at eight a.m."

He didn't ask me if I could make it or if the time was convenient. It was as if he assumed that I would be there because he wanted me to be there. At least he was correct about that. I did want to be there.

"Monday morning is fine," I said.

Seconds passed before I realized that he was no longer on the line. I stared at my cell phone for a moment before pressing END.

"Who was that?" Eugene said.

"Nathan Boles."

"Why did you tell him you were researching a book? You lied."

"It wasn't a lie. It's called a pretext. If you're going to work for a PI, you'll have to learn the industry jargon."

"Maybe I should have a pretext, too."

"Whatever," I said. "Let's get back to work."

A few minutes later, I was reading some general information about real estate development that Eugene had printed from a Web site when my cell phone rang again. This time it was Charley.

"Guess what," he said. "I located Rocky Kincaid's ex-wife. How about driving me over to interview her?"

"Now? What about the research you wanted me to do?"

"That can wait."

I ended the call and told Eugene that I had to pick up Charley in Manhattan Beach and I'd be gone for a while. I expected him to be anxious, but he took the news in stride.

"We both can't use the computer," he said. "Go do your thing."

"I hate to leave you alone."

"Tucker. I have it covered. You're acting like you don't trust me. I know what to do."

"Of course you do. Okay. Call my cell if you have any questions or if you find anything interesting." I grabbed my purse and walked toward the door but stopped before I got there. "And, Eugene? If you have time there's one more name I want you to check. Hugh Canham."

"Who's he?"

"Just somebody my attorney wants me to talk to," I said. "No big deal. Just check. Okay?"

# Chapter 11

Rocky Kincaid's ex-wife worked as a hairdresser at a six-chair shop located in a strip mall not far from Charley's office. As we arrived, an argument was brewing over a missing can of hair spray. All of the operators seemed to be talking at the same time, shouting to be heard over the noise of hair dryers, ringing telephones, and a radio tuned to a soft rock station.

Dorcas Kincaid was up to her elbows in rubber gloves, dabbing a dark-colored dye onto a male customer's roots. Long strawberry blond bangs nearly covered her eyes but they didn't obscure the impertinent expression on her round face. She was slouching, which only made her look more insolent.

Dorcas looked up from her work. "Be right with you."

When she was done with the dye, she inspected some gray

hairs sprouting from the guy's ears. For a moment I thought she was going to dye them, too, but instead she picked up a shaver that looked like a Lilliputian weed whacker and buzzed them off. She gave the man a tabloid magazine to read and directed him to sit in a chair near the door. Then she set a timer.

"Okay," she said to us. "Which one of you wants to go first?"

"I don't need a haircut," Charley said. "I want to talk about your ex-husband."

Dorcas looked over her shoulder to see if her customer had heard the exchange, but from what I could see from my vantage point, he seemed engrossed in a series of before-and-after photos of celebrity breast augmentations featured in the magazine he was reading.

"Why don't you guys leave me alone?" she whispered. "Rocky's dead, and I have to make a living. I've already told you all there is to tell."

Dorcas obviously assumed that we were from the police department. Charley made no attempt to correct her. I wondered if that was legal.

"How much do you charge for a cut?" Charley said.

"Twenty bucks."

"How long does it take?"

Dorcas looked at his close-cropped, thinning hair.

"For a guy like you? Fifteen minutes including the shampoo."

"So how about I pay you twenty bucks to come outside for fifteen minutes and talk about Rocky?"

Dorcas glanced at a clock hanging on the wall and then at the timer. A moment later she said, "Cash?"

Charley reached for his wallet, pulled out a twenty, and handed it to her. She inspected it for flaws and slipped it into her pocket.

"Okay," she said. "Why not?"

She took a cigarette from a pack she had stowed in a drawer, grabbed a lighter, and led us out to the sidewalk in front of the shop. She hunkered over to shelter the flame and lit up.

Charley took the lead. "First of all, I'm sorry to hear about the death of your ex-husband—"

She blew out a stream of smoke. "Skip the phony sympathy crap. You probably didn't even know him. I did. Nobody's sorry he's dead. He was a loser. He left me with two kids and a lot of bad memories."

"When did you and Rocky split?" I said. "Before or after his arrest?"

"Before."

"You mind telling us how it went down?" Charley said.

Dorcas paused as if she was considering whether accepting that twenty-dollar bill had been a good deal. She took another drag on her cigarette before answering.

"It's the same story I told you before."

"Why don't you tell us again?"

Dorcas rolled her eyes. "Rocky was sharing space with five other therapists. They each did their own thing until he got this brilliant idea that they should all chip in and hire somebody to answer phones, make appointments, and bill insurance. He said it would free them up to see more patients and make more money. Everybody liked the idea, so Rocky agreed to be the managing partner. He took care of everything."

"And did Rocky make more money?"

"If he did, I sure never saw any of it."

"Why did you two break up?" I asked.

She seemed reluctant but finally answered my question. "When I met Rocky, he had a coke habit. I told him I'd leave if he didn't clean up his act. He was okay for a long time. Then he started getting hinky on me. I thought he was doing drugs again. I told him I didn't want that shit around my kids. He swore he wasn't using, but it didn't get better, so I told him to get his ass out of my house. He left, and I hired a lawyer. When I heard he'd embezzled all that money, I couldn't believe it. He had his faults, but he wasn't a thief."

"What do you think he did with all the cash he took?" Charley said.

"How would I know? Like I said, he could have spent it on drugs, but he also liked to gamble. Maybe he lost it all. I was too busy working and raising two kids to pay much attention."

"When was the last time you heard from him?"

Her eyes narrowed as she studied Charley's face. "He called about ten days ago. Said he was finally going to pay me the child support he owed."

"Did he say where he was calling from?"

She hesitated. "No, and I didn't ask."

Charley kept pressing her for information. "He was carrying a Mexican tourist card when they found him. Could he have been calling from south of the border?"

"Like I said, I don't know."

"He said he was going to pay you child support. Where was the money coming from?"

"Doesn't matter. I never heard from him again, and I never got a dime." She glanced at her watch. "Your fifteen minutes are up."

Dorcas took one last drag on her cigarette and snuffed it out on the side of the building. "If you ever find any of the money, give me a call. My kids need new shoes." She threw the butt in a nearby trash can and strolled back inside the salon.

"Dorcas Kincaid sounded pissed off enough at Rocky to kill him herself," I said.

"Sounds like she may be standing in line behind a few other folks, like Kincaid's partners."

"Something's bothering me, Charley. A year ago Rocky skipped town after he was charged with embezzlement. Eve Lawson left LA around that same time. Do you think they were seeing each other back then? Maybe she was even involved in the theft."

"If Eve was charged, I think Meredith Lawson would have mentioned it."

"Are you sure about that?"

Charley shrugged. "I can check it out. If there was ever a warrant issued for her arrest, it'll be part of the public record. It's possible Eve just didn't get caught, except you said Meredith denied knowing anything about Kincaid. Seems like she would have at least heard that Eve was dating him."

I dropped Charley off at his house in Manhattan Beach.

When I got back to Tate Investigations, Eugene was at the computer.

"Somebody by the name of Neeva Moore called while you were out," he said. "She wanted to remind you about the block party today. And she found Fergie. She said you would know what she meant."

I had forgotten about Eve's cat.

"Where is Fergie now?"

"Neeva said she could crash at her place for a few days, but after that, you would have to make other arrangements."

I wasn't sure what to do. I couldn't keep a cat. Muldoon would never stand for a sister of the feline persuasion. Eugene might consider adopting her as a playmate for Liza, but I couldn't worry about that now.

"What else happened while I was gone?" I said.

Eugene smiled. "Come with me. I'll show you."

I followed him to the door of Charley's office. As I got closer, my nose began to tingle. A moment later I understood why. The air smelled a little too spring fresh. I stepped over the threshold and gazed around the room. Charley's desktop had been cleared of all debris and polished to a blinding patina. Even his sci-fi pencil sharpener was gone. The floor was bare except for the furniture. Files that had been stacked there earlier were nowhere to be seen.

Eugene waved his arms, beaming with pride. "Tah-dah!" He marched across the room to the cabinets and opened one of the drawers. Attached to the files were red plastic tabs in perfect alignment. They made a rat-a-tat-tat sound as he raked his finger along the edges.

"Active clients," he said.

He closed that drawer and opened the one below it. Those file tabs were blue.

"Inactive clients."

He continued opening drawers and pointing until he had taken me through the entire color spectrum. The only problem was that all the folders were empty.

I felt a sense of growing alarm. "Where are Charley's files?"

"In the closet. I didn't have time to sort through them. I'll do that later. Meanwhile, don't you think the place looks so much neater now?"

"Yes, much neater."

Charley would go ballistic when he saw it. I felt as if I had a brick in my stomach.

"I thought you were going to research the names I gave you."

"I did," he said. "I got a late start, so I didn't get far, but I did find out something about Wildwood Properties."

"That's great, Eugene. What did you find?"

"For one thing, the company has been sued up the ying-yang in the last year for everything from zoning violations to destroying the habitat of the *Stephanotis floribunda* vine. A guy named Austen Kistler filed three of those lawsuits. Three. That seemed like a lot. I wanted to find out why, so I found Kistler's business address and looked up his telephone number in the reverse directory. I was really nervous at first, but I just kept telling myself he couldn't see me, didn't know where I lived, and if things went bad, I could just hang up. I called him and used my new pretext. Then I lied and lied and lied. It was liberating, Tucker—so much better than knitting. Right now I feel almost serene."

The brick in my stomach was beginning to feel like the whole shithouse.

"What did you tell Kistler?"

"That I was a reporter for the *New York Times*. Boy, did *that* ever open the floodgates. Kistler lives in a town called Ladera Bonita. He's been there forever. I guess it's a horsey kind of place. Most of the houses are set on an acre or more. Lots of stables and riding trails. He says that's all about to change. Wildwood Properties has been buying up property like crazy. They're planning to tear down all the houses and build a development called Vista Village. The city council claims it will bring new jobs and stimulate the economy, but Kistler doesn't buy that. He thinks it will destroy the rural character of the town and turn it into yuppie central."

"What's Kistler's stake in all this?"

"He owns a feed and supply store in town. He thinks the development will drive away his customers and put him out of business. I think he has other issues, but he wouldn't go into specifics. He was pretty steamed. He went on and on about how he fought in Vietnam for justice and the American way of life and now he sees it all disappearing. Like . . . duh. He's just now finding that out?"

"So he filed the lawsuits to stop the project?" I said.

"Yes, or at least delay it until he thinks of something else."

"Like what?"

"He wouldn't say, but there's going to be a town hall meeting tomorrow afternoon. Maybe we should go and see what it's all about."

"We?"

"Of course. I'm not going to invent a perfectly good pretext and then let you have all the fun."

That took me by surprise. Eugene hated crowds. I couldn't believe he wanted to mingle with a group of cranky property owners.

"Are you sure?" I said. "Things could get dicey."

"Don't be negative. I bet if we go undercover we can collect all sorts of information."

For the next hour Eugene and I continued combing through Charley's databases, but we came up with little to show for our efforts. At three, I suggested that we take a break and go to Neeva Moore's block party. I doubted that Eve Lawson would show up as promised, but at least the event would serve as a dry run to see how Eugene withstood the pressure of a noisy troupe of picnickers.

By the time we arrived in Playa del Rey, the sun had burned through the marine layer. The air was sultry and heavy with the sounds of birds chirping and planes roaring out of LAX. The party was already under way on the street a block away from Eve Lawson's rental house. Orange traffic cones kept traffic at bay. Long tables were covered with bowls filled with salads, tuna casseroles, and chips and dips. Overhead, larcenous gulls flew in a holding pattern above the food. Children with helium-filled balloons tied to their wrists were playing under the watchful gaze of parents.

The submariner was talking to two uniformed LAPD officers near a table that supported a recruitment poster and a stack of brochures. The young *GQ* cutie from Le Tastevin was chatting up a girl in a bikini who had obviously been lured in from the beach by the heady aroma of tabbouleh. I watched as *GQ* discovered the cruel reality of a stand-up buffet—that it is impossible to eat while holding a drink in one hand and a plateful of food in the other.

"You want something to eat?" I said to Eugene.

"No, thanks. I've never been big on communal food baking in the hot sun. Salmonella can be fatal, you know."

Neeva Moore was standing at the far end of the block, talking to a Los Angeles City Council member who was rumored to be building a war chest for a state senate run. A moment later she glanced up and waved. Her billowing peasant skirt cast a wide shadow around her Birkenstocks as she headed toward us.

"Thanks for coming," she said. "Tyrone is not happy that Fergie has invaded his space. I'm glad she can crash at your place till Eve gets back."

"Well, here's the problem—" I said.

She interrupted. "Hold on. I'll get her."

Neeva sauntered away in the direction of her house.

"Who's Fergie?" Eugene said.

I put my arm around his shoulders and squeezed. "Just somebody I want you to meet."

Ten minutes later Eugene and I were alone, peering at a small gray kitty through the holes of a cardboard pet carrier.

"Poor thing looks totally freaked out, doesn't she?" I said.

"I know where you're going with this, and the answer is no. I won't take her. Liza would consider it a personal affront to our friendship if I brought home another cat."

I felt a wave of panic. What now? Charley was allergic to cats. Pookie and Bruce were too busy with the yoga studio to take a pet on a long-term basis. Deegan was more the golden retriever type. Venus? Forget it. She had her hands full with her boyfriend, Max. That left only me. The problem was, I'd never had a cat before. Muldoon was my first pet ever, and I was still learning how to take care of him. Plus he was a dog and a Westie to boot. I couldn't keep both of them in the same house. Terriers were bred to chase small furry creatures and the outcome was always uncertain.

My options were limited. Fergie was my responsibility until Eve came back or I could find her a permanent home. If I was going to take her home, I needed supplies. Food. Kitty litter. Catnip. Toys. Eve must already have those things. I wondered if her house was still unlocked. The entire neighborhood seemed to be at the block party. Her street should be deserted. I decided to walk over and have a look. While I was there I could check to see if her research notes were still on the table. Maybe they offered clues to where she might be.

"Here," I said, handing Eugene the cat carrier. "You and Fergie wait in the car. I'll be back in a minute."

I scanned the crowd to make sure nobody was watching. Then I strolled down the street and turned the corner. When I got to Eve's cottage, I noticed that her chalky red Nissan was no longer in the carport. I felt a pang of alarm. I wondered if Eve had come back to get the car or if something more sinister had happened. I climbed the wooden stairs, looking over my shoulder to make sure I was still alone.

I turned the knob. The door was locked. I peered through

the window at the kitchen table. Eve's research papers were gone, along with her computer. Alternate theories swirled through my head. Eve Lawson as fugitive. Eve Lawson as captive. Eve Lawson as corpse. I remembered Charley's admonition. *Don't jump to conclusions.* Maybe she took the notes with her when she picked up the car. Maybe she was at the library researching her book.

I studied the lock. It looked flimsy. Charley had told me a couple of things about how to pick locks, but that information was theoretical. It was time to move into the practice phase of my training.

I didn't want to ruin my Visa, so I took a plastic frequent flyer card from my wallet and slid it between the door and the jamb just as I had seen Charley do at the hospital. I worked it for a couple of minutes, but the lock wouldn't budge. I tried again. The sun's heat raised a slick of perspiration on my back, making my blouse stick to my skin as if a thin layer of honey had fused the two together.

"Ms. Sinclair?"

My heart slammed into my throat. I dropped the card and turned to see Detective Tony Mendoza standing at the bottom of the stairs. He looked hot and cranky in his suit and tie. There was a bulge under his jacket where his weapon was holstered.

"You scared the shit out of me," I said. "What are you doing here?"

His arms were crossed, and he was frowning. "I guess I don't have to ask you that question."

I picked up my mileage card from the landing. "It's not what you think."

"We hardly know each other and already you can read my mind."

"I was looking for kitty litter."

"Right." He stretched out the word as taut as a rubber band ready to snap.

"I'm taking care of Eve Lawson's cat. The kitty supplies are inside the house. Sometimes she leaves the door unlocked."

His gaze was fixed and intense. "Not today, I guess."

"No," I said. "Not today." I needed to change the subject. I walked a step or two toward him. "You live in the neighborhood?"

"No. You?"

"Nope. Just visiting."

Mendoza didn't move. He just stood there blocking my exit like some muscle-bound genie that had moments before been vapor in a magic lamp. Maybe he was waiting to grant me three wishes. I wanted only one. I didn't want to be arrested for attempted burglary.

I walked down another step. "Are you staking out Eve Lawson's house?"

"Why would you think that?"

"Because you're not in uniform, so you're not part of the recruiting team. You don't live in the neighborhood, so why would you come to the party? For the food? You don't look like a tuna casserole kind of guy to me."

"You have a curiosity problem, Tucker Sinclair."

I shrugged. "It's a mutant gene."

He smiled. "Too bad it's not a smart gene. Then you wouldn't be trying to break into a house that doesn't belong to you."

If Mendoza wasn't staking out Eve Lawson's place, I wondered why he was in the neighborhood. It was an odd coincidence, and I didn't believe in them anymore, either. Then I remembered our conversation at the police station. I'd told him about Neeva Moore. Mendoza had probably interviewed her and learned that Eve had promised to attend the block party. He had come to the neighborhood just like me, hoping to find her.

Mendoza was still blocking my path, but his smile made him seem less threatening. I continued walking down the stairs until I was so close to him that our bodies were almost touching. He didn't move, just watched me with a steady gaze as if he was considering his options.

"It's been nice seeing you again," I said, "but if you'll excuse me, I have to find catnip."

Mendoza didn't move right away. He was a big guy with a big gun who was playing the alpha-dog card because he could. When he sensed that he had made me nervous enough, he stepped aside and allowed me to pass.

By the time I slid into the front seat of the Boxster, Fergie was out of the box and nestled in Eugene's lap with her head buried in his armpit.

"She's shaking like a leaf," he said. "Maybe I should take her to my vet to make sure she's okay."

Fergie was trembling, but so was I. There was no need to worry Eugene about my encounter with Detective Mendoza, so I just said, "Stellar idea."

I dropped the two of them off in the parking lot at Charley's office building and watched them drive away. I trudged upstairs to finish writing the Web site copy. At some point that afternoon, my cell phone once again chimed out *La Traviata*. It was Charley checking in.

I told him about the legal problems surrounding the Vista Village project that Eugene had discovered. I also told him that we planned to attend the town hall meeting the following day to see what we could find out. He thought that was a good idea and suggested that I take a digital camera and a tape recorder with me.

"If you want," I said, "I can drop by your office in the morning before we leave and search through a few more databases."

"Nah, I'll come in and take a look myself."

"No!"

He paused, alerted by the hysterical tone in my voice. "What do you mean by no?"

My stomach was churning. All I could think of was Charley's files stacked in the closet and his uncluttered desk.

"I mean you should be resting. Why don't you wait for a couple of days?" *Or a couple of months*, I thought.

"Okay. What am I missing here? What did you do to my office?"

I hesitated. "Eugene sort of tidied it up a bit." There was silence on the line. "It looks good, Charley, and it smells . . . fresh."

More silence followed and then a sigh. "You're starting to remind me of Dickhead."

"Your son?"

"That's the one."

"At least I'm not a twin."

"I'll reserve judgment until I meet my new secretary."

"Administrative assistant."

"Don't press your luck, Sinclair."

After we hung up, I got my laptop and briefcase and locked Charley's office. Deegan wasn't due home until eight, which gave me plenty of time to polish the Lesco report. I stopped at a liquor store for a bottle of champagne and headed for San Pedro.

## Chapter 12

Deegan's Ford Explorer was parked in the driveway when I arrived. Under normal circumstances I would have assumed that he was at home, but Charley had made me realize that assuming wasn't an exact science. He could have driven to work in a police take-home car or maybe the Explorer wouldn't start and he got a ride to work with his partner or one of his sisters.

I let myself into the house with the key he'd left for me and set my files and the computer on the kitchen table. By six thirty I'd finished the Lesco report. The muscles in my neck felt tight and knotted and my skin was sticky with après-picnic perspiration. His bathtub looked too inviting to resist, so I decided to soak away the stress of the day. I found bubble bath on a shelf under the sink, and for once I didn't think about how it had gotten there. While the tub filled with water, I placed half a dozen candles around the tub. I poured myself a glass of champagne and scanned the radio stations until I found Gloria Gaynor singing "I Will Survive." I closed the door to contain the fragrant air and slid into the warm water. For what seemed like forever I did nothing but watch the candles flicker and my skin shrivel into a network of prunelike wrinkles.

I was startled by a knock on the bathroom door. My first thought was that Deegan had come home early. I felt vulnerable sitting in my birthday suit in a borrowed bathtub, even if it was in front of my hot date. I grabbed a towel from a nearby rack and clutched it to my chest.

"Come in."

The door opened. Standing on the threshold staring at me was Deputy DA Tracy Fields.

I let out a shriek. "What are you doing here?"

She stood motionless as if her feet were frozen to the floor. "Joe's SUV was in the driveway. I rang the bell. Nobody answered. I thought he was listening to music and couldn't hear."

"When that happens, most people leave a note on the door. They don't break into the house."

"I didn't break in. I have a key."

She held it up so I could see for myself. It looked just like the one Deegan had given me. I wanted to ask why she had it but decided to save that question for him.

"I didn't know he had company," she said.

"Now you know."

Fields was slowly regaining her composure. She cocked her head and stared at me. "You look familiar. Didn't I see you at the

police station last Thursday?" Before I could respond, a knowing smile appeared on her face. "You're the witness in the Rocky
Kincaid homicide."

"I'm not a witness."

"Yes, you are. I saw you talking to Tony Mendoza. I listened
to the tape of your interview when I got back to the station.
Your name is Tucker Sinclair, and you work for that PI. Maybe I
should ask what *you're* doing here."

If that wasn't already obvious to her, I wasn't about to
explain.

"Where's Detective Deegan?" she said. "I need to talk to him."

"He's out."

"Out where?"

"I'm not sure that's any of your business," I said.

In hindsight, it was probably the wrong thing to say.

Fields crossed her arms over her chest. "Then I'll just have
to ask his lieutenant. And while I have his attention, maybe I'll
tell him that his lead detective is screwing the star witness in a
homicide investigation."

I thought about trying to placate her because I knew she
could make trouble for Deegan, but I couldn't bring myself to
do it. She was clearly in the wrong to be there. Anyone could
see that. Ratting on Deegan would only serve to expose her
misconduct.

"Careful," I said. "Threats usually come back to bite you in
the ass."

She glared at me. "We'll see about that." She turned and
walked out of the room. A moment later, I heard the front door
slam.

The bathwater had cooled to an arctic chill. I got out of the tub and dressed. For a long time I sat on the couch in the living room, staring at Deegan's piano, the one he didn't play, waiting for him to come home. An hour and a second glass of champagne later, he walked through the door, filling the room with his presence.

He smiled. "You're here."

"Are you surprised?"

He pulled me toward him, encircling me with his arms. "Not really." His tone was teasing.

He held me like that for a while, adjusting the contours of his body to mine until it felt as though there was no air separating us. I savored the intimacy of the moment because Tracy Fields was about to come between us, and I didn't know what would happen then.

"We need to talk," I said.

He seemed to sense my somber mood and released his grip. "When a woman says that, it always means trouble."

"Did you know that Tracy Fields has a key to your house?"

He took a step back. "What happened?"

I told him that she had surprised me in the bathtub, that she had recognized me and threatened to tell his supervisor about our relationship.

His anger was quiet but palpable. It frightened me.

"Will she make trouble for you?" I said.

"Maybe."

"Is Tracy Fields the woman you were talking about the other night, the one you almost married?"

He shook his head. "She's just somebody I dated for a while."

I felt relieved because he'd answered my question without hesitation.

"What are you going to do?" I said.

"I don't know."

"I'm sorry. I should have handled the situation better."

"It's not your fault. Don't worry about it."

I put my arms around him and laid my head on his chest, feeling his heart beat against my cheek. "You're screwed, aren't you?"

He didn't reply for what seemed like a long time. Finally he leaned down and kissed me. "Not yet." The teasing tone was back in his voice.

There was a second kiss and a third. More followed until it was too late to stop them even if either of us had wanted to. I slid Deegan's jacket off of his shoulders and let it drop on the sheepskin rug. By the time we'd reached the bedroom, the floor was blanketed with our discarded clothing.

Tracy Fields was the last thing on my mind now. I felt as if I'd been transported beyond pleasure to some astral plane where heights and boundaries didn't exist. Wherever I was, I wanted to linger there forever. Afterward we lay in bed clinging to each other as though something had been unleashed and decided.

"Is that the best you can do?" I teased.

His touch was soft and sensual as he traced a line with his finger down my nose to my lips. "I'll keep trying until I get it right."

"Can I get that in writing?"

He smiled. "I think you can trust me on this one."

Even after Deegan fell asleep, I lay awake beside him, inhaling the commingling aromas of bubble bath and sex, wondering what disasters the following day might bring. I counted possibilities instead of sheep—Deegan, Tracy, Eve, Charley, Eugene, Pookie, Aunt Sylvia—until I fell asleep, too. When I woke up at seven thirty the next morning, Deegan's side of the bed was empty. I ran my hand over the sheet where he had slept. It was cold. I got up and searched the house, but he wasn't there. What worried me more than where he had gone was what he might do when he got there.

# Chapter 13

I didn't know if Deegan meant for me to keep his house key, so I decided to err on the side of caution. Before I went home, I left it on the kitchen table.

When I got back to the beach, I searched the Ladera Bonita Web site. The city's population was just over five thousand. Its main industry appeared to be the occasional tourist passing through on his or her way to someplace else. The town hall meeting was listed on the events calendar along with the address of the community center where the meeting was to be held. I printed out driving directions from an Internet map site, and as Charley suggested, I packed a tape recorder and a digital camera. I picked up Eugene at his apartment in Hancock Park and proceeded to the 10 Freeway.

The air was murky with smog in East Los Angeles County, making the distant San Gabriel Mountains look like a taupe smudge against the steel gray sky. By the time we neared Ladera Bonita, the mountains were looming large and the temperature was pushing ninety-five. The off-ramp was closed for roadwork, so I took the next exit and stopped at a hamburger stand to ask directions. The teenage girl working the counter, whose IQ and hourly wage were both minimum, was at least able to point me in the general direction.

Ladera Bonita was located in a valley at the base of the mountains. As Austen Kistler had said, the homes in the residential area were set on at least an acre of land. Most were small to medium-sized, one-story ranch houses with deep setbacks and fenced corrals or pastures in lieu of front yards. Horse trailers and RVs were parked in driveways, and oleander bushes and cypress trees acted as windbreaks and shade for the horses.

The small downtown area featured a main street lined with shops, a post office, a hardware store, and a café that had a sign draped above the front door that read NO VISTA VILLAGE IN LADERA BONITA. Aside from the hostile signage, the ambiance was pure Americana, bucolic and quaint.

The Ladera Bonita Community Center was located a short distance from Kistler's feed store. I turned off of the main drag onto a dirt road that arched like a rainbow for a hundred feet or so. At the apex stood a building that looked like an old barn that had been converted into a galleria. I waited while a middle-aged woman riding a palomino horse fitted with an English saddle passed in front of the car before I pulled into an open parking space. The rider wore jodhpurs and English riding boots. Her hair was gray, and her nose lay flat and wide against her face like a camel's. She tied the horse's reins to a hitching post with hands parched dry by years in the sun. She patted her horse on the rump, raising a cloud of dust. Then she strolled to the front door of the community center and stepped inside.

The meeting wasn't due to start for another fifteen minutes, but a crowd had already gathered in the parking lot. People were carrying placards with various messages, including DEVELOPERS SUCK and PROGRESS? JUST SAY NO! Despite the chaos, Eugene seemed calm. When we got out of the car, the odor of manure hung heavily in the air and flies buzzed around our heads. We approached a man carrying a sign that read SHAME.

"I guess the meeting hasn't started yet," I said.

He glanced at me. "No, but if they had any decency they'd let us in out of this heat."

Eugene extended his hand. "I'm Bix Waverly. My sister and I were thinking of buying—"

When the man heard the word *buying*, his expression turned sour.

Anticipating trouble, I completed Eugene's sentence. "A horse. We heard this was the place to get a good deal."

"There are no good deals here," he said, "only good horses."

"Of course," I said. "That's what I meant."

The man glowered and walked away.

I turned to Eugene, staring at him in disbelief. "Bix Waverly?"

He smiled. "It's my pretext name. It has a nice ring, doesn't it?"

Before I could say anything more, the doors were opened from the inside by two uniformed security guards. One held up his hand to stop the flow of people walking toward him.

"Hold on a minute," he said. "There are a couple of ground rules."

The crowd began shouting, "Free speech, free speech."

He held up both hands this time. "You'll all get a chance to have your say. Just keep it quiet and keep it peaceful."

Someone in the crowd shouted, "Screw you, Stillwell."

Several people laughed. The guard offered no further response except to wave us in.

"I wonder which one is Kistler," I said.

Eugene scanned the crowd. "I don't know. He didn't exactly say he'd be wearing a red carnation in his lapel."

The crowd moved into a small theater, filling the seats. The woman in jodhpurs that we had seen earlier was sitting in a chair on the dais next to two men in suits. The older of the two suits stood and introduced himself as Councilman Henry Menlo.

Menlo was a doughy white guy in his fifties with a toadying smile. He looked more like a smarmy telemarketer than a statesman. He gave an impassioned spiel about how Vista Village would revitalize the Ladera Bonita economy by creating jobs and businesses that would add to the tax base and improve city services.

The younger suit was the development's project manager. He gave a splashy PowerPoint presentation replete with charts and graphs that were projected onto a large screen located at the side of the dais. As a grand finale, he displayed drawings of how Vista Village would look when it was finished.

The proposed downtown area fit the description of a mixed-use development as defined by Sam Herndon. It was a synergistic European village with tree-lined boulevards and trendy lofts and condos above boutiques and outdoor cafés. Buyers with something more palatial in mind could choose from dozens of multimillion-dollar estates that would be carved out of the hill-sides in nearby Ladera Canyon. By the time the young suit finished his presentation, I was ready to move in.

The woman in the jodhpurs spoke last. Her name was Lea Brown. She represented a neighborhood group that supported the project. Her arguments seemed tepid and without conviction. Several times the audience booed her. By the time she finished her talk, her face was glistening with sweat. When everyone on the dais had finished, Councilman Menlo fielded questions from the audience. I braced myself, waiting for all hell to break loose.

A man in front of me stood. I reached into my purse and turned on the tape recorder. If it was Kistler I didn't want to miss what he had to say.

"I hear your so-called condos are going to cost five hundred thousand to two million dollars. Those are LA prices. Nobody here can afford that. Where are the working people going to live?"

Menlo's smile was ingratiating. "That's a good question, John. I was worried about that, too. Most of the condos were sold before a single nail was hammered. That's why I made sure the plan included plenty of apartments. Three hundred ninety of them to be exact."

"How much do they go for?" the man said.

"It varies. The average price will be eighteen-fifty a month."

There was a chorus of boos.

Menlo held up his hands to quiet the crowd. "Come on, folks. That's the average price. Some will be less. You know me.

I'm committed to affordable housing. We'll have plenty of that. But land and construction costs keep going up. That drives up prices. The thing to remember is that the shops and pedestrian friendly streets of Vista Village will be a focal point for residents and tourists alike. Visitors will come here, love it, and stay to raise their families."

"Who wants that? We moved out here to get away from those people."

Somebody else shouted, "Next thing you know, you'll make it illegal for a horse to take a dump on the side of the road."

The laughter lightened the mood, but only for a moment. The arguments continued. Either Vista Village would add jobs, shopping centers, and state-of-the-art medical facilities to the community or it would cause water shortages, traffic jams, and the erosion of the quality of life in Ladera Bonita. There seemed to be no middle ground.

At around three o'clock, I heard a cough coming from the back of the room. It was a rumbling sound that was fluid and mobile. A chair scraped against the floor. I turned around to see a man in his late sixties. He wore a dusty ball cap and an olive green shirt and trousers set. The deep wrinkles in his face could have come from the sun or a lifetime of scowling. He made his way to the aisle and began walking toward the dais. As he passed by me, an odor of sweat and horses floated to my nose on a faint breeze.

The councilman's smile was wary. "Austen, good to see you again. You got a question for us about the project?"

I checked the tape recorder. It was still whirring.

"Just one, Hank. You ever read Balzac?"

Henry Menlo looked puzzled. "Can't say as I have."

"He said, 'Behind every great fortune is a crime.' That was a long time ago but it seems like it still holds true."

"Now, Austen, be reasonable. Vista Village is going to help all of us."

"It won't help me a damn bit if you destroy everything that matters."

Menlo's laugh was uneasy. "I don't know what you're talking about. The development won't destroy your business. People are always going to need to feed their livestock."

"Enjoy that money while you can, Hank, because your evil ways will catch up with you sooner than you think. I know it. You know it. And pretty soon everybody will know it. In the end you and your partners will pay the price. Don't say I didn't warn you."

Kistler turned and walked out of the room. A nervous buzz rose from the crowd. Eugene and I used the distraction to make our way out of the auditorium. We caught up with Kistler just as he was climbing into a dusty green truck.

"Mr. Kistler," I said, "can we talk to you for a minute?"

"That depends. Who are you?"

"I'm Bix Waverly," Eugene said, "the reporter who called you yesterday. This is my"—Eugene paused as if he was thinking of a pretext name for me. I gave him the evil eye—"photographer. We can help get the word out about the Vista Village scandal. Just tell us what it's all about."

Kistler's eyes narrowed in suspicion. "I don't need your help. I got something better than the *New York Times*."

He slammed the door of his pickup and started the engine. As he pulled away, I groped for the digital camera inside my purse. I pulled it out, but Kistler was gone before I could take a shot.

In the car on the way home I asked Eugene what he thought about the meeting.

"It was okay except for that poor woman who looked like she was auditioning for *National Velvet*. What a terrible speaker. The horsey people weren't very persuasive, either. Their biggest concern was having to carry a pooper-scooper for Trigger."

"Do you think Kistler might be the person following Eve Lawson?"

"You mean because of all that 'you and your partners are going to pay' business?"

"Yeah," I said. "It seems to me he has a reason to hate Wildwood and everybody connected to it. Look at it this way. Kistler's old but he's still working. Why? I can think of only two reasons. Either he needs the social contact or he needs the money. The loss of social contact doesn't give him a strong motive for revenge but losing his source of income does."

"So he kidnaps a member of Lawson's family?"

"Maybe."

"Why didn't he grab Frank Lawson or Kip Moreland?"

"Because they live behind gates and layers of security. Eve Lawson is a much easier target."

"He's just one angry old man," Eugene said. "How could he pull it off?"

"I don't know."

"You're being melodramatic," he said. "A guy who quotes Balzac can't be dangerous. I feel sorry for him. He's eccentric, but he seems harmless."

Neither of us spoke for the next few miles. Eugene leaned back against the headrest and closed his eyes. I continued thinking about my Austen Kistler theory until it no longer made sense to me, either.

A short time later, Eugene said, "By the way, I forgot to tell you yesterday. I found Hugh Canham, and you're not going to believe who he is."

## Chapter 14

"He's a *what?*" I said.

"Please keep your eyes on the road," Eugene said. "You almost ran us into a ditch. I said Hugh Canham is a female impersonator named Peaches La Rue. He does an act called Tickle Me Peach at the Sizzle Lounge in Laughlin, Nevada."

For a moment, all I could think about was that my mother and father could be Pookie and Peaches. How could this be happening to me?

"Who is this Canham guy anyway?" Eugene said.

"My aunt claims he's my father."

"Oh, my . . ."

"It isn't true. Aunt Sylvia has a screw loose."

Eugene's breathing had become shallow. "What if it *is* true? What are you going to do?"

"Don't worry. I'll handle it."

"Maybe you should call Peaches and confront him. See what he says. Maybe he'll tell you that your aunt is lying, that he's never heard of Pookie Kravitz or Mary Jo Felder or Mary Jo Sinclair or any of the other aliases your mother uses."

Eugene was right. Maybe I wouldn't have to involve my mother at all. I decided to call the Sizzle Lounge and leave a message for Hugh Canham. I would explain the circumstances and ask if he'd ever slept with my mother. If he had, I would simply ask him to supply a DNA sample. Shelly would have it tested. It wouldn't be a match. End of story. Pookie would never have to know.

I'd just dropped Eugene off at his apartment when I remembered that I had a meeting with Nathan Boles the following morning. I called Pookie on my cell phone and asked her to keep Muldoon for a couple more days. She told me that Petal was spoiling him with back rubs and that he might never want to come home. I knew better. Turkey wieners at the beach trumped back rubs any day.

By five o'clock I was home. I called the Sizzle Lounge but my request to speak with Hugh Canham met with a frosty reception. I left a message, but I knew that he would never get it. Fifteen minutes later I called back. This time I made a reservation for the following Tuesday for the ten thirty p.m. show of Tickle Me Peach.

I checked my message machine. Deegan hadn't called. I wondered if he'd gone to confront Tracy Fields and, if so, what had happened. Several times I picked up the telephone to dial his number. Each time I chickened out. I finally decided that it was better to wait for him to call me.

The Lesco report was due in the morning, so I made a few last-minute edits and e-mailed a copy to the CEO. I decided to take the rest of the day off.

For the fun of it, I got my mileage card and practiced picking the lock on my bathroom door. It wasn't as easy as Charley made it seem. After fifteen minutes of trying, I could pop it open with the card but only from the inside and only if the door was closed but not locked. That was hardly progress. Next I tried to defeat the lock on the garage door. Nada. I found a couple of old bobby pins at the bottom of a junk drawer. I removed the plastic tips and tried to open an old bike lock that I couldn't remember buying and for which I had no key. Even though I visualized the pins in perfect alignment, I couldn't get that lock open, either. I felt like a failure.

After a while I got bored with lock picking. I selected a book from my to-be-read pile and strolled outside. The deck was covered with a thin layer of sand. I got a broom from the stand-and-throw closet and swept the planks until they were clean. The deck chairs and chaise longue sported green canvas cushions, so from a distance you could hardly tell that the furniture was plastic. I dusted off the two chairs with my hand, the one that rocks and the one that doesn't. Then I swept the chaise.

The sun was setting on the purple-flowered sand verbenas growing on the nearby dunes. A lone beachcomber sat watching the waves break in one of the three Adirondack chairs that stood between Mrs. D's house and mine. My mind wandered. Maybe I needed a barbecue grill like Deegan's. I could throw parties and invite my friends. I tabled the idea for the moment and sprawled on the lounge chair, Muldoon's favorite outdoor retreat, and opened the book, a crime novel by T. J. McGinn. It was still light enough to read but somewhere in the middle of chapter two I fell asleep and dreamed of case-hardened detectives in peach feather boas.

Santa Monica is a single runway airport located approximately five miles inland from the beach in the middle of a densely populated residential neighborhood. As instructed, I arrived at eight o'clock on Monday morning for my meeting with Nathan Boles, CEO of N.B. Construction. A woman stood near the front door of the Typhoon Restaurant wearing navy blue trousers and a light blue shirt with epaulettes. She was in her early forties, five four or so with dimples in her cheeks. She introduced herself as Captain Gordon and led me onto the tarmac to a private jet. Once we were inside, she disappeared into the cockpit.

A male flight attendant took me on a tour of the Gulfstream IV, which was outfitted with everything a successful executive needed, two bedrooms, showers, fax, Internet, grand salon, etched glass conference room with leather seats. Van Gogh's *Sunflowers* was displayed on the wall. It looked real but turned out to be an image on a plasma TV.

"Where are we going?" I said.

"The Sequoia Club. Ever heard of it?"

I had. It was a private club located somewhere on the Sonoma coast, and it was as exclusive as you could get. The waiting list to get in was at least twenty years long. According to rumor, its members were the movers and shakers of the U.S. economy and included at least two former presidents and the leaders of several European nations. I was intrigued by the place and willing to play along as long as Captain Gordon got me back at a reasonable time.

We had been in the air a little more than an hour when the plane began its descent into a small airport in the middle of nowhere. A limo drove me along a narrow serpentine road that was lined with hairy pampas grass, thistles, and redwood trees bowed by the weather. Just over the cliff a thousand feet below, cows grazed on a grassy plateau above the rugged coastline. As the highway passed beneath the limo, I watched as the sun sliced through the trees, stenciling lacy patterns on the pavement.

The driver let me out in front of a rustic lodge. I waited in the great room under the watchful eye of the woman concierge while a runner was sent to find Nathan Boles. The room featured a two-story stone fireplace and tasteful furniture upholstered in leather and fabric in shades of forest green and wine. Stuffed animal heads with glassy eyes hung on the walls. The aroma of cigar smoke, leather, and dusty fur made it a place in which only men could be content.

I was just conjuring up a scenario in which the relatives of all those animals had formed a hit squad bent on revenge when Nathan Boles walked through the door. Tall and lean, he moved with the fluid grace of an athlete. His gray hair and unlined face were a contradiction, but I guessed that he was somewhere in his late forties.

"I assume you haven't been here before," he said. "Let me show you around. Dina, could you fit Ms. Sinclair with the appropriate footwear?"

Dina glanced at my feet and disappeared into a back room. She returned a moment later with a pair of hiking boots and a lightweight jacket. I slipped them on, feeling clumsy and overdressed.

"Let's take a walk," he said.

We traveled along a narrow path that had been cleared through the brown grass and continued through a stand of sequoias to a cliff striated with tan and gray sedimentary rocks that looked like layers of lasagna.

"I haven't seen Eve in a while," he said. "How is she?"

I hesitated, not wanting to reveal that I didn't know how she was.

"I didn't realize you knew her."

"We met through her father, Frank Lawson."

I nodded to acknowledge the connection. "She's working hard on her book."

"That's what you said on the telephone. What possessed her to start writing?"

"She thought it would be cathartic."

"That sounds like a tall order. What exactly is she writing about?"

"The Los Angeles real estate boom after World War Two."

His smile seemed strained. "That's it? Doesn't sound very sexy."

"To each his own, I guess."

I wanted to ask him about Eve, who her friends were, who

she trusted, why she had left Los Angeles a year ago, but I was supposed to be collaborating with her on a book about World War II. If I asked those kinds of questions Boles might get suspicious about my motives for wanting to speak with him.

"Is she staying with her father in Bel Air?" he said.

"No. She rented a place near the ocean."

"If Eve wanted information, why didn't she contact me herself?"

I wasn't sure how much to tell him, so I said, "I think she's awfully busy right now. I could ask her to call you if you'd like me to."

He shook his head and then looked away. The beach below was silent except for the sound of waves crashing on the rocky shoreline. Brown pelicans and gray gulls rested on the sand near a shelter built from driftwood. A family of three black-tailed deer grazed in a meadow about a hundred feet away. Their ears twitched in response to every sound we made.

Boles gestured toward the sequoia-covered hillside. "I'm working with the coastal commission to develop two hundred one-acre luxury estates up here. The project will include a resort and spa. The setting is beautiful, don't you think?"

I nodded. "It almost seems a shame to spoil it."

Boles didn't seem at all annoyed by my comment. In fact, he smiled. "I see that you're one of *them*. I'm sorry to say you're not alone. We were due to break ground a month ago until somebody raised a stink. The project will proceed, but it will cost everybody more money now. Such a waste."

"Kip Moreland's Ladera Bonita project is having similar problems. It's a mixed-use development called Vista Village. Are you familiar with it?"

He paused as if waiting for me to say more. When I didn't, he said, "I know about the project."

"What can you tell me about it?"

Boles stopped walking and looked at me. "Did Eve tell you much about her family?"

I noted that he'd changed the subject, but I decided to let him tell the story in his own way.

"Not really. I know that her father was a successful developer."

Boles resumed walking. "Do you know how he got that way?"

"No, but I'd like to."

"Frank Lawson lived in Ladera Bonita many years ago with his first wife, Dorothy. Eve was born there. He made a comfortable living as a pharmacist in a retail drugstore, but he wasn't rich by any means. When Dorothy died, he sold some farmland in Ventura that she'd inherited from her father and went into partnership with a developer to build a three-hundred-thousand-square-foot shopping mall. That's how Wildwood Properties was born."

"How did you meet Lawson?"

"My father started N.B. Construction after the war. He made good money, but he didn't care much for the business side of construction. He was a carpenter at heart, a real craftsman. When I got out of college, he brought me in as a partner. My first project with Frank was a strip mall in San Fernando. I finished on deadline and under budget. That got his attention."

"So other projects followed."

"Yes. It was a successful alliance."

"What about Kip Moreland? Have you worked with him, too?"

"Only once."

"What happened?"

Boles's gaze was tilted downward, watching his feet move along the path. "Look, I agreed to speak with you for a couple of reasons. First, Sam Herndon and I go way back. He asked me to tell you about real estate development so you could help Eve with her book. I'll give you what I can, but if you tell anybody you got the information from me, I'll deny it, and I'll make you regret that you accepted my hospitality today."

Boles smiled again, which softened the threat somewhat, but there was little doubt in my mind that he was dead serious about me keeping whatever secrets he had to tell.

I nodded to indicate that I understood.

"When Kip took over the business, he had no clue what he was doing, and he was too arrogant to admit it. He lost a lot of money and pissed off a lot of people, including investors I brought into the deal. My father and I spent too many years building the company's reputation to throw it all away because of a screwup like Kip Moreland."

"Why did Frank Lawson give him the job?"

"Why don't you ask Eve that question?"

"Because I'd like to hear the answer from a neutral party."

"Frank is a stubborn guy," he said. "He thought he could beat the Alzheimer's. When he realized the disease was getting to him, he was forced to start succession planning. He wanted to hire somebody from outside the family, but Meredith pressured him into giving Kip a chance."

"Had Kip worked in development before?"

"I don't think Kip had ever worked anywhere before." Boles's tone seemed brittle. "He's spent most of his life as a member of the idle rich."

"He must be doing okay now," I said. "The Vista Village condos have sold out, and they haven't even been built yet."

"Everybody lucks out once in a while."

"Would you ever consider working with Moreland again?"

"No."

"I gather you two parted on less than friendly terms."

"If you want dirt on Kip Moreland, I suggest you talk to Eve. She could tell you more than enough to fill a book. If you want information about the housing boom after World War Two, I'll tell you what I know. That's why you're here. Right?"

"Right," I said.

His gaze met mine and lingered there for some time. He seemed forthright enough, but there was a shrewd look on his face that made me wonder if he knew much more than he was willing to tell.

On the way back to the lodge, Boles regaled me with stories his father had told him about his early years in construction. If he wondered why I wasn't taking notes, he didn't ask.

Just before we reached the front door, Boles said, "I'm looking to buy a small travel wholesaler based in Chicago. They package adventure tours that might fit in nicely with a development I'm building near the Colorado River. I need somebody to check out the company and see if it looks as good in person as it does on paper. Would you be interested in the job?"

I was surprised and flattered. "Yes, I would."

"Good. Captain Gordon will fly you to Chicago in the morning. Seven sound okay?"

I found it curious that Boles would offer me a job without preamble and doubted that the move was spontaneous. He had probably checked my background before I ever stepped onto his corporate jet. He was a powerful man who could refer me to other powerful clients if he liked my work. If I turned down his offer I could be giving up a chance at real success. If I said yes I would be abandoning my other clients, including Charley Tate. I couldn't do that, especially with Charley injured. He needed my help more than Boles needed my services.

"I'd love to work with you," I said, "but I can't leave tomorrow. What about next week?"

He shook his head. "Maybe another time."

I was disappointed to lose the opportunity but annoyed by his lack of flexibility, which seemed more like a macho power play than a time crunch problem.

Boles opened the door and gestured for me to go inside. "I have a meeting in a few minutes, but you're welcome to stay for lunch. Our chef is French. The special today is sole en pipérade with a cold pumpkin soufflé for dessert. I guarantee you'll remember the experience for a long time."

"You sound like a gourmand."

He chuckled. "I know the names of some of the dishes but that's about it. I took a cooking class once. The most important thing I learned was that I should stay out of the kitchen."

I turned down the lunch offer. Instead, I returned the shoes and jacket to Dina and asked her to call the limo to take me back to the airport. While I waited in the room full of dead animal heads, I thought about what I'd just learned. Kip Moreland had pissed off a lot of people. Nathan Boles was one of them. I was curious to know if there were others and if they were the type of people who would take their revenge on Eve Lawson. I wondered where she was. If Charley wasn't able to find some viable clues soon, the chances of finding her might disappear forever, just like the pristine Sonoma coastline.

On the flight back to Los Angeles, I remembered that Boles had told me there were two reasons why he'd been willing to talk to me. One was his friendship with Sam Herndon. I wondered what the other reason was.

# Chapter 15

That night, at around six thirty, I heard a knock at my side door. I peeked through the shutters and saw Joe Deegan standing on the deck holding a couple of grocery bags. He was wearing denim jeans and a teal T-shirt that fit tight across his chest. A pair of sunglasses hung from the neck of his shirt.

I pointed to the bags. "You moving in?"

He raised his eyebrows in a suggestive way. "You making me an offer?"

I smiled. "Let's see what's in the bag. Then I'll decide."

He reached in and pulled out a blue Frisbee that he'd bought for Muldoon. He put his hand back in the bag and brought out a bottle of Dom Pérignon champagne. "Does this win me any points?"

"When does the moving van get here?"

He smiled. "How did I know that's what you were going to say?"

Deegan walked past me into the kitchen, where he unloaded groceries from the bag, an onion, a zucchini, fresh basil, Parmesan cheese, and something green and leafy.

"What's all this?" I said.

"I'm going to make you a frittata."

"What's that green stuff?"

He folded the bag and set it on the counter. "Swiss chard."

To tell the truth, I wasn't at all sure what a frittata was, much less Swiss chard.

"Got any eggs?" he said.

"I don't know. What do they look like?"

He grinned and opened the refrigerator to see for himself.

"You disappeared on Sunday," I said. "Where were you?"

"Taking care of business."

I took a frying pan from the cupboard and set it on the stove. "Business with Tracy Fields?"

He shot me a glance.

"Sunday isn't a workday," I continued. "She must have been at home."

He ran water over the zucchini. "She was."

"Did you put out any fires?"

"Let's just say it didn't go as well as I hoped it would."

"Why? Because she wanted something you weren't willing to give her?"

He opened a drawer and pulled out a chopping knife. "You might say that."

"And what did she want?"

He handed me the onion and the knife. "Something I'm saving only for you." He was teasing me, but there was an edge beneath the banter.

After dinner we went out to the deck to watch the sun set on the water. We both squeezed onto the chaise longue. I put my head on Deegan's chest and breathed in the aroma of laundry soap and olive oil.

"I've been trying to reach Charley Tate," he said. "I want to talk to him about Eve Lawson. He's never in his office."

"He was in a traffic accident the night Eve disappeared. He injured his back and spent a night in the hospital. He hasn't been going in to the office every day."

"Is he having any luck finding her?"

"Not yet."

"You'll let me know when he does. Right?"

"I'll tell Charley to keep you posted."

I felt him pull away from me. "That's not what I asked."

I responded in kind by rolling onto my back, pretending that I was looking for stars in the opaque sky. "Eve is Charley's client."

"She's a person of interest in a homicide investigation."

I didn't like it when he pulled rank on me, so I didn't answer right away.

"Okay," I said. "I'll let you know when he finds her." I waited to let that digest before asking my next question. "Any suspects in the Rocky Kincaid case?"

"I have a couple of theories."

"Care to share them with me?"

"How about we share dishwashing duties instead. I have to

be at work early tomorrow for a meeting with the captain, so I should get on the road."

Deegan was always meeting with the captain, so my pulse was only slightly elevated. "Everything okay?"

He nodded.

"Does this meeting have anything to do with the task force?"

He seemed puzzled by my question. "No. We only have one task force operating at the moment. The vice unit is investigating bookmaking at a local sports bar."

I felt relieved, because that meant Tracy and Deegan wouldn't be working together anytime soon.

Neither of us made a move to get up. We lay together like that for a few more minutes, lost in our thoughts.

"How did you leave it with Tracy Fields?" I said.

He leaned in close and brushed the hair away from my forehead with a gentle sweep of his hand. "I got my key back."


The following day was Tuesday. Charley worked from home all day because his back was bothering him. Eugene had returned to work the reception desk at Aames & Associates under the watchful eye of Harriet in HR. He called during his break and reported that the vet had found Fergie dehydrated and infested with fleas but otherwise healthy. She was confined to his bedroom until she and Liza could bond under supervision. I held my breath, but he didn't say a word about returning Fergie to me. Just to make sure he didn't bring it up, I told him I would be out of town until Wednesday afternoon.

I didn't have to leave for the airport to catch my flight to

Laughlin until three, so I finished writing the text for the Tate Investigations brochure and e-mailed it to the graphic artist so she could prepare it for printing. I also called the Web designer to discuss the launch date for Charley's Web site.

If Charley found Eve Lawson in the next week or so, my work for Tate Investigations would be finished. I needed to move forward, so I made a few calls to line up start dates for other clients who were waiting for my services, including a woman who planned to open a shop that sold gourmet bonbons made from recipes she'd inherited from a great-grandfather who had been a Belgian chocolatier. I'd have to do further research before I was convinced that candy alone would generate enough revenue to warrant the cost of rent, furnishings, and labor.

After that, I turned my attention to the marketing plan I'd promised to write for Kismet Yoga Studio. When it first opened, Bruce had refused to charge for his classes, preferring instead to accept voluntary donations. Even my mother realized that the idea was a nonstarter.

The problem was, in Los Angeles yoga teachers were a dime a dozen. They taught in studios, gyms, offices and private homes, on the beach, in the air, everywhere. There was chair yoga for seniors, weight-loss yoga, kids yoga, goal-setting yoga, chakra-awakening yoga, Christian yoga, and I had no doubt that some entrepreneur would soon come up with a yoga class to help us deal with the high price of gasoline. If Bruce was going to succeed, he had to distinguish himself from the pack. Either he needed a tabloid photo of an A-list movie star walking into his studio, or he had to come up with a unique twist on an old art.

I had located the results of a recent study by a nonprofit health care facility in Seattle. It showed that the control group that had taken classes featuring a gentle form of yoga reported more pain relief than the other two control groups who took no yoga classes. Based on the health benefits, I was hoping that Bruce could get some local physicians and chiropractors to participate in a series of free lectures about the benefits of Downward Facing Dog. I had already targeted the five most successful yoga classes in the city. As soon as I had some time, I planned to take a class at each one in order to find out what made them so popular. All that was on the back burner. First I had to convince Hugh Canham aka Peaches La Rue to help me prove to my aunt that he wasn't my father.

Laughlin, Nevada, is a small resort town located at the intersection of the Mojave Desert and the Colorado River, about two miles west across the bridge from Bullhead City, Arizona. It's a place where people can water-ski and lose their child's college fund all in the same weekend.

There were no direct flights from LAX. I had to change planes in Las Vegas and rent a car in Lake Havasu City for the forty-mile drive. It was getting late and halfway there I started to feel sleepy. I was scanning through the local radio stations looking for some lively music to keep me awake when I heard the announcer mention Vista Village. I cranked up the volume. He was inviting interested buyers to take a virtual tour through the model homes at either of the Wildwood sales offices, which were located in Beverly Hills and Las Vegas. I was curious to know why Wildwood Properties had a sales office in Nevada. I decided to find out. I pulled to the side of the road and jotted down the address. There was a two-hour layover in Vegas on my return trip. That left me ample time to taxi over to the Wildwood office and see what they were up to.

# Chapter 16

I was staying at the Laughlin Edgewater, one of the high-rise hotels and casinos that snake along the edge of the Colorado River. I parked the car and entered by the front door, ambling past the blue Kokopelli painted on the column supporting the entrance portico. I'd been to the Southwest before and knew that Kokopelli is a mythical Native American flute player who brings good luck and good health. From the miserable expressions on the pasty-looking people I saw leaving the casino, Koko was going to be working overtime.

The lobby was filled with people either milling around or lounging on cushy chairs, looking bleary-eyed from too much booze or too little sleep. I could almost tell the gamblers from the vacationers by the degree of their sunburns. Dorcas Kincaid had told Charley and me that Rocky had a gambling problem. I wondered if he had ever lost money in Laughlin.

I checked into my room and spent some time enjoying the panoramic view of the river and the mountains, watching powerboats and Jet Skis navigate the water below as boaters enjoyed the remnants of fading sunlight.

Hugh Canham aka Peaches La Rue appeared four nights a week in Tickle Me Peach at the Sizzle Lounge in a hotel just down the street from the Edgewater, where I was staying. I arrived early for the ten thirty show. The lounge hadn't opened yet, but there was a hostess at the door. I asked her if I would be able to get Canham's autograph. She told me nobody was allowed backstage, but if I hung around the lobby after the show I might be able to catch him before he went up to his room.

To pass the time, I wandered around the casino for a while, people watching. Thirty minutes before the performance started, I was seated in a medium-sized nightclub, sharing a table for four with a gay couple from Denver and a schoolteacher from Omaha. In front of me was a glass of white wine, one half of the two-drink minimum. The schoolteacher told us the trip was a present she'd given herself for her sixtieth birthday. Brett and BJ were in Laughlin for a family reunion.

At exactly ten thirty the house lights dimmed. A combo that included a drummer, a bass player, and a pianist began to play. A throaty purr cued a spotlight that illuminated a tall, thin figure with a long, narrow nose. He was wearing a glittery peach-colored sheath, a matching peach wig, and enough makeup to stucco a small hacienda. The guy had a better figure than I did. A moment later he belted out, "Whatever Peaches Wants, Peaches Gets."

Canham was not lip-synching, and his voice was surprisingly pleasant. The audience clapped and whistled their approval.

The show was bawdy and funny and I laughed in spite of myself. Peaches clowned around with his four male backup singers until the crowd was screaming with laughter, especially during one of the more strenuous dance numbers when his false boobs began gravitating toward his navel and had to be rescued by his able assistants. There were two short intermissions, during which Peaches changed into different wigs and a variety of outfits decorated with glitter, rhinestones, sequins, and fur, all in peach. An hour and a half later it was over.

The schoolteacher left two unfinished cosmopolitans on the table and went up to her room. Brett and BJ invited me for drinks at the Flamingo, but I declined. Instead, I waited around the lobby.

Forty-five minutes later, I saw Hugh Canham heading toward the elevator wearing sneakers and a black nylon warm-up suit. His peach wig was gone, exposing a shiny dome rimmed by a band of brown hair.

"Excuse me, Mr. Canham. Can I talk to you for a minute?"

He pushed the elevator UP button. "Sorry. I'm late for a meeting. Perhaps some other time."

He had an accent. It was faint but it sounded Australian.

"I'm Tucker Sinclair, Mary Jo Felder's daughter. I'm not sure if you remember her. You two dated thirty years ago."

He turned to look at me with a probing stare. Up close I could see that he still had a glob of makeup on his neck and that his eyes were blue. Pookie's eyes were blue, too. Mine were brown. My grandpa Felder said they were the color of Old Grand-Dad

Kentucky bourbon. Two blue-eyed parents didn't prove anything. I remembered studying a recessive gene chart in high school science class. Brown eyes could pop up when you least expected them.

"Of course I remember Mary Jo." He glanced around. "Is she here?"

I told him no and thought I saw disappointment in his expression. If so, it was fleeting. The elevator door opened. A heavyset couple and their young son moved over to make room for Canham. He stepped inside.

"Please send her my regards," he said.

Before the door closed, I blurted out, "Are you my father?"

Canham held out his arm to keep the door from closing. He stared at me for a moment without speaking. Finally he said, "Standing up all night in high heels is a bitch. I need a drink."

The woman in the elevator gasped. Her husband scowled and nudged her with his elbow. The kid yelled, "Stop hitting Mommy!"

Canham took me to a small lounge in the hotel and offered to buy me a cocktail. I declined. I had already consumed my two-drink limit. He sipped a Scotch and soda while I explained the situation with my aunt Sylvia and the house and her most recent claims about my parentage.

"So if you'd be willing to provide a DNA sample," I said, "I could at least prove that you're not my father and maybe my aunt would leave me alone."

"Did your mother tell you how we met?" he said.

"No. She doesn't know about my aunt's allegations. In fact, she doesn't know I'm here."

Canham went on as if I hadn't spoken. "We were in an acting

class together. The coach paired us up to do an on-camera cold reading. When he played back the tape, I looked like a clod, but your mother had an amazing blend of spontaneity and naïveté that was pure magic. I was quite smitten with her."

"How long did you date?"

"Not long."

"But long enough to have sex."

He smiled. "Yes, my knowledge of your mother was definitely carnal."

"Why did you break up?"

Canham agitated the ice in his glass and took a drink. "That's a sad but all too common story. She met somebody else."

"My father?"

He set his glass on the coaster, adjusting it until it was perfectly centered. "That seems to be in dispute at the moment. Let's say she met the man who became her husband."

"Did you have any reason to believe that my mother was pregnant when you two broke up?"

He frowned. "No. I would have never let her leave me if I'd known that."

"Would you be willing to provide a DNA sample?"

Canham again swirled the ice around in his glass and downed the last of the Scotch. "In truth, I'd rather not know. It gives me something interesting to think about." He stood. "It's been a pleasure, Tucker, but I have to run. I'm meeting my wife for a nightcap, and she doesn't like it when I'm late."

I felt my eyebrows arch. "You're married?"

His smile was wry. "Yes. I also have a daughter. Her name is Mary Jo. In some ways you remind me of her."

He threw a twenty-dollar bill on the table and walked out of the room, leaving me to wonder why he had named his daughter after my mother.

For the rest of that night, I thought about what I would do if my aunt Sylvia arrived at my door with an eviction notice. Even if she failed in her efforts to get the beach cottage, I would still be saddled with the cost of defending myself. It made me angry that my aunt thought she could make false claims against innocent people and not be held accountable. There had to be a way to stop her. I just didn't know what it was. Yet.

I left Laughlin early the next morning and drove to Lake Havasu City to catch my flight. When I arrived at McCarran International Airport in Las Vegas, I made sure that I had my boarding pass for the second leg of the trip. Then I exited the terminal and found a taxicab driver who would take me to the Wildwood Properties sales office. I told him that I was on a tight schedule and negotiated the price for him to wait for me while I was inside.

The high-rise hotel-casinos along the Strip were already doing a booming business with vacationers from Boise to Baltimore, trying to recoup their losses before heading to the hotel swimming pool.

The cab cruised past the Eiffel Tower, the Statue of Liberty, the Pyramids, and an erupting volcano before stopping in front of a three-story building on a side street about a mile from Las Vegas Boulevard. There was a sign in the window that read VISTA VILLAGE IN BEAUTIFUL LADERA BONITA. HOMES NOW AVAILABLE.

The lobby was tastefully decorated with travertine marble floors and modern furniture that looked angular but still comfortable. The walls were covered with modern paintings. A few well-placed plants made the place look attractive but staged.

A young Asian woman wearing a push-up bra and a straw cowboy hat sat at a desk. Her hand was propping up her head. She looked like she would rather be anyplace but where she was.

"How's business?" I said.

She smiled as she tucked some silky black hair behind one ear. "Great. We just opened our offices, and we've already sold eighty percent of the condo units. We're offering a hundred dollars if you watch a promo about the development."

Councilman Menlo claimed that all of the condos had been sold. Now I was hearing eighty percent. If sales were so brisk, I wondered why Wildwood was bribing people to go on a virtual tour. Perhaps Kistler's lawsuits had been causing problems for the development.

"I hear the project has some detractors," I said.

That didn't set well with her. "Look, if you're not interested, don't waste my time."

"I'm interested. I'd just like to know what I'm getting into."

"My boss is a partner. If you go on the tour, he'll answer all of your questions."

I wrote my name on the contact card that she provided, and as instructed, I took the elevator to the third floor. When the elevator door opened, I felt as if I had stepped into somebody's living room. There were a fireplace and furniture, a wide-screen TV and a DVD player. French doors opened onto a patio. There weren't many people interested in buying a condo in Ladera Bonita that morning. In fact, I was the only person there, which made me feel unsettled.

A man in his fifties greeted me. He had a high forehead and wide-set eyes. His suit looked well cut and was probably expensive, but the buttons didn't close in the front. It looked as if he had gained weight but refused to buy the next size up. He introduced himself as Vince Cimino and offered me a self-assured handshake.

"Looks like a slow morning," I said.

Cimino's expression seemed neutral as he sized me up. "That doesn't matter. We're always ready to deal."

He took the contact card out of my hand and studied it. I noticed that his fingernails were beautifully manicured.

"Do you own property now?" he said.

"Yes, a house."

"Where's it located?"

"On the beach at Zuma," I said. "Just north of Malibu."

He set the contact card on the end table as if that was all the information he needed and handed me a brochure. It featured the artist's rendering of a completed Vista Village that I'd seen at the town hall presentation plus a sketchy map of the area.

"I was surprised to find a sales office in Vegas. Isn't Ladera Bonita a small town in California?"

"Vista Village has multimillion-dollar estates and a central village with the ambience of Aspen or Gstaad but warmer and more luxurious. It's going to put Ladera Bonita on the map. Wait till you see the place. You're going to love it."

He picked up a DVD and laid it on the machine's tray.

"That won't be necessary," I said. "I've already seen the plans.

I like the concept, but some people say Vista Village may not be a good investment."

He smiled with forced patience. "Then some people are wrong."

"I heard that several lawsuits were filed against the project, and the neighborhood has become a war zone."

He waved his hand as if he was brushing away a pesky fly. "Those are nuisance suits. Any nutcase can file one. They'll go away. You can trust me on that one."

"So you plan to settle before they go to trial?"

"What does it matter? They'll be settled one way or the other."

"Is that what Kip Moreland told you?"

Cimino was no longer making any attempt to mask his annoyance. "You know Moreland?"

"We've met."

He picked up the contact card from the table and studied it. He moved so close to me that I could smell his heavy citrus cologne. "Look, Tucker, you don't want to watch the movie, and I get the impression that you're not here to buy, so let's call it a day. Just put your address on the card, and we'll send you your hundred bucks."

A sinister tone had crept into his voice.

"Forget the money," I said, slipping the brochure into my purse. "I wouldn't want to take advantage."

Cimino was an intimidating figure. I wondered what kind of pressure he could bring to bear if the Vista Village development ran into a snag. He'd been so certain that Austen Kistler's lawsuits would disappear. It made me wonder if Kistler might be in danger of disappearing along with them.

When the elevator door had opened again, I glanced back. Cimino was leaning against the fireplace, arms crossed, watching me like a leopard scrutinizing a baby gazelle. All the way to the airport, I kept peering through the back window of the cab until I could no longer feel Cimino's predatory glare boring into my back.

I flew back to Los Angeles and picked up my car from airport parking. Since it was still early, I stopped at a computer store to buy an accounting program so Charley could produce invoices and keep track of his clients and his bottom line. After I made my purchase, I drove to his office to install the software on his computer.

Eugene hadn't been at Tate Investigations since Saturday, but the air still smelled of cleansers and floral air fresheners. I set the program on the reception desk and looked around for the computer. It was gone. Charley must have wheeled it back to his office.

I strolled into the back room to have a look and found Charley lying on his back on the floor with his eyes closed. I felt a rush of panic. I ran over to where he lay.

"Charley?"

He opened his eyes. "Relax. I'm just resting."

I looked up and noticed that the closet door was open and some of his files were once again stacked on the floor around his desk.

"You're not supposed to lift anything. You should have asked for help."

"It doesn't matter. I found what I needed."

Lying on the floor like that, he reminded me of a sunbather

on the beach at Maui. I crossed my arms, adopting what I hoped was a stern demeanor.

"You're going to cause permanent damage to your back. Do you want to spend the rest of your life in a wheelchair?"

"Can it, Sinclair. You're starting to sound like Lorna. Ask me what I found."

I blew out a frustrated breath of air.

"Okay. What did you find?"

"Eve Lawson's buddy at the suicide hotline. Christie Swink. I was just about to go talk to her. How about you and me take a drive?"

## Chapter 17

Christie Swink worked for the publishing industry as a media escort. Her job required her to pick up out-of-town authors from the airport, take them to the hotel, and ferry them to book signings and radio and television interviews. When Charley had called to set up the meeting with Swink, he'd told her that Eve was missing and that her family had hired him to locate her. After hearing that, she seemed eager to help.

We caught up with her on the second floor music section of the Borders store on Westwood Boulevard. Her author du jour was nearby, sitting at a table on a raised platform. He was alone with a stack of books and a pen, trying with limited success to look optimistic.

Christie was in her midtwenties with thick tendrils of tangerine Medusa-like hair. Her makeup was too heavy and the colors too harsh for her age, including the hooker red lipstick that had leached onto her teeth. Her eyes were a shade of washed-out olive green that even Crayola couldn't name.

"If you don't mind me asking," I said, "why did you leave the Sanctuary?"

"Nick kicked me out of the program," she said. "He thought I was too flippant to be counseling people who wanted to kill themselves."

Her gaze darted from Charley to me as if judging our reaction to her words. Were they too glib? Too cynical? Past experiences must have taught her to be cautious.

"Eve left town around that same time," Charley said. "Do you know why?"

"I think it was a lot of things. For one, the training bummed her out. I don't think she was cut out for suicide prevention. Plus, she told me that living in LA was too expensive."

"I thought Eve was living off a trust fund," I said.

"She was, but when her dad got sick, he turned over control of everything to her stepmom. She changed the trust so Eve got less money each month and she couldn't get control of the balance until age fifty. After that, Eve really had to watch her pennies. That's why she was living in her dad's guesthouse."

Eve had given a lot of personal information to a relative stranger. She had also given Neeva Moore details about her life that she hadn't shared with Charley. Maybe she felt more comfortable talking to other women. Still, it was curious, so I asked Christie to explain how the conversation had come about.

"She was only at the Sanctuary for a week or so, but every

day we went to lunch at this Mexican restaurant down the street. They had a little old lady out front making homemade tortillas. She looked like she was straight out of a Mexican market in Chiapas. Eve lived in Spain for a while, so she spoke Spanish. She liked to talk to the woman while we waited for our table. Eve never ordered anything without obsessing about the price. I thought that was odd for a rich girl, so I asked her why."

Our conversation was interrupted by an announcement over the public address system alerting customers that the author was signing books on the second floor. In this case, signing books was a euphemism. The author was sitting alone at the table reading a book—his own.

"You know where Eve went after she left LA?" Charley said.

"Not really. She traveled a lot, so it could have been anywhere."

"Who else would she have told about her plans?"

"I don't know."

"Does the name Rocky Kincaid mean anything to you?" I said.

She thought for a moment. "Huh-uh."

"Did Eve ever mention any hobbies she had?" I said.

Christie's expression brightened as if she had finally been presented with a question she could answer. "She liked to cook."

*Big deal*, I thought. Deegan liked to cook, too, but that wouldn't help me find him if he went missing.

"In fact," Christie went on, "she was taking a French cooking class with her boyfriend."

"Do you remember his name?" Charley said.

"She never said. I got the impression they were keeping the

relationship a secret. I just assumed it was because the guy was married."

"Where was the cooking class?"

"I don't remember the name of the place, but I think it was somewhere near the Helms Bakery."

"Is there anything you might know about Eve that we haven't asked?" Charley said.

A potential customer had drifted to the author's table. He picked up a book, opened it to the flap copy, and started reading.

"I can't think of anything else," Christie said, "and I can't talk any longer. I have to go back to work."

Christie Swink hurried back to her author. Charley and I took the elevator down to the parking garage. We were both quiet until we got in the car.

"What's the likelihood that anyone at that cooking school would remember one of their students from a year ago?" I said.

"Very unlikely."

"So what are you thinking?"

"That we're getting nowhere fast."


Charley was in pain from lifting all those files out of his closet, so as soon as I dropped him off at his car, he headed for home. I volunteered to stay at the office and follow up on the cooking class angle.

I logged on to the Internet and typed in "French cooking classes in Los Angeles" and came up with a list of names. I narrowed the search to two schools that were near the Helms Bakery. I called both and told them that Eve Lawson had recommended their curriculum. I asked if they could look up her name and verify which classes she'd taken. Once I'd gotten that far, I hoped they would give me the name of Eve's boyfriend.

One administrator flat out refused to give me the information. The other confessed that a few months back the school's computer had been infected with a virus that destroyed the hard drive. There was no information to verify.

I massaged the facts again. Eve took a cooking class with a boyfriend whose name she was keeping a secret. Christie Swink thought it was because he was married. Eve's last known boyfriend was Rocky Kincaid. Rocky had been married a year ago. We still didn't know when Eve had started dating Rocky. If they'd been together back then, maybe their relationship had been a factor in the Kincaids' divorce. I wasn't sure if the information was important, but I decided to ask the only person that might be able to answer that question, Rocky's ex-wife, Dorcas Kincaid.

When I arrived at the beauty salon, Dorcas looked too busy for the impertinence she had shown on my previous trip to visit her. She was cutting the hair of a toddler sitting in a booster seat, screaming in an earsplitting pitch. Most of the other customers were grimacing, except the older ones, who I suspected were too deaf to notice. The kid's mother ignored the tantrum as she collected locks of her daughter's hair from the floor where they'd fallen and tucked them into a pink envelope.

When Dorcas saw me, she scowled.

"Wait over there," she said. "I'll be done in a sec."

I sat in a chair under a broken hair dryer. Five minutes passed, and I was getting bored. I picked up a magazine from a stand next to the chair. On the cover was an unflattering photo of the latest

Hollywood celebrity to check into rehab. I thumbed through the pages and looked at the pictures. When I returned the magazine to the stand, I noticed the label on the cover. It listed Dorcas Kincaid's name but the magazine hadn't been sent to the shop. The address was different. The subscription must have gone to her home address. I glanced around to make sure nobody was watching. Then I peeled the label off the magazine and slipped it into my purse.

A few minutes later Dorcas motioned for me to step outside. "You lied to me," she said. "You aren't a cop. I checked. My lawyer said to tell you to stay away from me or he'll file charges."

"We never told you we were cops," I said.

"You can't keep coming here. You'll scare off my customers."

"Look, Dorcas, I need your help. It's important. I just have a couple more questions."

I reached into my wallet and took out a twenty. She grabbed it and jammed it into her pants pocket.

"My prices just went up," she said. "You have five minutes."

"A woman named Eve Lawson is missing," I said. "Did Rocky ever mentioned her name?"

"No."

"Where did he go when he left LA? Did he give you any hint where he was when he called you ten days ago?"

Dorcas stood silent with her arms crossed in defiance. I wasn't getting anywhere being pleasant. I had nothing to lose, so I confronted her with my suspicions.

"Was Rocky cheating on you? Is that why you divorced him?"

Her brow furrowed. She pointed her index finger in my face. "Fuck you. You think I'm not good enough to satisfy a man like Rocky?"

I held her gaze, didn't step away. This was no time to appear timid.

"No," I said. "That's not what I think."

"Time's up." Without another word, Dorcas turned and walked into the salon.

I'd handled that like a pro.

Dorcas seemed overly defensive when I suggested that Rocky was straying from the marriage bed. In a moment of Shakespearean clarity, I thought, *The lady doth protest too much.* If her husband had cheated on her, I doubted she would relish admitting that fact. Again, I wondered who had killed Rocky Kincaid. Dorcas seemed none too pleased with him at the moment. He'd screwed up her life royally, which gave her a possible motive for murder. If she knew he was back in town and where to find him, she also had opportunity. When I got back to the car, I pulled out the magazine label from my purse and checked the address in my Thomas Guide map book. The house was in Westchester, a neighborhood just north of the airport. I decided to drive over and take a look around.

## Chapter 18

The address on the magazine's mailing label led me to a quiet residential street lined with jacaranda trees in full bloom. The delicate flowers created a profusion of purple against the muted blue sky. The scene reminded me of an establishing shot in a movie that was meant to illustrate how beautiful things could be before they turned ugly. I made one pass by Dorcas Kincaid's small Spanish bungalow but had to park down the street because most of the curb space was taken by city-issued blue, black, and green garbage cans ready for pickup.

The Kincaid house featured a flat roof and paint peeling from the wood on the eaves and window frames. Behind the gated driveway were a small bicycle and a child's plastic wading pool deflated by a puncture wound. Water had pooled at the whim of gravity and stagnated into green pond scum. From the age-related toys, I guessed that Dorcas's kids were still young. Maybe they were young enough to be at home with a babysitter.

No one responded to my knock. I didn't want to draw attention to myself by walking behind the gate. You never knew who might be snooping around. I was about to leave when I heard a noise coming from somewhere near the street. I turned and saw a woman rummaging through Dorcas Kincaid's blue recycling container, picking out aluminum cans and plastic bottles. She pulled out a pink cake box, set it on top of the black trash bin, and continued searching through the blue one.

The woman must have sensed that I was watching her, because she glanced at me.

"I'm just recycling," she said.

*Like hell,* I thought. Stealing from LA's recycling bins was a cottage industry. I kept staring until she grew uncomfortable and closed the lid. Then she walked across the street and got into a brand-new Scion xB.

The cake box was still on top of the trash container. If I didn't throw it away, it would end up in the gutter, so I walked over to toss it back in the bin. White frosting was clinging to the insides of the box, leaching grease through to the outside and creating a gooey mess. I pinched the edge of the lid with my thumb and index finger to avoid getting my fingers sticky. As I lifted the box, it fell open and four pink candles dropped to the ground. From all appearances they were birthday candles—a child's birthday candles. The trash was picked up every week, so the cake box had probably not been in the bin for long. I gathered that one of the Kincaid children had had a birthday recently.

Dorcas claimed that Rocky had called her promising to pay the back child support he owed. That meant he still cared about his kids. I wondered if he cared enough to send his little girl a birthday card. If so, there might be a return address on the envelope or at least a postmark.

There was a slight breeze, but it had little effect except to blow the hot air around. I moved toward the blue recycling bin and opened the lid. Hot sour air swirled around my face. I stepped back, waiting for it to dissipate. There weren't any newspapers inside the bin. Either Dorcas couldn't afford the paper or she wasn't interested in current events. The can contained empty macaroni and cheese TV dinner boxes, junk mail, and old magazines. It was unwise to draw attention to myself by searching through the contents in full view of the neighbors. I decided to take the stuff back to Charley's office where time and privacy were on my side.

In order to do that, I needed plastic bags. There were two inside the black bin, but they were full of garbage. I opened them and dumped the garbage loose inside the bin, which already smelled like hell. I stuffed the papers from the blue container into the bags and turned to leave. An elderly man stood on the sidewalk glaring at me. A wisp of long white hair fluttered in the breeze. One leg of his trousers was bunched up in his sock, but he seemed oblivious to that fact.

I smiled. "I'm just recycling."

His gaze followed me as I walked down the street and slid into my Porsche Boxster. By the time I got to Charley's office, my car smelled like a hot day at the Puente Hills landfill. I took the bags to the Dumpster behind the building and started weeding out the detritus.

Dumpster diving is a tedious endeavor, not to mention mal-odorous. I'd been at it for forty-five minutes before I found the corner of an envelope with a handwritten number on it. I kept digging and found several more. People tear paper into tiny pieces for only one reason. There's something on that paper they don't want anybody to see.

I gathered all the bits of the envelope I could find and took them upstairs to Charley's office. I began laying them out on the front desk, fitting them together as if I was working a jig-saw puzzle. Some parts were missing. Others were smeared with greasy stains. Fifteen minutes had elapsed before I pieced to-gether enough of the envelope to see that a series of numbers had been scrawled across the face of it.

The first three numbers were 011. That looked as if it might be the international area code for the United States. Next came 52, probably a country code. I opened the telephone book to the page for Long Distance and International Calling. I skipped past Afghanistan, Bangladesh, and French Polynesia until I found 52. It was the country code for Mexico. I used Charley's telephone to dial the number on the envelope, keeping my fingers crossed that my rusty high school Spanish wouldn't fail me.

A woman answered. *"Buenos dias, Hotel Camino Real."*

*"Perdóneme,"* I said. *"Por dónde queda el Hotel Camino Real?"*

The woman paused before answering. *"En Todos Santos, México."*

I wondered if Rocky had been a guest at the hotel. If so, I wouldn't be surprised. The police had found a Mexican tourist card on his body. He must have been there at some point.

Dorcas claimed that he hadn't told her where he was, but she could have lied. Maybe she wanted him to stay free until she got her child support money. If I could confirm where Rocky had been living ten days ago, I might find some clue about Eve Lawson and where she might be now.

I asked the operator to connect me to Rocky Kincaid's room. I heard a tapping sound as if she was typing on a computer keyboard. After a short pause, she told me the hotel had no record of a guest by that name.

Then I remembered Deegan telling me that the tourist card had been issued under a phony name. I gambled and asked the operator to connect me to the room of Brian Smith. Again I heard clicking. A moment later she told me that Mr. Smith had checked out of the hotel.

*"Quiere usted hacer una reservación?"* she said.

I didn't need a reservation, so I said, *"No, gracias,"* and hung up.

At least I knew one thing. Dorcas Kincaid was a liar. Rocky had called her from Todos Santos, Mexico, shortly before returning to Los Angeles. Maybe he'd been there all along. I imagined it would be easy for a fugitive to hide in Baja. Rocky called from a hotel, but that didn't mean he'd stayed there for long. He wouldn't need an address. He could camp out indefinitely on a stretch of deserted beach. Use disposable cell phones. Live an anonymous life. He might have stayed in Mexico forever, but he came back to LA and ended up dead in a motel on Lincoln Boulevard.

I wanted to see if Todos Santos had a Web site and if the hotel might be posted there. I went to Charley's computer and typed the city's name into the search box. The home page gave a short description of the city's history. Todos Santos had been founded as a mission in 1724. Its amenities and charm had drawn many artists and foreign residents to set up housekeeping there, including Rocky Kincaid, I suspected. I browsed under accommodations but couldn't find the Hotel Camino Real. I searched through travel information and weather statistics. I clicked my way through Special Services, Clubs and Associations, and Things to Do Locally. The city boasted of art galleries, a cooking club, a writing workshop, and AA meetings, but I found nothing that would connect Rocky Kincaid to the place. I wasn't sure what I expected to find. Community services for fugitives?

The more I looked, the more Todos Santos sounded like an appealing place to live. I clicked on a community events directory and found a page announcing an annual prize awarded by the city to people who had grown the largest sunflowers. I scanned down the list of winners and stopped. I blinked to make sure that my eyes weren't failing me. The prize for the second best sunflower had been awarded to none other than Eve Lawson.

As of a few months ago, Eve Lawson had been living in Todos Santos. Rocky had called Dorcas from that same city shortly before he was murdered. I didn't know if Eve had met Rocky Kincaid there, but I was certain of one thing. If I snooped around long enough I would probably find out.

I called Charley but got his voice mail. I left a message, telling him about my discovery. Then I drove to Santa Monica to pick up Muldoon. When I arrived at Kismet, soft music played in the background. The lights in the yoga studio had been turned low. The air was sweltering. Several people sat on mats, waiting for Bruce's seven o'clock to start.

Petal was perched on a stool behind the counter, looking blissful. Muldoon lay at her feet with his stomach on the hardwood floor, trying to stay cool. His yellow cashmere sweater had been temporarily abandoned. He sat up when he heard my voice. His expression read, *Serenity sucks. Let's rock and roll.*

Pookie and Bruce emerged from the back office. Bruce said, "Yo," as he walked past me and took his place at the front of the class. He closed his eyes and flared his nostrils as he inhaled a bottomless breath that threatened to suck up all the oxygen in the room. Simultaneously, his arms swept skyward. The class followed suit.

"Did you find your lost sales figures?" I said to Pookie.

She shook her head.

"You want me to take a look?"

She sighed. "Maybe some other time."

"How about some tea?" I said.

She looked at her watch. "It's sort of late for tea."

"A glass of wine?"

Her mood brightened. "I'll get my purse."

We left Muldoon with Petal and headed down the street to an English pub. A group of guys was clustered around a television set at the bar, watching the Dodgers lose to the Colorado Rockies. There wasn't a cocktail waitress on duty, so Pookie claimed an empty table while I ordered two glasses of pinot grigio from the bartender. For a time we watched the male bonding antics being played out at the bar. We also discussed Muldoon's eating habits. Pookie thought I spoiled him with too much fatty food. She was probably right, but lately I'd made a concerted effort to offer him healthier cuisine.

"Pookie, there's something I need to talk to you about."

She must have picked up on the serious tone in my voice, because her spine stiffened.

"What's wrong?"

"Nothing," I lied. "Do you remember a guy named Hugh Canham? You dated him for a while before I was born."

She wrinkled her brow as if searching her memory. "I vaguely remember him. That was a long time ago."

"I guess you two got it on a few times."

She frowned. "Don't be crude, Tucker. How do you know about Hugh, anyway?"

A chorus of groans interrupted our conversation. The Dodgers had just allowed a two-run triple in the top of the sixth. I waited for the noise to die down before telling Pookie about Aunt Sylvia's allegations that I wasn't a Sinclair and therefore I wasn't eligible to inherit the beach house. Even inside the dark bar, I could see her face go pale.

"It's not true," she said. "Hugh and I dated for a while, but we only slept together once."

"That's pretty much all it takes, Pookie."

"Hugh had a problem. He was a little quick on the draw, if you know what I mean. I doubt if any of those bullets ever made it to the target."

"But you don't know for sure."

"Yes, I do." She put her hand on mine. "You look just like your father, Tucker. After you were born, the first thing I checked was your toes. They were so beautiful. That little one next to the pinkie, it was crooked, just like his. When I saw it I cried. I couldn't help myself. He would have loved you so much."

Pookie blinked as she tried to control her emotions. Maybe she was thinking back to all the tough times she'd had after my father died. There had been a lot of them, and they weren't over yet.

I couldn't watch my mother's pain. Instead, I stared at the TV. A wild Rockies pitch had just hit the Dodgers' batter on the wrist. The boys at the bar shouted things like, "Shit, man! Did you see that?" and "Throw that fucker out of the game!"

Pookie stood. "I've had enough of this crap. I'm not going to let her get away with it any longer."

"Where are you going?"

She grabbed her purse and headed for the door. "To throw water on a wicked witch."

After Pookie left, I sat in the bar for a few minutes. I was gawking at the TV, but my mind was envisioning what she planned to do and how it would rock my world. When I got back to Kismet, my mother was gone.

I picked up Muldoon and his cashmere sweater and headed home. The sky was overcast and a faint breeze swayed the upper branches of the trees. Muldoon was whining for me to open the window so he could hang his head out and let the air ruffle his whiskers. I ignored him, because it wasn't safe. Rush hour traffic had thinned, which is probably why I noticed the car behind me. Its headlights were on high beam. I drove a few more blocks, glancing up periodically, waiting for it to turn off in another direction. Ten blocks later, the lights were still piercing the back window of the Boxster.

I took a detour into the Santa Monica mall garage and waited to see if the headlights followed. They didn't. Still, I drove all the way to the top floor and back down before heading for home.

Eve Lawson's paranoia was becoming contagious.

## Chapter 19

Thursday morning I fielded a call from Lesco's CEO, questioning me about the report I'd e-mailed to him on the previous Sunday. He seemed both pleased with my work and troubled by some of my findings. We agreed to meet early the following week to discuss the company's next step.

I had just hung up the phone when Mrs. D stopped by the house in a tizzy. She'd stepped out to get the newspaper and locked herself out of the house. She couldn't rouse her husband, so I walked next door and tried but failed to trip the lock with my mileage card. I ended up calling Mr. D on my cell phone and letting it ring until he woke up.

Eve Lawson had been missing for a week, and we still didn't know if she'd run away as she had the year before or if somebody had kidnapped her. The problem was it was hard to separate truth from fiction where Eve was concerned. She'd told different stories to different people. Charley and I didn't know if she was writing a nonfiction book about real estate or a tell-all memoir. We didn't even know if there was a book.

All we knew for sure was that Eve claimed she was being followed. Then she disappeared and her boyfriend was found murdered. Her family thought she'd gone off the deep end. The police suspected she might have killed Rocky, which also fit into the family's theory. The other possibility was that somebody seeking revenge against her father or stepbrother may have seen Eve as an easy target and kidnapped or killed her. There had been no ransom demand so far, but there was certainly some evidence to support the retribution theory. The Vista Village development had stirred up strong feelings in the community with people like Austen Kistler. Ladera Bonita was a small town and Kistler had lived there forever. He must have at least met Frank and Dorothy Lawson during the time they were in residence and may have held a grudge against them for some reason.

On the flip side, I hadn't been able to make a connection between Austen Kistler's anger and any threat he might pose to Eve Lawson. To complicate matters, the Lawsons hadn't lived in Ladera Bonita for over thirty years. Eugene may have been right about Kistler, that he was just an old man tied to the past, but I still wanted to speak to him.

I knew that Kistler had a feed store in Ladera Bonita, but he must own a house in the area, as well. Wildwood was buying acres of land to make room for Vista Village. I wondered if they had tried to buy Kistler's property. If so, surely he would have refused to sell. A holdout could cause problems for the project, especially if the land was in a strategic location.

I decided to go back to Charley's office and search through his databases to see if I could come up with Kistler's home address. I asked Mrs. D if Muldoon could come over to play. Of course, she said yes. I dropped him off with a few of his favorite toys and headed to Culver City.

When I got to the office, I wasn't sure where to start looking. I didn't know where Kistler lived, but I knew where Vista Village was located. I opened my purse and pulled out the brochure that Vince Cimino had given me in Vegas. The map of the site was sketchy, so I ran downstairs and got a California map from the glove compartment of my car to get a better perspective.

I logged on to the county tax assessor's database. It gave me two options. Search for property by street address or by intersection. There were only two cross streets listed on the Vista Village brochure, Lateral A and Ladera Canyon Road. I typed them into the empty boxes and pressed SUBMIT.

A map appeared on the screen that showed a series of rectangles representing lots near that intersection. I clicked on one of them and got a page of information, including address, tax rate, and recent sales figures. I continued checking. All of the properties had been recently sold for between three and four hundred thousand dollars. The buyers' names weren't listed, but I assumed Wildwood had purchased most if not all of the lots. The names of the owners weren't listed, either, so I skipped from lot to lot, jotting down addresses, hoping to find the information in another of Charley's databases.

Lot 84 was one of the properties bordering Ladera Canyon

Road. It looked larger than the others, and when I checked the county's database, I found no recent sales data posted. I wondered if the land belonged to Austen Kistler. There were no elevations on the assessor's map or on the brochure, so I consulted the more detailed California map to get my bearings. I held the map up to the screen, lining up the streets. I couldn't be sure, but it looked as though Lot 84 overlapped the Vista Village site. That had to be a mistake. I searched several other databases, looking for the name of the owner of Lot 84. After a tedious twenty minutes, the information appeared on the screen. I stared at it in disbelief. The owner was Eve Lawson.

Something was wrong. The map in the sales brochure clearly showed that Lot 84 was part of the Vista Village development but in comparing the maps, I didn't see how that could be possible. There was no evidence that Lot 84 had been sold recently, so it still belonged to Eve Lawson. Even if she had once agreed to sell the house to Wildwood, she couldn't have gone through with the deal. She'd been estranged from the family and out of contact with them for at least a year. Perhaps Kip Moreland had assumed Eve would sell once he found her. After a year of looking for her without success, he figured she wasn't coming back and went ahead with his plans to build Vista Village.

But Eve *had* come back. I remembered something Sam Herndon said at dinner the previous Friday. He told Venus and me that a faulty title could destroy a development project. Something else buzzed around in my head: Austen Kistler's accusation at the town hall meeting. He'd said something about how Menlo's lies would catch up with him. If there were title problems with Eve's property, it might explain why Kip Moreland would pay a hundred thousand dollars to hire Charley to find her. He needed legal control of Lot 84 or he risked upending a multimillion-dollar development deal.

Again I wondered what would happen to Moreland if the Vista Village deal fell through. Wildwood had already started construction. There would be millions of dollars lost. Investors would be angry. Investors like Vince Cimino. If that happened, all sorts of folks could find themselves in jeopardy, perhaps even Austen Kistler, whose lawsuits against the development might have already eroded sales. I wondered if his life insurance policy was paid up. I decided to drive to Ladera Bonita and ask him.

An hour later I pulled into the parking lot in front of Austen's Feed and Seed, which was located just outside of Ladera Bonita proper. The store was painted barn red and had a bleached cow skull mounted above the door. A Western saddle was thrown across a hitching post near the front porch, which also displayed an old barrel and the requisite wagon wheel.

A middle-aged man in jeans and a Western-style shirt came out of the store carrying a fifty-pound sack of grain over his shoulder. He threw the sack into the bed of a pickup truck and drove away. I waited for the dirt cloud to settle before getting out of the car. I walked under the cow skull and into the store, inhaling the aroma of hay and horse chow. Hanging from the ceiling above the counter was an orange tube that was dotted with the carcasses of hundreds of flies. I called, "Hello" and "Mr. Kistler" several times but nobody answered.

There was a room behind the counter. I peeked inside, but it was empty. The store was open, so I assumed Kistler was close by. I wandered around, checking out the shelves to see what I might need if I ever decided to get Muldoon a pony. There were horse brushes, currycombs, salt spools, metal feed scoops, cans of pine tar, and horse stall refresher. Taking care of a pony seemed much more complicated than taking care of a dog. All Muldoon need-ed was a water dish and a periodic nail trim. Perhaps the pup would have to settle for a stuffed toy instead.

Kistler had obviously stepped out. Only a trusting kind of guy would leave his store open and unattended like that. He may have been one of those people, but the odds were against it. Something felt wrong.

I walked outside. The parking lot was empty except for the Boxster. A horse trailer was parked at the side of the store un-der the shade of a jury-rigged canvas sunshade. Hundreds of flies buzzed in and out of the trailer's vents, ignorant of their compadres hanging from that orange pole inside the store. The more I watched the flies the more I thought about Eve Lawson and where she might be. Needles of dread prickled my neck. The last thing I wanted to do was to look inside that trailer, but if I didn't look I would torture myself forever wondering if I'd missed something important.

The vents were too high for me to see into the trailer, so I went back inside the store to look for a ladder. There were no ladders. Instead, I found blue plastic buckets and a basket of small metal flashlights on one of the shelves. I took one of each and went back to the trailer. I turned the pail upside down, using it as a step stool. The flies were unrelenting. The stench of ma-nure was overpowering. I flipped the switch on the flashlight and swept the beam of light along the bottom of the trailer—back and forth, again and again, dreading what it might reveal—until I had searched the entire area.

There were no dead bodies, only piles of semifresh horse biscuits. I was relieved that the trailer was empty and worried why Austen Kistler had not come back to the store. I waited around for a few minutes but the store remained deserted.

Eve Lawson's house on Lot 84 was near Ladera Canyon, just a few miles from Kistler's store. I decided to drive to her place and see what I could find out. I'd check back with Kistler on my way out of town. The flashlight I'd borrowed was small but sturdy, so I left enough money on the counter to cover the sticker price plus sales tax and headed for the car. As I drove out of the parking lot of the feed store, I imagined Austen Kistler in the trunk of Vince Cimino's car, wearing a new pair of cement shoes.

Ten minutes later, I was parked across the road from Eve Lawson's modest house. Lot 84 had a well-trimmed lawn and a large sycamore tree in the front yard. There were no corrals or barns on the property, no toys in the yard, not even a bone that would indicate a dog might be in residence. In the distance I saw cranes and wooden skeletons that would eventually become the trendy neighborhood of Vista Village.

I was about to get out of the car and go exploring when I saw a woman in jodhpurs riding a palomino horse along the shoulder of the road. I recognized the horse first and then the rider. It was Lea Brown, the woman I'd seen at the town hall meeting representing the town's pro-development contingent. I rolled down my window and waited for her, hoping she wouldn't recognize me.

"Nice horse," I said. "What's his name?"

"*Her* name is May."

"I was driving around looking at property," I said, "and I noticed that some of the houses on this street look empty. Do you know if any of them are for sale?"

"Most of the places have already been sold to a developer. They'll eventually be demolished to make way for a big housing project."

I gestured toward Eve Lawson's house. "Too bad. A couple of them are in good shape, like that one with the big tree in the front yard."

She turned to look. "It hasn't been officially sold, but I suspect it's just a matter of time. The developer's family owns it. It's funny. I didn't think he would ever allow that place to be torn down."

"Ever? That's a long time."

She shrugged. "Not for Frank Lawson. His wife died in there, and I get the impression he has trouble letting go of the past."

"Looks like it's been empty for a while."

"Yeah. He rented it out a few times, but I guess he got tired of people painting the walls purple and clogging up the plumbing. One guy even started digging up the backyard to put in a spa. That was the final straw. Frank evicted him. The house has been empty ever since. I hear he transferred the title to his daughter a while back but made her promise not to sell the place until after he died. I guess he changed his mind or his company wouldn't be building Vista Village."

"Maybe I should contact the daughter. See if she'd reconsider and sell the house to me. When was the last time you saw her?"

"Gosh, I haven't seen Eve since she was a kid. The gardener comes once a week to mow the lawn. Ida Miller used to clean every couple of weeks, but about six months ago she moved back East to be near her son. I haven't seen anybody else around the place since then."

May did a nervous dance. Lea Brown pulled on the reins to regain control. "Good luck house hunting." She nudged her heels into the horse's sides, and May set off cantering down the road.

I decided to check out the house. The windows were closed and the curtains drawn. Lea claimed that the house was vacant, but I knocked on the door anyway. As expected, no one answered. I stepped off of the porch to take a look in back. There was a detached two-car garage, but there were no cars inside. The curtains in the kitchen were an inch shy of meeting the sill, so I was able to peek inside. The house was empty. A beam of sunlight exposed a layer of dust on the floor and what looked like a set of footprints leading into the room beyond. I wondered who had been walking around inside the house and if the person had left any clues that might tell us where to find Eve Lawson.

I turned the knob, but the door wouldn't open. I took out the mileage card and fiddled around with the lock for a while with zero success. It looked solid. Probably seven pins. The most difficult kind to pick. And it looked new. That was odd. The house was going to be torn down. I wondered why it needed a new lock. There was nothing inside the house to steal.

There was a gold seal affixed to the glass pane in the kitchen door. It read GOLD-E-LOCKS, AZUSA, CALIFORNIA. There was a telephone number listed. I took the cell phone out of my purse and dialed. The owner answered. His name was Ed. I told him I needed new locks, and that he had come highly recommended. He didn't bother to ask by whom.

"I saw the locks you put on a house out in Ladera Bonita," I said. "I can't believe it. They still look new."

"They are new. Just put them in a few weeks ago."

"The owner has good taste."

"It wasn't the owner. It was the Realtor who called in the order."

"The house is for sale?" I said, surprised by the news. "I was just out there. I didn't see a sign."

"I wouldn't know about that. The Realtor told me the owner lost the key and needed me to change the locks so she could show the place. The house was empty when I got there. Looks like it's been that way for a while. The place was sort of dirty."

That explained the dusty footprints on the floor. They must have been Ed's.

"Sounds like the Realtor was taking care of business," I said. "I may be selling my place soon. Maybe you could give me her name."

"Hold on. I got her number right here." I heard the receiver bang against a hard surface. A moment later Ed was back on the line. "Madeline Fallbrook is her name. She's with Premier Homes in Pasadena. I never met the woman, but she has a nice voice."

He gave me the number, and we ended the call.

By the time I got back to Ladera Bonita, the sign on Austen Kistler's feed store read CLOSED. For a moment I thought about calling the sheriff's office, but what would I tell them? That the store was open, and then it was closed? I was overreacting. Kistler had probably run out of horse chow and had closed the store until new inventory arrived.

There was nothing more I could do in Ladera Bonita, so I decided to check out the real estate market in Pasadena.

# Chapter 20

Pasadena is located about ten miles east of downtown Los Angeles. It's the major city in the San Gabriel Valley and the home of the Rose Bowl, Caltech, the Jet Propulsion Laboratory, and stately old homes that were built when people had both money and good taste.

Premier Homes Realty was located on the second floor of a brick building on Arroyo Parkway. I caught Madeline Fallbrook just as she was leaving the office to meet with a client. When I told her that I was a first-time home buyer looking for a Realtor, she eagerly led me back to her workstation and gestured for me to sit in one of her cushy guest chairs.

Fallbrook was around sixty years old with chiseled features and long graceful fingers. Her gray hair was cut in two-inch chunks and moussed to spiky perfection. The color made her look wise. The style made her look hip. I told her I'd driven by the house on Lot 84 in Ladera Bonita, and I was interested in buying it.

"I'm sorry," she said. "That place has been sold."

Ed at Gold-E-Locks was right. Fallbrook did have a lovely voice. It was rich and low like an old-time radio announcer. I pegged her as a smoker.

"Is it possible that the deal will fall through?" I said.

"No. Escrow closed this morning."

"I wish I'd known about the house earlier," I said. "I read the 'Homes' section of the *Times* every week. I guess I missed the ad."

"There wasn't an ad. The owner wanted it kept quiet. She felt no pressure to sell. She wanted a certain price so she asked me to send out feelers to see if I could generate any interest. I asked a few of my colleagues to quietly put out the word."

"How interesting," I said with greater enthusiasm than necessary. "Is that usual?"

"Sure. Happens all the time. We call it a pocket listing. Sometimes the seller just wants to test the market. Sometimes they don't want looky-loos traipsing through their house. I usually turn down listings so far from my home base, but the owner was willing to show the place herself. It was an easy sale. The buyer paid more than the asking price. All cash. That's why escrow closed in thirty days."

"How much did it go for?"

"One-point-four million." She must have noticed my surprise, because she added, "I know it sounds like a lot for that little place. The house is small but the property is extensive. It basically spreads across the entrance to Ladera Canyon. There was no mortgage, so it was pure profit for the seller. The buyer can flip the house tomorrow for double the amount he paid. Everybody was happy with the deal."

"I thought Vista Village was being built in Ladera Canyon."

"That was the plan, but it's not possible now. Ladera is a blind canyon. It only has one entrance. Before proceeding, the builders have to get an easement from the new property owner. If the owner refuses, there's no way into the canyon without burrowing through a mountain. The cost would be prohibitive."

"So whoever owns Lot 84 has the developer over the proverbial barrel."

Madeline shrugged. "It's the nature of the business. I have clients who spend every day of their lives looking for deals like this. The buyer and seller both knew about the development, so everybody went into the sale with their eyes wide open."

"Who's the buyer?" I said.

There was an uncomfortable pause. "I'd rather not say until it becomes part of the public record."

"Sorry. I don't mean to pry. As you can tell, I'm new at this game. I'm just happy to learn everything I can from an expert like you."

She smiled. "Glad to be of help."

"Let's say you can find me another house I like. How do I get to the part where money changes hands?"

Madeline checked her watch. "I'll give you the short version. The buyer makes the offer. The seller accepts. The property goes into escrow. A title is requested. The escrow officer prepares a new deed. The buyer wires money to an escrow account. The new deed is sent to the county recorder's office. The money is wired to the seller's account."

"Jeez," I said. "Sounds complicated. You guys really earn your commissions. I'm just curious. Are there rules about where the money is sent? For example, could it be wired out of the country, like to Mexico?"

"Mexico. The Caymans. Switzerland. Anywhere. The account doesn't even have to have the seller's name on it."

I felt my eyebrows arch. I wanted to ask her where the money for Lot 84 had been sent, but if she had refused to tell me the name of the buyer, she would certainly balk at telling me what happened to the money. Plus she might become suspicious, if she wasn't already. I needed to remain on good terms with her in case I had more questions later. I took her business card and told her I'd be in touch.

So Eve Lawson wasn't missing after all. All the time Charley and I had been searching for her, she'd been sneaking around negotiating a secret deal to sell Lot 84 to the highest bidder. Her father had given her the house with the stipulation that she would keep it in the family until after his death. She had broken that promise, maybe to get back at her stepmother or maybe because she needed the money. Perhaps she felt that given her father's deteriorating condition he would never find out what she'd done.

According to Eve's fellow volunteer, Christie Swink, Meredith Lawson had changed the terms of Eve's trust, basically limiting her monthly income and delaying for years her control over the balance. Now Eve had gotten her revenge. She'd sold

Lot 84 and walked away with one-point-four million dollars and she'd done it by screwing over Meredith Lawson's son, Kip Moreland.

I wondered how Rocky Kincaid fit into the scheme. Maybe Eve had met him in Mexico and solicited his help with her plans. When the sale looked solid, perhaps she'd killed him rather than share the profits. On the other hand, maybe Rocky had been killed by somebody who wanted to stop the sale of Lot 84 to anybody but Wildwood Properties, somebody like Kip Moreland or his cronies.

I thought, *Why kill Rocky? Why not kill Eve?* Eve Lawson had hired Charley because she thought she was being followed. Maybe a killer had been watching and waiting for an opportunity to get her, too. I wondered where that one-point-four million dollars was and if Eve would survive to spend it.

On the drive back to town, I called Charley Tate and told him what I'd discovered about the sale of Eve Lawson's house. He complimented me on a job well done. Said he was proud of me.

"I may have a lead on Rocky Kincaid's accomplice in the embezzlement scheme," he said. "I was looking up arrest warrants in county court records to see if I could find anything on Eve Lawson. I didn't find a warrant for her, but I found one for a woman by the name of Mikki Sloan. Turns out Sloan was the person Kincaid hired to work at his therapy practice. She was arrested along with him. The judge issued a bench warrant for both of them when they failed to appear in court. It's possible that she and Rocky skipped town together."

"There goes my theory," I said. "If Rocky left town with

Mikki Sloan, he didn't leave town with Eve. That means Eve was probably not involved in the embezzlement scam. She must have hooked up with him in Mexico."

"That's my guess, too."

"Then who was Eve Lawson dating a year ago?" I said. "If we could find him, he might know something. Maybe he's still in contact with her."

"I'll check it out, but right now I'm on my way to talk to Meredith Lawson. While I'm doing that, I'd like you to meet with Mikki Sloan's probation officer."

"She was on probation?"

"Yeah. She had a cocaine habit. About a year before she hooked up with Kincaid she was arrested on a DUI."

Dorcas Kincaid claimed that Rocky used cocaine, as well. Maybe that was where all the stolen money had gone—up their noses.

"No probation officer is going to talk to me about one of their cases," I said.

"She will, if I ask her to."

"Charley, don't you think we should call the police?"

He remained silent for a while. "And tell them what? They don't care about Eve Lawson's house. She had every legal right to sell it. All they want to know is where she is so they can question her about Rocky Kincaid's murder. I don't know where she is. Neither do you. We have nothing to tell them."

His logic seemed solid, but my intuition told me we were making a mistake.

• • •

Charley instructed me to meet Mikki Sloan's probation officer in front of the Santa Monica courthouse on Main. He told me her name was Sue.

"What's her last name?" I said.

"She'd rather you didn't know. Just call her Sue."

Just Sue was a petite woman with mousy brown hair and a pair of eyeglasses that had worn a groove into the bridge of her nose. Her sleeveless blouse exposed a jagged scar on her upper arm that looked like the mark of Zorro. Hiding her legs were a pair of those billowy clown pants you sometimes see at the beach or at the gym. I assumed she dealt with some pretty tough characters in her line of work. I wondered if she was trying to keep them from learning that there was a woman's body under that yardage.

Just Sue voted against hanging around the courthouse to talk, so we snaked through the parking lot to Fourth Street, stopping at the wire fence in front of Santa Monica High School. The girls' track team was in the field, practicing their pole vaults under the watchful eye of their coach.

"Let's get one thing straight," she said. "I shouldn't be talking to you, and I wouldn't be talking to you if I didn't know Tate from the old days. It's unprofessional. Besides, my colleagues think every PI is a lying sack of shit. I tend to agree with them. So here are the rules. Don't lie to me. Don't ask for anybody's home address, telephone number, or Social Security number. And don't share any information I'm about to give you with anybody but Chuck."

I listened to the barrage of rules without interruption. I could have told Just Sue that I was a business consultant, not a

PI. The lying sack of shit part was less easy to defend. I let it all slide because all I could think of was . . . Chuck?

I glanced toward the field and saw a young woman with a long springy pole running toward a crossbar. She planted the pole on the ground and lunged skyward. She landed on her ass in the sawdust.

"Maybe you could just tell me what Mikki was like," I said.

"She's smart but lazy. That's why she lies. It's easier than the truth."

"I'm interested in the guy she was with. Rocky Kincaid. Do you know how long they were together?"

"No. Mikki was always with a man but never for long. She used them, threw them away, and went on with her day. Short, fat, old, young, rich, poor. Didn't matter. She found something to take from all of them."

"How did she manage? I can't seem to keep even one guy."

My attempt at female bonding did not resonate with Just Sue. She didn't even pause to share a tepid girlfriend smile.

"Mikki is a master manipulator," she said. "She could sell beer to a teetotaler. It's such a waste. She could have used her talents for good."

Out on the field, the budding track star had brushed the dirt off of her butt and was at it again. This time she made it to the crossbar, knocked it down, and landed with a thud on the bordering grass.

"What will happen when Mikki is caught?" I said.

"She's already in violation of her probation for not checking in with me. When they find her, she'll be tried on the embezzlement charge. If she's found guilty, she'll do time. Lots of it. Once she gets out of state prison, I'll transfer the file to her parole officer."

"Do you have a photograph of Mikki?"

Just Sue put her hands on her hips and cocked her head. "Not that I'd give you."

"Can you at least tell me what she looks like?"

She hesitated. "She's a skinny blonde."

The description was generic enough to be useless. I had a feeling Just Sue had planned it that way.

"Do you have any idea where Mikki might be now?" I said.

"If I knew that I wouldn't be working here," she said with poker-faced delivery. "I'd have my own TV show. *The Psychic Probation Officer.*"

"Sounds like a winner."

Mikki Sloan had probably left Rocky as soon as they got out of town. She could be anywhere, likely with a new man. If that were the case, she wouldn't have any information about Eve Lawson. Maybe she never had any to offer. I hated to admit it, but Sloan was probably a dead end.

Just Sue headed back to the courthouse. I lingered a while to watch the track team. The pole vault star was psyching herself up for another run. This time she soared over the bar. Her teammates and the coach applauded. Success. I could use a little of that myself.

# Chapter 21

Just Sue had disappeared around the corner of the Santa Monica courthouse by the time I arrived at the parking lot where I'd left my car. She was probably already at her desk, ordering a few bench warrants to appease her conscience for talking to me.

Joe Deegan hadn't called me in three days. Under normal circumstances I wouldn't have worried about his silence. We didn't always talk everyday, especially when he got busy with work. However, there was that unresolved Tracy issue to fret about and the meeting with his captain. I was hoping that the deputy DA was busy doing her job and that Deegan was no longer focusing on Eve Lawson as a suspect in Rocky Kincaid's murder. Neither of those scenarios seemed likely.

I hate not knowing things, so before I left the parking lot I called Deegan's cell phone and left a message. Then I called his home, but the answering machine didn't pick up. Finally, I dialed his number at work and was told that he was "out in the field," which is police speak for "We wouldn't tell you where he is even if it was any of your business." I waited a few minutes and called again. This time I posed as Deegan's mother and learned that he had called in sick.

If Deegan was sick, he should have been at home in bed, answering his telephone. Something was wrong. He wasn't the type to ask for TLC and chicken soup. He'd tough it out on his own. The only problem was viruses could turn deadly. I imagined him lying in bed too weak to call for help. I had to make sure he was okay.

When I arrived at Deegan's house, his Explorer wasn't parked in the driveway, but it might have been in the garage. I knocked on the front door, but nobody answered. I was prepared to walk to the back door and peek inside the kitchen window when I heard a small voice behind me.

"Joe's not here. He's on his boat. He's going to take me for a ride sometime but not today, because I have a temperature."

A blue-eyed girl of about six stood a few feet away from me. Her sandy hair was swept into pigtails. Her nose and cheeks were covered with a cluster of freckles that looked like planets in a faraway galaxy. It was late in the day, but she was still wearing a pair of cotton pajamas emblazoned with cats that all looked like Fergie.

"Sounds like fun," I said. "What kind of a boat does Joe have?"

Her tongue was poking out of a large gap where a front

tooth used to be. "A sailboat." It came out sounding like *thailboat.* "It's called a sloop because it only has one mast. It used to be his daddy's, but it's his now."

I acknowledged this information with a nod, but even as I did, it felt as if an unseen hand was squeezing the air out of my lungs, not because Deegan hadn't called me in three days and I was beginning to think he was avoiding me, but because a six-year-old neighbor kid knew the name of the marina where he kept a boat that I didn't even know he had.

I arrived in Marina del Rey and located Deegan's slip number with the help of the dockmaster. The sun was low but still bright against the western horizon. I'd left my sunglasses in the car, so I squinted to read a sign posted on one of the pilings to verify that I was in the right place.

Deegan was at the end of the dock, hosing off a sailboat that looked to be around thirty feet long. The boat had one mast, just as his pint-sized neighbor had said. Laid out on the dock were a bucket of soapy water, brushes, and terrycloth towels.

The gate leading to the gangway was locked. I waited until a man came by with a key, and I slipped in behind him. The gate clinked closed. Deegan heard the noise and glanced up. His hair was tousled. He was wearing knee-length surfer shorts and wraparound sunglasses. His shirt was off, exposing a six-pack bronzed by the sun. When he saw me, he paused for a moment, frowned, then turned his attention back to the hose.

An onshore breeze ruffled my hair as I walked along the dock. As I got closer to the boat I noticed that the fiberglass hull was a chalky white and the varnish on the teak railing was chipped and peeling. I stopped a few feet away and waited through an uncomfortable silence.

"You have a boat," I said.

Deegan turned off the hose and dipped a large sponge into a bucket of soapy water. His efforts had raised a film of perspiration on his back. There was stubble on his face as though he hadn't shaved that morning.

"I heard you were sick," I continued. "What's going on?"

He applied sponge to teak. "I'm taking a few days off."

"In the middle of a homicide investigation?"

His scrubbing was aggressive. I almost felt sorry for the wood.

"I've been taken off of the Kincaid case," he said.

I felt as if the air had been knocked out of me. I looked down at the water, because I couldn't stand to see Deegan trying but failing to mask his sense of loss with soapsuds.

"Tracy Fields filed a complaint?" I said.

"Yup. She claims I've been sharing confidential information about the Kincaid homicide case with you and your PI friend. There's more, but I'll spare you the details."

I wasn't completely surprised, but I'd hoped that Fields would think twice about risking her reputation and perhaps her job by making spurious accusations against a police detective. Obviously, my judgment of human nature was faulty.

"That was fast," I said.

"It usually takes a couple of weeks after the paperwork goes to IA. They arrange an interview. I ask for a defense rep. But Tracy has juice with the captain, so he decided to speed up the process by handling it at the division level."

My chest was filled with that special brand of anger that grows from powerlessness. "They bounced you off the case on Tracy's word alone?"

"Not totally. They know you're working for Tate. They know Eve Lawson is his client and that she's also a suspect in a homicide investigation. Now they know about us. What they want to know is if I'm leaking confidential information to a PI. They've asked the Department of Justice to audit every time I've logged on a government computer in the past year. They'll make me justify all the names I've looked up, and they'll ask me to prove that the search was connected to a case I was working on. If I can't do that, I'm screwed. Even if I'm exonerated, the beef stays in my package forever."

"That's crazy. How can they do that?"

"They can do anything they want to do," he said.

Deegan put the sponge back in the bucket and picked up the hose again. The hair on his arms shimmered in the sunlight like fine bronze threads.

"That really burns my ass," I said. "A pissed off ex-girlfriend can make false accusations against you and ruin your career. Just like that. Nothing you can do about it."

Deegan turned on the water and began hosing off the soap. I saw his calf muscles flex and heard his flip-flops slap against his heels as he moved.

"There are things I can do," he said, "and I'll do them."

"How can I help?"

"Quit working for Charley Tate."

"You know I can't do that."

He turned to look at me. "Can't?"

"I need clients or my business fails."

"Do something else."

"Like what?" I said. "Sit in a windowless office posting numbers to a ledger like Scrooge?"

The ghost of a smile appeared on his lips.

"I'm serious, Deegan. What can I do to help you?"

He pulled the hose around toward the stern and continued washing. "Nothing. I just need time to think things through."

"How much time?"

The soapsuds were off the boat and floating in the water around the hull. A chamois lay on top of the dock box. Deegan picked it up and began wiping down the stainless steel stanchions.

"I'll let you know," he said.

I looked at the boats tied up at the slips and listened to the groan of dock lines straining against the current. Masts swayed gently with the breeze like old people at a sing-along.

"You think this is my fault, don't you?" I said.

"No."

"Then why are you pushing me away?"

He stopped to wring water from the chamois. Then he laid it out to dry on top of the dock box. I sensed that there was something he wanted to say that he couldn't yet put into words. I waited. He stood there for a moment with his hands on his hips—tall, tanned, and ripped. His face was an enigmatic mask.

"Look, Tucker. It's just better if we don't see each other right now."

For what seemed like a long time I stood as inert as one of those pilings at the end of the dock. My throat felt thick. He had called me Tucker. He never called me that. He called me Stretch because I was tall like a stretch limo. It had been his nickname for me from the very beginning.

"I understand," I said.

I conjured up a smile, because I wanted Deegan to know how mature and evolved I was, even though his words had punched a hole in my heart.

Maybe Charley was right. Maybe all relationships eventually turned to shit.

I had no food in my house, so when I got home from the marina Muldoon and I went to the market. I bought ground lamb for him and a package of frozen macaroni and cheese for me. I realized when I got home that it was the same brand I'd found in Dorcas Kincaid's recycling bin.

After dinner I took Muldoon for a walk along the beach. Several times the pup stopped and looked at me as if to say, *What's up? We don't usually go this far.* Nonetheless, we kept walking until I no longer found comfort in the sound of the waves breaking on the shore.

It was probably inevitable that my relationship with Joe Deegan would end. I just never imagined how agonizing it would be when it happened. He and I were different in so many ways. He'd come from a stable family with two parents and three sisters who adored him. I'm the only child of a single mom who may have conceived me with a female impersonator named Peaches La Rue. By contrast with Deegan's, my growing up years had been uncertain and unconventional.

There was no reason to get maudlin about Deegan. I had been through the pain of breakups before. I knew the drill. You cry. You feel you won't survive another day. You get angry, and then you get over it. After my divorce, I hadn't worried about finding somebody else. I moved on and put my energy into building my career. I knew what I wanted out of life—success, friends, and my independence. I now realized that I had never been too clear about what I wanted from a relationship. I didn't know what Deegan wanted, either, which was part of the problem. That was the sort of intimate conversation we never had.

That night, sleep eluded me. The bedroom window was open, but the air inside and out was hot and still. Muldoon opted to bed down in the living room on the cool tiles near the French door. My hair felt lank and abrasive against my neck and a thin film of perspiration covered my face. I kicked off all the covers and thrashed around for a while, seeking comfort where none existed.

The truth was I'd lost a relationship that meant more to me than I cared to admit, and I might finally lose my house, as well. I avoided speculating about life without Joe Deegan. Instead, I imagined my life without the beach cottage. I didn't have any idea where I would go if I had to move. Since I'd given up the security of my corporate salary, I couldn't afford to buy in the high-priced Southern California real estate market. I'd have to live in an apartment. It would be small and cramped and expensive. That is, if I could find any place that would take Muldoon.

At three a.m., I gave up all hopes of sleeping. I got out of bed and went into the living room to my grandmother's steamer trunk. It was trimmed with canvas and wooden slats and had come with the house, along with the wrought iron headboard on my bed. The trunk's past was a mystery, but it looked old. I'd found it on a shelf in the garage when I moved in. The locks were pitted with rust. I suspected that it was so beat up that none of the renters who had lived in the house before me had bothered to steal it.

I opened the trunk and began to sort through the relics of my grandmother's past, pictures of strangers I would never know, and an ornate box that held a comb and brush set. A couple of my father's old cameras were in there, too, though I suspected they no longer worked. As I sifted through graduation announcements and funeral programs, I came across an old photograph of my grandparents Anne and James Sinclair and their children Jackson, Donovan, and Sylvia. I'd seen the picture before, but this time I carefully studied each of their expressions.

My grandfather looked handsome but stern. Anne Sinclair's expression was enigmatic. Without knowing her I couldn't tell if the emotion on her face was the result of happiness or hemorrhoids. My father looked to be around twelve, dark-haired and already tall, full of piss and vinegar, as my grandma Felder used to say about me. I couldn't tell if his toes were crooked, because his feet were outside the frame.

My aunt was the oldest of the three children. In the photo she appeared to be around eighteen or so, gangly and unsure of herself. She stood with her arms crossed as if she didn't know what to do with them. She looked miserable. I studied the distress in her expression and remembered my own gawky youth when I'd been teased for being the tallest girl in my second grade class. My ego had survived, and for the millionth time, I wondered what had turned my aunt so bitter. If I snooped around long enough, I might find the answer to that question, as well.

I thought about Eve Lawson's difficult childhood and what it must have been like to lose her mother at such a young age. Meredith Lawson claimed that Eve had no friends left in LA, but I found that hard to believe. She must have had somebody she confided in.

Eve had been seeing a man just before she left town a year ago. I couldn't shake the feeling that if I could locate him he might be able to tell me why she ran away and perhaps offer some idea about where she was now.

The information I had about that relationship was sketchy. Christie Swink thought Eve was keeping her boyfriend's identity a secret because he was married. I thought of three other possible reasons. They might have worked at a company that didn't allow employees to date. Except Eve had never worked at a real job. She had only spent a brief time as a volunteer for the suicide hotline. The Sanctuary's executive director, Nick Young, was married. He was a potential suitor, but his dour personality made that seem unlikely. A second possibility was that Eve knew her family would disapprove of the man she was dating, either because they would think he was after her money or he was beneath her social station. The third option was that the family already knew the man and disliked him on his own merits.

Christie said that Eve liked to cook and that she had been taking a cooking class with her boyfriend before she left town. Somebody else had recently told me about taking a cooking class, but I'd spoken to so many people in the past few days I couldn't remember who it was.

I was lying in bed in that state of semiconsciousness when creativity often breaks through the haze when I finally remembered. It had been Nathan Boles who told me that he took a cooking class and learned that he should stay out of the kitchen. Boles had known the Lawson family, including Eve, for years. He had flown me on his private jet to Sonoma County in order to help her with research on her book, had seemed so eager to find out where she was. Boles had severed his business relationship with Wildwood Properties because Kip Moreland's inexperience and arrogance had lost Boles and his friends a great deal of money. After that, I suspected he had become persona non grata around the Lawson house.

It was difficult to imagine Nathan Boles and Eve Lawson as a couple. They seemed so mismatched. Boles was handsome and sophisticated. Eve cut a dowdy figure in her dated clothes and that ancient handbag she carried. On the other hand, a lot could happen to a person in a year. Eve may have been a hot babe back then. I also thought about Charley and Lorna and was reminded that people are drawn together for reasons I didn't always understand. If Boles and Eve Lawson had been lovers, I was convinced they would have kept their relationship a secret from her family.

Charley always accused me of assuming too much, but this time I decided to go with my gut. First thing in the morning, I was going to ask for another audience with Nathan Boles.

# Chapter 22

The next morning I called Nathan Boles at his corporate office in Century City. He was reportedly busy, so I left a message with his executive assistant. After that I made a few cold calls to drum up business. At noon I started researching the business plan I'd promised to do for Pookie and Bruce.

I pulled the Kismet Yoga Studio folder from my file cabinet and found the list of the top five LA yoga classes that I'd ripped from the pages of a magazine. One of the instructors was scheduled to teach a class at seven p.m. at the Sports Club/LA on Sepulveda. The club was private, but I'd called a couple of weeks before and a sales associate had sent me two seven-day guest passes, along with a classy brochure outlining their various services, including the yoga program. I needed some moral support, so I called Venus and talked her into going with me.

The Sports Club is an ultratrendy gym and day spa on the Westside of Los Angeles that features everything the health-obsessed Angeleno could possibly want in a one-hundred-thousand-square-foot building, including cutting-edge exercise equipment, a swimming pool, a basketball court, a rooftop driving range, and a bevy of white-clad valets at the ready to park your Lamborghini. It's where buff and beautiful Westsiders and their wannabe counterparts go to work out and be seen. That is, if they can afford the steep initiation fee and pricey monthly dues.

At five thirty, I rolled into the parking garage and made my way to the front desk. Venus was already there, gym bag in hand, staring at a hunky guy in line at the smoothie bar.

"So what do you think?" I said.

"I think if Max starts giving me grief, I know where to find a replacement."

We took a table at the club's restaurant. I ordered penne and broccoli and Venus ordered steak and a baked potato. During dinner I told her about Tracy Fields and the trouble she was causing for Deegan.

"That woman needs her ass kicked," she said. "If I ever run into her, I just might do it myself."

I smiled at the thought.

"Better yet," she went on, "you should sue her for messing with your love life. When the jury takes a look at Deegan, they're gonna give you millions."

I smiled. I could always count on Venus to cheer me up.

"How's it going with Max?" I said.

"Things are heating up, Tucker. He wants me to go on vacation with him. To Europe."

"Sounds romantic," I said. "Where in Europe?"

"France, of course. He's got a bike tour all picked out. We're gonna ride by day and eat by night. My kind of trip, except the ride by day part."

I nodded but this time I couldn't dredge up a smile. I was happy for Venus, but hearing about her trip made me feel adrift in a world full of happy couples. She seemed to sense my mood change.

"I've got an idea," she said. "Come with us."

"A ménage à trois?"

"Sure. It'll be fun. You and I can take the sag wagon into town every day and shop while Max hangs out with the jocks."

"No, thanks. It would feel too weird."

She set down her knife and fork and rested her arms on the table.

"Don't pine away for him, honey. It won't do either of you any good. You gotta get right back on the horse. Find somebody who'll take your mind off of Deegan."

It sounded like good advice, except if that person existed I wasn't in the mood to go looking for him.

Venus fiddled with the carcass of her baked potato. "So what's with this yoga class?"

Glad to be off the subject of Joe Deegan, I handed her the brochure. She read down the page until she came to the class description.

"Tucker, it says here, 'It is recommended you do not eat two to three hours before practice.' I just ate a side of beef and a spud as big as Idaho. I think we should cancel."

I looked at the brochure. The class was listed as level four. I wasn't clear on what that meant. I probably should have consulted Bruce.

"That's just a recommendation," I said. "Don't worry. We'll be all right."

Venus raised her eyebrows to register her skepticism but voiced no further objections. We paid the bill and headed toward the locker room. We checked out locker keys from the attendant and changed into our workout gear. Venus put on the gold sweatsuit she'd bought at Wheelz. I donned a pair of black tights and a souvenir T-shirt from Scales and Shells restaurant that I'd bought a few years before on a trip to Newport, Rhode Island. Fashionistas we weren't.

When we got to Studio Two, Venus and I found some yoga mats stacked in a corner of the room. We each took one and laid them side by side on the floor near the exit. The lights dimmed. The air was blistering.

Venus fanned herself with her hand. "I ate too much."

"Me, too."

The teacher was a vision of serenity in her aqua sweats and matching tank top. She had pale skin, auburn hair, long and graceful limbs, and a voice that could melt ice floes.

She started the music and took her place on the dais in front of the class. She raised her arms to the ceiling and inhaled deeply. The class followed her lead, thirty sets of nostrils sucking up oxygen. A moment later the air came back out from the depths of thirty sets of lungs. OMMMMMMM. The sound was deafening.

Venus slapped her hand to her chest.

"What the hell was that?" she whispered.

"Deep breathing."

"They should warn people."

Five minutes into the workout, we knew we were in over our heads. The session was not about gentle stretching. It was more like a toad-jumping contest.

"I thought this was supposed to make me serene," Venus said. "This is more like combat training, and right now my stomach is at war with that steak I just ate."

"Do you want to leave?"

Venus rolled her eyes. "Yes, Tucker. I want to leave. I suggest we find the shower and then we find alcohol."

We waited until the class was in a sustained stretching pose. When everybody's eyes seemed closed, we skulked out of the studio, abandoning our mats and one of LA's premier yoga teachers.

Venus and I made our way to the women's dressing room. I wrapped a skimpy gym towel around my body and put on a pair of old flip-flops. Venus's towel didn't quite reach all the way around her ample figure, but that was no problem. Most of the other people in the locker room hadn't bothered with towels at all. Naked women were everywhere, using hair dryers, curling irons, straightening irons, and cell phones. It was like being in a sweltering female-only indoor nudist colony.

"Let's take a Jacuzzi," Venus said. "All that yoga stressed me out. I need to relax."

"Eugene says Jacuzzis are breeding grounds for bacteria."

"Eugene is a bony-assed germophobe."

I followed Venus toward the sound of jets blowing full

throttle, whipping the water into a frothy cascade. The air in the Jacuzzi room was warm and moist and smelled of chemicals. There were two people already in the spa, a heavyset woman in her fifties and a buff young hottie who was spread out along one side of the pool, claiming the territory of two people.

Venus dropped her towel and stepped into the water, wading to an unoccupied corner of the underwater bench. She laid her head back against the edge of the pool and closed her eyes. I scanned the space, looking for a place to sit. The hottie's eyes were closed. Her hair was pinned on top of her head with a butterfly clip. It was honey blond with multiple-colored chunky highlights. She was nude and mostly underwater, but I could still recognize the buff-a-licious body of a gym rat. This one belonged to Deputy DA Tracy Fields.

It seemed fitting that the tables were now turned. Tracy was naked in the water, and I was looming over her wearing a look of stunned surprise. A moment later she opened her eyes. She recognized me and bolted to an upright and sitting position.

"What are you doing here?" she said. "If you think you can harass me and get away with it, think again."

Venus opened her eyes and looked at me with a questioning frown. A moment later her gaze swept past me and fixed on Tracy Fields.

"Stay away from me," Fields said, "or I'll get a restraining order against you."

Venus's mood darkened. For a moment I fantasized about a two-against-one catfight in the roiling water of a hot tub. It was a tempting thought, but I restrained myself before a judge could do it for me.

"Don't flatter yourself, Tracy," I said. "I'm not following you."

"Oh, really? Don't you think it's pretty coincidental that you just happened to show up at my gym?"

"It's not your gym," I said. "Even people like me can join, although I'm not sure I want to work out next to somebody who tries to destroy a man's career just because he refuses to sleep with her anymore. I have some advice for you: Move on."

"Fuck off," she said.

Venus sat up straight. I could see her fists clenched under the water. The gaze of the other woman in the spa tracked the volley of words as if she was a judge at a tennis match.

"I just hope your past is squeaky clean, Tracy," I said, "because I'm going to make it my personal mission to dig into the darkest corners of your pathetic little life and expose you as the liar and fraud that you are."

Tracy stood. "I don't have to listen to this shit."

She moved toward the steps of the spa. Somewhere midtub she lost her footing and did a belly flop in the bubbling water. By the time she stood upright again, she looked like a cat that had just stepped out of the shower, bedraggled and irate.

"Oops," said Venus. "You must have tripped."

The older woman in the spa clapped.

"I give that dive a five," she said.

Tracy Fields was fuming as she got out of the pool. She pushed passed me and ran toward the locker room. I remembered the first night I'd seen her in the hallway at the police station. Detective Mendoza told me that Tracy had problems with a lot of men. I assumed that included men at work, men at play, and maybe even men she had met at the gym. I decided to use every day of my seven-day pass to see if I could find just one dis-gruntled former lover that might be willing to dish about a dirty deputy DA.

Muldoon had been cooped up in the house all evening, so when I got home from the gym, I drove him to Mickey D's and bought him a Quarter Pounder. I was still trying to limit his in-take of fatty foods, so I ordered the burger without cheese, bun, or sauce. He gobbled down the meat patty and ruffled his nose in the bag.

"Sorry, pup," I told him, "no fries for you. Gotta watch your waistline."

He cocked his head and let out a high-pitched whine.

"Yeah? Well, no one said life was going to be easy."

When we arrived back home, I found a message from Nathan Boles on my voice mail, telling me to meet him at eleven o'clock the next morning at a construction site in West Los Angeles. Again, it seemed more like an order than an accommodation.

# Chapter 23

Saturday morning I drove to West Los Angeles to meet Nathan Boles. N.B. Construction was the general contractor for a new office complex that was being built on Olympic Boulevard. I was surprised to learn that there was room for another skyscraper on the congested Westside, but there it was, a massive hole in the ground surrounded by a fence that sheltered the public from the noise and dust of tower cranes, bulldozers, and jackhammers working their magic. Men, equipment, rebar, lumber, and blue portable bathrooms dotted the landscape. A security guard issued me a hard hat and pointed me toward a double-wide mobile construction trailer a few yards away. A black pickup with the N.B. Construction logo painted on the back window was parked in front of the door.

I found Nathan Boles in the trailer, sitting at his desk looking through a stack of photographs. Viewing them from my upside-down point of view, they appeared to represent various stages of the construction process. Aerial shots documenting building progress. Dignitaries cutting a ribbon during some kind of groundbreaking ceremony. Dump trucks filled with debris. Men conferring over blueprints.

A plate of doughnuts on the corner of the desk was providing a sugar fix for a colony of ants that had marched through a crack under the door. Boles did nothing to stop the assault. Maybe he didn't see it or maybe he preferred to choose his battles.

It seemed counterproductive to continue lying to him about helping Eve research a book on World War II, so I told him the truth, or as much of it as I felt he needed to know: Eve Lawson had disappeared and I had to find her.

Boles stared at me. His jaw twitched with tension. A couple of times I thought he would say something, maybe chastise me for deceiving him and wasting his time, but instead he returned to sorting through the photos, pulling a few out and stacking them in a separate pile.

"I haven't seen Eve in a year," he said. "Why don't you ask her stepbrother where she is?"

"I suspect Kip Moreland would be the last person she'd contact if she was in trouble."

He looked up from the photos and frowned. "Trouble?"

"Did you know that Eve Lawson owned a house in Ladera Bonita?"

Boles laid the photos down and leaned back in his chair as if he wanted to create distance between us. "Yes."

"Did you know she sold it recently?"

"Yes."

That surprised me. "How did you find out?"

"Because I'm the buyer."

I was dumbstruck. It took a moment to assemble my thoughts. When I did, I pressed Boles for details. He explained that one of his colleagues had heard through the grapevine about the pocket listing. The colleague was interested but couldn't come up with the cash. He called Boles. Boles offered more than the asking price, because he figured Eve was selling the house because she needed the money and he wanted to help her out.

"Kip needs that land for Vista Village," I said. "Now that Eve has sold it out from under his nose, he must be pissed."

"That's his problem. He can have the property for the right price."

"And that price will be high. Right?"

Boles smiled. "Very high."

I suppose Boles looked at the deal as payback for the losses he'd suffered because of Kip Moreland. He acted as though he was manipulating pawns on a chessboard with the Ladera Bonita transaction, but while he had been checkmating Kip Moreland, he may also have put Eve Lawson in danger. I told him that Eve feared she was being followed and that somebody close to her had already been murdered.

Boles looked like a man sitting outside a hospital room, hoping for good news. "What do you want to know?"

"Were you and Eve lovers?"

Boles looked down at his hands. While I waited for him to respond, I glanced at the doughnuts. The chocoholic ants had scored big-time and were already heading back to the farm, but the ones that had gone for the jelly were in trouble. The heat had turned the centers into jiggly quicksand and several of the ants were mired in red goo.

"Eve and I dated for a while," he said. "I ran into her last year at a party. We had dinner. We laughed. One thing led to another. We kept the relationship quiet because I wasn't exactly on Kip Moreland's VIP guest list. Eve was afraid he'd cause problems for her if he knew we were seeing each other."

"She left town about that time," I said. "What happened?"

He looked away from me and gazed out the window. "I wish I knew. Things were good between us. At least I thought so. One day I came home from work and found a message from her on my answering machine. She told me she was leaving town. Just like that. I never heard from her again. If I did something to upset her, I don't know what it was."

"What else was happening in her life at that time?"

"Her father's Alzheimer's was progressing, so he turned the Ladera Bonita house over to her. Kip was livid because he was counting on that property to build Vista Village. He already had partners signed on, and they were not the type of people you want to disappoint."

"You mean people like Vince Cimino?"

He seemed surprised that I knew Cimino's name. "He's one, but there are others. Kip was under a lot of pressure to make the deal work. It was stressful for Eve because she'd promised Frank she wouldn't sell the house until after he passed away."

"Why didn't she just tell Kip to go to hell?"

"It wasn't her style. She wasn't confrontational. Plus she depended on Meredith Lawson's largess to survive and that meant Kip's, too. I suspect she left town because she couldn't stand the pressure anymore."

"Why didn't Frank Lawson want her to sell that house?"

"I don't know," he said. "It seemed completely irrational to me. Frank told me he had a recurring nightmare that he was going to lose everything. The Ladera Bonita house was paid for. Maybe he thought it would be his ace in the hole if something catastrophic happened."

I continued questioning Boles about the Lawsons and Wildwood Properties, but he didn't have any more answers. It was frustrating, but given his past relationship with Eve, I assumed he would have helped me if he could have.

"Eve must have confided in somebody about what happened," I said.

Boles paused as if to think. "She might have told Beulah."

"Beulah?"

"Beulah Judd, the Lawsons' cook."

I remembered something Meredith Lawson had mentioned in our interview. When Eve was a child, she had forged friendships with various members of the household staff. Her relationship with the cook had become a disruption, a nuisance. Meredith had put a stop to it. From what Boles had just said, it appeared that Eve might have kept the connection going for all these years despite her stepmother's interference.

"Where can I find Judd?" I said.

"I wish I could help you, but I just don't know."

I thanked Boles and followed the line of chocoholic ants to the door. I imagined them cruising back to the farm, high-fiving each other. Chocolate. Yeah. I liked the feeling of being in the winner's column, but in some ways I felt more akin to the other ants, the failures. It reminded me of where Charley and I were in the search for Eve Lawson. Mired in goo.

As soon as I got to Charley's office I went straight to the computer. As it turned out, invading Beulah Judd's privacy was alarmingly simple. Not only did I learn that she had sold her house and moved into an assisted living facility in Torrance, but I located her telephone number, as well.

I didn't know if Beulah could offer any insights into where Eve Lawson was, but she might know why Eve had left town a year ago. According to Meredith Lawson, Beulah had retired about that same time. I doubted that the two events were connected but it was worth the time to ask.

I dialed Beulah's number and told her that Eve had asked me to stop by and say hello. I expected her to be hungry for visitors. Old people are supposed to be lonely and needy. Not Judd. She told me she was competing in a bingo tournament for the rest of the day but would call me when she was available to talk. She asked for a number where I could be reached. I got the feeling that she was stalling until she checked my references. I hoped she didn't plan to check them with Kip Moreland.

I still had no idea what I was going to do about Tracy Fields. My threat to uncover the sins of her past was probably not a realistic goal. I didn't have time to cruise the juice bar at the gym, looking for disgruntled ex-lovers. Maybe there were none to find.

Instead, I checked the Web site for the California Bar Association, hoping to see if any grievances had been filed against her. There was a charge for obtaining the information and the request had to be submitted in writing. That could take weeks. I wanted immediate action. I did the only other thing that made sense. I called Eugene and asked for his help.

"So you think she's done this sort of thing before?" he said. "Like maybe she's a serial man-eater?"

"Could be. If you have the time, would you search the Internet and see what you can find out?"

"Don't worry, Tucker. Bix Waverly is on the job."

I was glad that Eugene couldn't see me slap my forehead with the palm of my hand. I couldn't help but believe that I'd created a monster with that pretext business.

"How's Fergie?" I said.

"She's awesome. She has this whole amazing language. At first she just did the silent meow thing, but now she's verbalizing. She says 'ak' when she's asking a question and howls when she wants her box cleaned. Liza isn't thrilled. She's acting out, but she'll adjust in time."

In time. Those words were music to my ears.

"So you can keep her for a while?" I said.

"Of course. It would be cruel to uproot her again so soon." His tone became frantic. "Omigod! Liza's chewing on my schefflera. I have to go."

Late that afternoon I received a call from my attorney, Sheldon Greenblatt. He told me he had arranged an informal meeting with my aunt and her attorneys for Monday morning at ten. I asked what was so urgent about the meeting to compel him to call me on a Saturday to tell me about it. He declined to go into the details, only saying that my mother had provided him with some information that he was pursuing. He didn't want to get my hopes up, but it looked promising.

Later I called my mother, but she refused to tell me anything about what she and Shelly had planned. No amount of coaxing, pleading, or threatening would sway her from that position.

I spent the rest of the weekend in limbo. Muldoon and I played on the beach with the Frisbee that Deegan had brought for him, but mostly I had to retrieve the thing myself. Muldoon isn't the type of dog that flies through the air to fetch anything unless it's a Ball Park Frank.

I practiced picking locks and actually managed to defeat that old bike lock with a bobby pin. I also went to another yoga class on my top-five list. The teacher wasn't bad, but he wasn't as good as Bruce. The rest of the time I just lounged around. It was too hot for any strenuous activity like weeding out decades-old outfits from my stand-and-throw closet. So I read. I watched reruns of my favorite TV shows. I took walks. I thought about the woman that Deegan had almost married and wondered if he was already making frittatas for somebody else. When I couldn't take any more wondering, I sat around waiting for Monday and the showdown with my aunt Sylvia.

Shortly after ten on Monday morning I arrived at the Beverly Hills law offices of Heller, Greenblatt, and Hayes for the legal powwow with my aunt Sylvia and her phalanx of high-priced lawyers. My stomach fluttered with anxiety. I was five minutes late because Mrs. D was pup sitting for Muldoon again, and I couldn't find the spare key to my house. I wanted her to have somewhere to go in case she locked herself out of her place again.

Shelly was already in the posh conference room, impeccably dressed and wearing a gold monogrammed ring on his pinkie finger. He was sitting at the imported Brazilian mahogany table across from Aunt Sylvia and her posse, which included four attorneys and a secretary who had been dragged along to take notes. Each member of the opposition had turned down cappuccinos. I figured it was an intended slight, but it was their loss. Shelly's paralegal was so good at frothing milk she could have been a professional barista.

Pookie hadn't arrived yet, which made me nervous wondering where she was. I sat next to Shelly on the defense side of the table, feeling outnumbered and vulnerable. Sylvia seemed fidgety and bored and refused to look at me.

A few minutes later, Shelly began the meeting by stating that he had called us all together for the purpose of informally discussing ways to settle this "heartbreaking family misunderstanding" and avoid "further costly legal wrangling." His speech sounded sincere, but everybody in the room knew it was total bullshit. This was the opening salvo in an all-out posturing war.

My aunt's lead attorney was a woman in her fifties who had made a name for herself by representing corrupt politicians. Her presence in the room almost made me wonder if my aunt was planning to run for office. She spoke without moving her lips, which was great for a ventriloquist but bad for a lawyer. Her voice lacked authority. I leaned forward, straining to hear.

"This issue can be easily resolved," she said, "if Tucker agrees to sell the beach house and accept a reasonable one percent of the proceeds as a relocation fee."

"I won't sell the house," I said.

Shelly put his hand on my arm to shut me up. Before responding he adjusted his tie, holding his ringed pinkie finger out as if he was drinking tea from a dainty porcelain cup at the Hotel Ritz.

"That's an interesting offer," he said, "but a nonstarter. Your client's allegations that Tucker is not a Sinclair are baseless."

"We have affidavits confirming that shortly before she married Jackson Sinclair, Tucker's mother had an affair with a man named Hugh Canham. As you know, we believe she conceived a child with Canham and that he is Tucker's biological father. Tucker and her mother deceived the probate court by purposefully withholding this information."

"He was a premature ejaculator!"

This stentorian blast came from the direction of the doorway behind me. I turned to see my mother cradling an accordion file in her arms. If her anger had been a gun, it was loaded for bear. Sylvia grimaced. The members of her legal team responded with various expressions of shock and disgust, except for the secretary, who looked sympathetic.

Pookie handed the file to Shelly and sat in the empty chair next to me. Shelly waited for the murmuring to quiet down before resuming his presentation.

"The matter is simple to settle," he said. "My client is willing to submit to DNA testing. That should resolve the issue."

"We have been unable to locate Mr. Canham," the attorney

said. "We believe he has left the country and returned to his native Australia."

"I'm afraid you didn't look hard enough," Shelly responded. "He's living in Nevada and has already met with my client about submitting a sample."

Aunt Sylvia's attorney frowned and began thumbing through the pages of her yellow legal tablet as if she was consulting some kind of oracle. A moment later I could almost see the cartoon lightbulb clicking on above her head.

She looked up and smirked. "If he agreed to DNA testing, then why are we having this meeting? If the results supported your position, I assume you would have already presented them to us."

She'd called Shelly's bluff. I wondered what kind of rabbit he planned to pull out of his hat now.

"Mrs. Branch," Shelly said, addressing my aunt directly, "you have spent the past two years making your niece's life miserable and depleting her limited resources. I am appealing to you one last time. In the name of decency, stop your reckless behavior before the damage to this family is irreparable. Let Tucker live in peace in the house your mother intended for her to have. Surely you can't need the money."

"It's not about money," Sylvia said. "It's about justice."

"For whom?" Shelly said. "For you? For your brother?"

Sylvia fidgeted in her chair. "My brother was a golden boy. He wanted for nothing, including justice."

"I'm just trying to understand your point of view, Mrs. Branch," Shelly said. "Please tell me—"

Sylvia glared at her attorney, who, in turn, interrupted Shelly midsentence. "My client isn't interested in responding to this line of questioning. Move on."

Shelly sighed. "Very well. Anne Sinclair's will states that the beach house was the only asset that was to be passed down to Tucker. Am I correct?"

The attorney nodded.

Shelly continued. "She left the balance of her estate to her surviving children, her daughter, Sylvia, and her son Donovan and any heirs they might produce. Also correct?"

"What are you getting at, counselor?" the attorney said. "There are no other heirs."

Shelly's expression looked grim as he reached into the accordion file and pulled out a photograph. I glanced over his shoulder and saw a studio portrait of a handsome woman in her thirties with dark hair and brown eyes. Shelly held it up for a moment and then skittered it across the polished wood table toward Sylvia. My aunt glanced at the photo but made no move to touch it.

Her attorney looked puzzled. "Is this picture supposed to mean something to my client?"

Shelly stared at Sylvia. "If she studies the image carefully, I think she will see that there is a striking family resemblance. Of course, the young woman has changed considerably since you last saw her, Mrs. Branch. You did see her, didn't you? Or did they whisk her away before you had a chance? You'll be happy to know that your daughter turned into a beautiful young woman, both inside and out."

Sylvia blanched. "This is nonsense."

"No," he said, "I'm afraid it isn't. Before he died your brother Jackson Sinclair confided to his wife, Mary Jo, that you had gotten pregnant in your senior year of high school. You spent the summer in Maui recuperating from the birth. He made her promise never to tell anybody, so for all these years, she kept it a secret. Until now. Just yesterday I located your brother Donovan at his home in France. I explained the situation. He confirmed the story. Family secrets so rarely remain hidden forever. I assume that you will want to notify your daughter of your existence. If so, I can provide you with an address. I understand that her circumstances are modest, so I'm sure she will be most interested in her inheritance."

With each word, Shelly slapped photo after photo on the table in front of Sylvia until he had a montage spread out in front of her. Throughout his entire presentation, Sylvia remained stony. Her gaze never dipped to look at the pictures. Instead, she kept her focus on the wall in front of her.

The photos were an indictment of sorts, but I wasn't sure of whom. My mother and Shelly were doing what they thought was best for me, but they had colluded to use a family secret as a tool of blackmail. I felt awful for everybody involved, including my aunt. Poor Sylvia. She had been harassing me for all those years when all that time she had her own daughter to torment. What a wasted opportunity.

Shelly had implied that he might contact my cousin to inform her of her status as an official Sinclair, but I didn't believe he would interfere in her life that way. I wondered if she would ever learn about her relatives. If so, I was certain that the information wouldn't come from my aunt.

Once Shelly had laid down the last photograph, Sylvia

pushed her chair back from the table like a polite dinner guest. Without saying a word, she stood and marched out of the room. Her entourage stuffed papers into briefcases and followed.

A few minutes after I left Sheldon Greenblatt's office, I got a call from the Lawsons' ex-cook, Beulah Judd. She was ready to talk.

## Chapter 24

Beulah Judd told me she would be going to lunch at eleven thirty, but that I was welcome to visit her after that. She suggested two p.m. It was a waste of time for me to drive all the way out to the beach only to come back again, so I spent the time in Charley's office, entering data into the new accounting program I'd purchased for him.

Charley's financial records were a train wreck, poorly documented or nonexistent. Most of his clients either hadn't paid his fees or hadn't yet been billed. For the next couple of hours, I sorted through files, entered client information, and did my best to create organization from chaos.

At around one o'clock, the telephone rang. I was in the middle of auditing a page of numbers, so I decided to let the answering machine pick up. The sixth ring activated the message recording. I waited but didn't hear anybody speak. I thought maybe the volume was turned down, so I walked over to have a look and found nineteen calls, mostly hang-ups. I wondered who it was and why they had chosen not to leave a message.

At one fifteen I left the office and headed for my appointment with Beulah Judd. The Lawsons' former cook lived at Villa Roma Retirement Village, an upscale three-story apartment building on a quiet street in Torrance. I navigated through the security checkpoint at the garage level and took the elevator up one floor to a tastefully decorated room that featured a grand piano and a birdcage filled with yellow finches. A man in his mid- to late seventies was using a putter to bang golf balls over green Astroturf and into a cup. The front desk gatekeeper made me write down my name, time of arrival, and the name of the person I was visiting. The White House had less security than this group of seniors living the good life.

I took the elevator up to the third floor and walked along the deserted hallway until I spotted Judd's apartment number on the door. When she finally answered my knock, she was out of breath.

"You must be Tucker," she said in a deep, throaty voice that commanded attention. "Come in."

She was wearing a gold-and-black caftan embellished with a primitive design and long, dangling earrings. Her hair was mostly gray and pulled back into a knot at the nape of her neck. She walked with the help of a deluxe four-wheeled walker that was fitted with a basket and a seat. Her gait seemed off kilter as though she had something wrong with her hip.

The apartment was small but cozy and featured a living room, a kitchenette, and a separate bedroom and bath. Her TV was tuned to the Food Network, but the background sound came from a radio playing classical music.

"All I have for cooking these days is a microwave," she said, "but at least I can still heat water for coffee."

I waited on a blue floral love seat across from her recliner as she filled a container with water from the kitchen faucet.

"You said you'd heard from Eve," she said. "She usually calls every few weeks, but the last time I heard from her was three months ago. When did you see her?"

"A few days ago. We were supposed to meet later that afternoon, but she no-showed. I haven't heard from her since. I was hoping she might have contacted you."

Judd seemed hurt by the news. "I didn't even know she was in town. She usually calls me right away. Maybe she wanted to get settled first."

I hesitated to tell her that Eve had been in town for weeks, and if Charley didn't find her soon, she might never get around to visiting Beulah, because she might be in jail or in the wind.

Beulah set the timer on the microwave and scooped grounds into a French press coffee maker, working effortlessly with long thin fingers the color of cumin.

"I understand you've known Eve for a long time," I said.

"I worked for Frank Lawson from the time Eve was a baby till my hip went bad. When I couldn't get around so good anymore, Frank found this place for me. The people here are nice, but the food is bad. Sometimes I want to go down to that kitchen and show them how it's done."

"Mr. Lawson sounds like a good employer."

She answered without hesitation. "He's more than that. He's a good man."

"Did you know Eve was writing a book?"

She shook her head. "I didn't know. She's good at a lot of things, though. I guess she'd be good at writing a book, too."

"It's a memoir," I lied. "Eve wants me to help her write it. She thinks I can bring objectivity to her story. She asked me to talk to you. She thought you would be able to fill in some blanks about her childhood. Would you mind if I asked you a few questions?"

Beulah paused as if considering my request. "That depends on what you want to know."

"For example, Eve can't remember much about her mother. What was she like?"

Beulah closed her eyes and took a deep breath as if she was trying to dredge up a painful memory. "She was delicate like a flower and always sick. She took pills for this and pills for that. I hear she spent most of her time in bed before that baby came. Doctors said it was morning sickness, but I think she was afraid."

"Afraid of what?"

"Afraid of the delivery. The pain. Being a mother. When Eve was born, she just couldn't cope. That's why Frank hired me. Nobody was eating right. I cooked and looked out for the baby, too, but that was before he got rich and hired a full staff. Mostly he wanted me there to make sure Eve was taken care of."

"What happened the day Eve's mother died?"

Beulah poured hot water over the coffee and placed six

chocolate-dipped madeleines from a nearby cookie jar onto a plate.

"I wasn't there. It was my day off. They said she took too many pills and drowned in the bathtub. Seemed odd to me. Wouldn't you wake up when the water got in your nose?"

"Was Eve there when it happened?"

Beulah shook her head. "She was at school. When she found out her mother was dead, she ran away. Took Frank hours to find her. In some ways I think she's still running, afraid to stop because she'd have to face all that pain."

"Why did Mr. Lawson send Eve away to boarding school?" I said.

She gave me a sharp look. "Because of Meredith. She set out to get rid of Eve from the start and she agitated till she got her way."

"Why didn't Frank stop her?"

Beulah drew in a deep breath that elevated her into perfect posture.

"I guess you never had to choose between two people you love. When that happens, somebody has to lose. Eve didn't help her cause by acting out the way she did, even if she had a good reason for it. All things considered, Frank did the best he could."

She pressed the grounds to the bottom of the glass receptacle and poured the coffee into cups. She loaded everything onto the seat of her four-wheeler and shuffled toward me.

"How did Eve get along with Kip Moreland?"

She handed me a cup, took the other one herself, and settled into her recliner. "About how you would expect under the circumstance. She hated him and the feeling was mutual."

"They must have patched up their differences, because I spoke with Kip a few days ago. He seemed worried about her. He thinks she's on the verge of a mental breakdown. He's afraid she may try to kill herself just like her mother did."

Beulah's face was partially obscured by the coffee cup but her eyes were not. They were dark with suspicion. "That's a lie. Eve is not suicidal, and she's not crazy."

"What happened to make Eve leave town a year ago?"

Beulah looked at me as though I had asked one nosy question too many. "Why are you asking me? Eve can tell you that better than I can."

I was walking a fine line with her now, but I needed to get some concrete information before I left. At the risk of alienating her, I had to press her for more.

"Frankly, I'm worried about her. She seemed nervous when I saw her on Thursday. She thought somebody was following her. It sounded crazy at the time, but then she no-showed for our appointment. Do you have any idea what was going on in her life?"

The cookies were still lying untouched on the plate. Beulah set her coffee cup down on a tray near the recliner.

"No," she said, "but if Eve is in some kind of trouble, you should call the police."

"I'm sorry," I said. "I didn't mean to worry you. She's probably just busy researching her book and forgot that we were supposed to meet."

The tension in her face eased but the suspicion didn't. "I'll stop worrying when I hear her voice. You tell her to call me as soon as you see her."

I assured her that I would. When I was ready to leave, Beulah pressed a button on the remote control connected to her recliner and waited for the chair to tilt her forward. She accompanied me to the door with the aid of her walker.

On the way out, I paused for a moment by an étagère near the front door. It was filled with knickknacks and family photographs. I recognized a young Beulah in front of a small clapboard house with her arm around an older woman. Beulah surrounded by copper pans in what I assumed was the Lawsons' kitchen. Beulah unpacking boxes in the living room of her Villa Roma apartment with the help of a young woman with dark hair and a tentative smile. It was difficult to make out the woman's facial features, but the body type was almost identical to mine, tall and thin.

Beulah noticed me staring. "That was the day I moved in here," she said. "It wasn't easy to leave my house. I had to get rid of most of my things. Not enough room here for memories."

"Who's the woman with you?"

Beulah seemed puzzled by my question. She picked up the photo and studied it as if to refresh her memory. "It's Eve, of course."

My heart began to race and my hands felt cold and clammy as I stared at the photo in Beulah Judd's hand. I waited for a wave of nausea to pass before echoing her words.

"Of course."

The only problem was that the woman in the photo with Beulah Judd was not the same person who had hired Charley Tate a week ago. So who was she and where was the real Eve Lawson?

## Chapter 25

As soon as I left Beulah Judd's apartment, I called Charley Tate's cell phone but got no answer. When I called his home, Lorna claimed he was sleeping and couldn't be disturbed.

"I have to talk to him," I said. "It's an emergency."

"I'll let him know as soon as he wakes up."

"No!" I said. "Now."

"He has to rest."

"Look, Lorna. Don't dick around with me. Okay? Go get Charley."

There was a moment of silence long enough for her to consider my request. Then she hung up on me.

I'd had enough. It was time to storm the Bastille. I made it to

Tate's gingerbread house in Manhattan Beach in record time. It took me even less time to turn Lorna's face purple with rage.

"I told you," she said. "He can't be disturbed."

I formed a megaphone with my hands and shouted through the crack in the front door. "Charley!"

"Be quiet. The whole neighborhood will hear you."

I raised my voice a decibel or two. "It's Tucker. I need to talk to you. It's important."

A moment later, Tate limped into the foyer. He was dressed in a pair of cotton pajama bottoms and an old Cal State Long Beach T-shirt. He seemed sleepy-eyed and disoriented.

"What the hell is going on?" he said.

"Eve Lawson is not Eve Lawson," I blurted out. "The person who hired you is an impostor. I've been trying to reach you but Lorna wouldn't put me through."

"You were sleeping, honey," she said. "I didn't want to bother you."

Charley's expression soured. Lorna spotted trouble. She turned and stamped up the stairs. A moment later I heard a door slam.

"Follow me," he said.

Charley led me to a large room jammed with overstuffed furniture, a pool table, and a wide-screen TV. We sat in cushy chairs across from each other, and I filled him in on details of my visit with Beulah Judd.

"So is the real Eve Lawson missing or not?" I said. "I suppose this could be a case of identity fraud, but it seems much bigger than that."

"I agree. If it's just identity fraud, then why did this woman hire me? Seems risky."

I got up and started pacing, trying to organize the jumble of facts in my head. "Maybe she wanted to establish that Eve Lawson was in some kind of danger, or maybe she killed Rocky Kincaid and she thought you'd be her alibi."

"That sounds a little iffy."

"We need to go back to the beginning," I said. "Fit as many of the puzzle pieces together as we can. See if a picture emerges."

Charley put his hands behind his head and settled back into the chair. "Be my guest."

I pressed my palms to my temples, hoping to squeeze out a few creative thoughts. "A year ago Eve Lawson was camping out in her father's guesthouse. She stayed longer than usual, so things must have been going okay for her. For one thing, she was hot and heavy with Nathan Boles. Then one day she left town and cut off all contact with her family. No one claims to know why. Boles thinks Kip Moreland wanted her to sell the house to Wildwood, and she left because she couldn't take the pressure anymore. That's just a guess. So what really happened?"

"Maybe she didn't need a reason," Charley said. "Crazy people do crazy things."

"I don't buy that argument at all. Eve was in therapy. That doesn't mean she was mentally ill. Sometimes people feel lonely and isolated and need somebody to talk to. Beulah confirmed that Eve didn't exactly have the support of her family. She felt wounded by her childhood."

"Beulah Judd is hardly an expert on the subject."

"No, but she was as close to Eve as anybody was."

"Keep going," Charley said.

I continued to wear a path in the carpet. "So Eve leaves town. Where did she go? Arizona for sure because the Lawsons received a letter from her postmarked in Phoenix. Boles never heard from her again. She kept in touch with Beulah but only by telephone. We know that as of three months ago Eve was growing sunflowers in Todos Santos, Mexico. That was about the last time Beulah heard from her."

"Jeez, sit down. You're making me dizzy."

I ignored Charley's request. The pacing was helping me think.

"Eleven days ago somebody claiming to be Eve Lawson comes into your office," I said. "She tells us she's being watched. She tells Neeva Moore that she's got a boyfriend named Rocky. Rocky turns up dead. So what connection do Rocky and this woman have to Eve?"

"You tell me."

Charley was more than capable of following the logic and coming up with his own theories, which might have been better than mine, but I could tell by the thinly veiled smile on his lips that he was enjoying watching me sort through the confusion.

"Rocky called his ex-wife from a hotel in Todos Santos," I said, "so let's assume he was living there."

"Or he was just passing through."

"For the sake of argument, let's assume that I'm right. Eve lived in Todos Santos and so did Rocky. We think Rocky skipped town with Mikki Sloan, his partner in the embezzlement scam. Let's say they went to Mexico together. They hooked up with Eve at some point and stole her identity."

"And how did they do that?"

"Easy," I said. "Rocky and Mikki were on the run. They needed money. What's the one thing they know how to do?"

"Steal money from suckers?"

"No. They know how to run a therapy practice. So they hang out their shingle but keep the business low-key, because they don't want to draw attention to themselves. Todos Santos is a small town. Word travels. Eve hears about this new therapist in town, and he's an American to boot. She's been in therapy most of her life, and something upsetting has just happened to her in LA. Something that made her leave a comfortable life in her father's guesthouse and a promising relationship with Nathan Boles. She needs to talk to somebody. She makes an appointment. On that first visit, she fills out paperwork, including her Social Security number and date of birth. Once Mikki assumes Eve's identity, the sky's the limit. Her credit is rock solid. She can do almost anything."

"Sounds good even if it is total speculation."

"Maybe, but what do you do when you go to a shrink?"

"You're asking me?"

I ignored his sarcasm. "You tell him what's bothering you. You tell him things that you don't tell anybody else about people who've hurt you. About your stepbrother who's putting impossible pressure on you to do something against your father's wishes. You tell him why you left LA."

"So who killed Rocky Kincaid?" he said.

I sat in the chair like a deflated party balloon. "I don't know. I haven't figured it all out yet. If it was Mikki Sloan who hired you, I don't understand why she'd want to attract the attention of a former cop."

"Because she's stupid?"

"Or because she's setting you up for something," I said. "We need a photograph of Mikki Sloan. Can you get a copy of her driver's license?"

"Probably not, but I may be able to get the mug shot from her DUI arrest."

"Do it," I said. "Then we can show the picture to the Realtor who sold Eve Lawson's property. At least we'll know for sure if it was Mikki Sloan who was posing as Eve to sell Lot 84."

Charley made a call to somebody he chose not to identify and arranged for the photo to be faxed to his office. Then he telephoned Madeline Fallbrook, the Realtor in Pasadena. He identified himself and explained that he suspected the sale of the Ladera Bonita house was a scam. He asked if she would be willing to confirm the identity of the seller if he faxed a photograph to her. That must have made her palms sweaty, because she agreed without hesitation.

I left Charley and drove back to Tate Investigations. Mikki Sloan's mug shot was waiting for me in the fax tray when I arrived. In the photo her face looked gaunt, her gaze vacant, her rosebud lips flaccid. Her hair had been shoulder length and dark when she first came into Charley's office posing as Eve Lawson, but in the photo it was cut short and bleached to a flaxen hue. Just Sue had nailed the description. Mikki Sloan was indeed a skinny blonde. If she had used Eve's identity to sell the Ladera Bonita house, I only hoped that Madeline Fallbrook would be able to look beyond the disguise to finger a con artist and maybe a killer.

I slid the mug shot photo into the fax machine, dialed Fallbrook's number, and pressed SEND. Sometime later Charley called to tell me that the Realtor had confirmed it was Mikki Sloan who had come to her office with several pieces of ID, including the original Deed of Trust to the Ladera Bonita house. She claimed to be the owner, and Fallbrook had no reason to doubt her. Fallbrook also told Charley that the escrow funds had been wired to a bank account in Mexico City, opened in the name of Mikki Sloan.

Mikki had told Fallbrook that the house had been empty for some time and that she'd lost the key. The property was a long drive from Fallbrook's office. That was why she was relieved when the seller agreed to show the place herself. As a courtesy, Fallbrook arranged with Ed at Gold-E-Locks to replace the locks. However, Mikki never showed the place, because Nathan Boles snapped up the property sight unseen. She lucked out. If he *had* wanted to look at the house, he would have exposed Mikki as an impostor and the deal would have fallen apart.

"So where's Eve?" I said to Charley.

"I'll be damned if I know, but I have to tell Meredith Lawson what's going on."

"Maybe I should come with you."

"Not a good idea."

"We still don't know what happened to Eve. No one has heard from her in three months. What if she *has* disappeared? What if Kip Moreland had her whacked because she wouldn't give him that house?"

"You've seen one too many gangster movies, Sinclair. There's no evidence that she's been murdered, but if it makes you feel any better you can monitor your cell phone. If you don't hear from me in a couple of hours, send out a posse."

For the next hour or so, I wandered around the office, conjuring up horrific scenes of Meredith Lawson confronting Charley with an Uzi on the dance floor of her guesthouse or of Charley floating faceup in the koi pond with the end of a sterling silver dessert fork protruding from his heart. Charley talked a good game, but he couldn't fend off trouble in his current condition. He was vulnerable, even if he chose to deny it.

I was still in my reverie when I heard footsteps on the stairs outside Charley's office. Not a heavy stride but a light tread as if it belonged to a woman. Maybe it was Manny Reygozo's paralegal. Charley claimed they had a nooner every Sunday while his wife was at church. This was Monday, but maybe Reygozo's wife was out rolling bandages for the mission fields and the two lovebirds saw an opportunity for a roll of their own on the old office couch.

It was after five. Charley's office was officially closed, so I ignored the footsteps until they stopped outside his door. I held my breath for a moment, listening for clues in the silence. Tension prickled along my jawline, because I couldn't remember if I'd locked the door. The knob turned. I watched and waited. The lock held. A moment later the telephone rang. I couldn't pick it up. Answering it would give away my position, so I let it ring. The sixth ring activated the message machine. Again, the caller waited on the line while the message played and then hung up.

For the next fifteen minutes, I waited around the office listening, but I heard no further sounds to indicate that anybody was still standing in the hallway. I eased open the door and stepped out. Once outside, I kept in the shadows of the building, watching cars pass by on the busy streets. None slowed or stopped. None looked suspicious. I glanced around but saw no one lurking around the bushes. I sprinted for my car. All the while, I had the distinct feeling that I was being watched.

# Chapter 26

I was reaching to put the key into the ignition when the passenger door opened and Eve Lawson aka Mikki Sloan slid into the seat beside me. She looked disheveled and wild-eyed. She was wearing shorts and a denim jacket and hugging that ancient Louis Vuitton purse of hers.

"I've been calling and calling." Her voice was vibrating with a desperate kind of rage. "Nobody ever answers the telephone. What kind of business are you running anyway?"

I thought back to all those hang-ups. It must have been Mikki. I didn't want to let on that I knew she was an impostor, because she might freak out if I backed her into a corner. I wanted to keep her engaged in case she knew where Eve Lawson was.

"We were out trying to find you," I said.

"I changed my mind. I don't need a PI anymore. I want my money back."

"Okay," I said. "I'll see that you get a check—"

"No checks! I want cash just like I gave Tate."

"Charley won't be back in the office until tomorrow. Give me your telephone number, and I'll have him call you."

"I need the money now. I saw him put it in his desk drawer. Maybe it's still there."

She seemed frantic about a measly thousand dollars. I wanted to ask her why she didn't use some of the one-point-four million she'd gotten from the fraudulent sale of Eve's house, but she probably didn't have access to it yet.

"That was a week ago," I said. "I'm sure he's deposited the cash by now."

"How much money do you have in your purse?"

"Forty bucks at the most."

"Why don't you use your ATM card? He can pay you back tomorrow."

"The machine won't let me have that much money in one day."

She narrowed her eyes. "Bullshit."

"I'm just being honest with you. The most I can get is five hundred dollars. I'll lend you that, but you'll have to get the rest tomorrow from Mr. Tate."

Mikki gnawed on the cuticle of her thumb as if that would help calculate the shortfall in her budget. My stalling ploy was not working, so I shifted to another tack. My purse was lying on the floor under her feet. I reached for it.

"Let me try to call Charley," I said. "I'll see if he can get the cash and meet us here."

She stamped her foot down on my hand.

I yelped. "What did you do that for?"

"You just said he wasn't available. Now you say he is. Which is it?"

"I don't know if he's available or not. I was going to try to reach him because you seem a little stressed out right now."

Mikki's gaze darted between my purse and me. She seemed unsure of what her next step should be. I yielded to silence, hoping she would realize that I was a lousy financier and decide to move on. Instead, she picked up my purse from the floor and threw it on my lap. I had expected her to take the ATM card and my PIN number and get out of the car, but she surprised me.

"Let's go to your bank," she said.

There were probably branches closer to Charley's office, but I decided to go to the one in Westwood, because I knew the area from my UCLA days. There would be people around if I needed help. As I steered out of the parking lot, I saw a red Nissan parked on the street about a block away. The finish was chalky. It looked just like the car I'd seen in the carport of Eve/Mikki's house in Playa del Rey. It had a dent in the front bumper that hadn't been there before. Seeing it made me glad she hadn't asked to drive the Boxster.

I took Sepulveda all the way to Wilshire and made my way into Westwood Village. During the drive I tried to engage Mikki in conversation, but she was unresponsive. I arrived at Bank of America and double-parked in a loading zone in front of the

ATM machine. I switched off the Boxster's ignition and pulled out the key.

"Leave that with me," Mikki said, "in case I need to move the car."

I hesitated. "Okay."

I grabbed my purse and started to get out of the car.

"Do you have a cell phone in there?" she said, pointing to my purse.

I nodded.

"Leave it here, too. I need to make a call. In fact, I'll watch your purse. All you need is your ATM card."

Now I knew Mikki's game plan. She was going to drive off with my car, my purse, and my identity and head for her bank account in Mexico. With one-point-four million dollars tucked away, she could disappear for a long time, maybe forever. I had a plan, too. As soon as she pulled away from the curb, I was going to run into the bank and scream bloody murder.

I waited in line at the ATM machine behind three other people. They all looked like students. I periodically glanced over my shoulder, each time expecting to see the Boxster's taillights disappearing into traffic, but Mikki had my cell phone up to her ear and made no attempt to move into the driver's seat.

When it was my turn at the machine, I took out five hundred dollars. I thought about sprinting into the bank to safety, but the facade of deception was still in place between Mikki and me. If I kept it that way, she might let something slip. Maybe I still had a chance to learn information that would help Charley find Eve Lawson.

I walked back to the car. Mikki looked more relaxed now.

Perhaps the person she had spoken with on the telephone had soothed her fears. She rolled down the window, and I handed her the money.

"Thanks," she said. "I really appreciate this. I'm sorry I was such a bitch before. If you take me back to my car, I won't bother you anymore."

She seemed to have gained a new attitude and maybe a new game plan, too. If so, it sounded reasonable. I said, "Sure."

I slid into the driver's seat and turned the key. The Boxster growled to life. I glanced down the street and waited for a break in traffic. Mikki was rummaging in her purse. I turned to find out why. For a moment everything seemed blurry and languid as if I was swimming underwater. Then my vision cleared, and I saw the barrel of a gun pointed at my chest.

Mikki pressed the weapon to my side and said, "Drive."

My breathing felt shallow. I fought to control the tremor in my hands as I pulled into traffic on Westwood Boulevard. "What's the deal, Eve? I'm on your side. Remember?"

She glared at me and pressed some buttons on my cell phone. The next thing I heard was Charley's voice coming over the speakerphone.

"Hey, kid," he said, "guess what. I was on the way to the Lawsons' place when West Traffic called to tell me they made the car that ran me off the road. Remember when I wrote down all those license plate numbers the day we were in Playa del Rey? Eve's red Nissan was one of them. I gave the list to the detectives, and they matched her number to the partial license from the witness. The car is registered to a woman in San Diego. She says she sold it about six weeks ago to Eve Lawson, but from the description she gave detectives, it looks like Mikki Sloan was the buyer. Obviously Sloan didn't change the registration. And get this, I just got off of the phone with Detective Mendoza. He says Sloan matches the description of a woman seen running out of Rocky Kincaid's hotel room shortly after the desk clerk heard shots fired. He's going to show her mug shot to the wit to see if he can get a positive ID." The message ended with "She's dangerous, Tucker. If she comes anywhere near you, run."

Charley must have left the message on my voice mail while I was standing in line at the ATM. Too bad my cell phone didn't have a secret access code. Dread burned my stomach like acid. I thought about stopping the car and bolting, but there were pedestrians everywhere, mostly young, probably students. Mikki would shoot me and probably take out a few other innocent people as well.

It seemed futile to continue the pretense now. "You killed Rocky," I said.

Her expression was defiant. "It was an accident but so what? I did all the work. Why should I share the money with him?"

"Why did you hire Charley?"

"I told you. Somebody was following me. I had to know who it was. If it was the cops, I needed to disappear."

"Then why leave Playa del Rey before Charley arrived to place the cameras?"

"Because I found out who it was before he got there."

"So who was following you?"

"Rocky. He knew I had to stay in town until escrow closed on the house in case something went wrong. He was supposed to sit tight in Mexico, but he got suspicious when he didn't hear from me. He thought I was double-crossing him, so he came back to town and started hanging around the neighborhood."

"How did you find out it was him?"

"When I got home from Tate's office, he was waiting for me in a taxi. Said we needed to talk. I couldn't let Tate see him there, but he wouldn't leave. So I got in the cab and we went back to his motel. He told me he'd given all of his cash to his ex-wife, and he needed money to pay a debt to a bookie. Stupid asshole. What did he think? That the bank was going to give us cash for the house? I told him I didn't have any extra money because I just blew a thousand bucks to find out if the cops were tailing me. Instead, I find out it's him. I told him to go to Dorcas's house and get his money back so we could get out of town. He wouldn't do it. We had a big fight. I thought he was going to kill me, so I pulled out the gun so he'd leave me alone. He grabbed for it, and it went off."

"So you left the motel and went to Charley's office to get your thousand dollars back."

"I had to. I was running low on cash, and I sure wasn't going to get any back from Dorcas. Tate was just leaving, so I followed him. I thought I'd wait till he stopped. Then I'd ask for the money."

"But he didn't stop, so you tried to run him off the road and ended up with that dent in your fender."

"That was *his* fault. He spotted the car and tried to run *me* off the road."

"Where's Eve Lawson?" I said.

"How should I know?"

"Is she okay? Can I talk to her?"

"I told you, I don't know where Eve is. I haven't seen her in months. Just drive. I'm getting sick of your stupid questions."

"Where are we going?" I said.

"The 405. North."

I headed for the freeway. The sun was just descending below the buildings in the west. As I passed Veteran, I saw on my right the war statue that stood before a semicircular stucco wall in front of the Los Angeles National Cemetery. Just inside the cemetery grounds were four palm trees that looked like the backup singers in Hugh Canham's Tickle Me Peach show. An overturned metal shopping cart lay on its side near the wall. It was filled with plastic grocery bags and dirty blankets. A homeless man was asleep near the cart with a folded newspaper over his face.

To my left was the Federal Building that housed the FBI. The offices would probably be closed by now, but there must have been guards on duty. I wondered if I could jump out of the car and survive the sprint across multiple lanes of rush hour traffic or if I should pull into the parking lot and start screaming for help.

I did neither. Instead, I turned onto the freeway and drove north as instructed. I tried to get Mikki to talk but every time I said anything, she told me to shut up. By the time we transitioned onto the 118 traveling inland, the sun had set. Darkness seemed to settle her nerves. She used my cell phone again, dialing from memory.

"Hey, it's me," she said. "I'm on my way but I'm running late." There was a pause while she seemed to be listening. "Okay, I'll meet you there."

She turned off the phone and slid it into the pocket of her denim jacket.

So Mikki had a partner. I wondered who it was.

"Where are we going?" I asked again.

I hoped she would say anywhere but the desert. That was the dumping ground of choice for dead bodies.

"I told you to shut up."

"Come on, Mikki. Here we are. Alone in the car. Just you and me. Why don't you loosen up?"

"You loosen up."

"Okay," I said. "I think I have most of the pieces put together. Tell me if I'm right. You met Eve Lawson in Mexico. Eve came to Rocky for a few therapy sessions. She told him about inheriting the Ladera Bonita property. So you and Rocky cooked up a plan to steal her identity and the house. I'm not sure about the book, though. Did Eve really plan to write one or did you make that up?"

Mikki was slumped in the seat with the gun resting on her thigh, sulking. "I hope you're having fun."

*Yeah,* I thought, *being here with you is a real kick in the head.*

"Eve told Rocky about a lot of shady development deals that went down in LA," she said. "Her father did bad things to get rich. I thought all those stories would make a great book, and the Lawsons would probably pay a lot of money to keep us from publishing it. I wanted Rocky to get Eve to write everything down as part of her therapy, but she wasn't interested. Writing it ourselves was too hard, so I came up with the house idea."

"Is Eve Lawson alive or did you kill her just like you killed your boyfriend, Rocky Kincaid?"

"You're full of shit. I didn't kill Eve. We were taking her money, but that was legit. She loved spilling her guts to Rocky about her evil stepmother and her asshole stepbrother. One day she missed an appointment and we never saw her again. We figured she left town."

"Did Eve tell you why she left LA?"

"It was because of that house. Her stepbrother wanted it but she wouldn't sell. One night they had a big fight, and he threatened to kill her. She was afraid. So she left town. I figured she'd never come back to LA, at least not for a long time."

"So where is Eve now?"

She raised the gun and placed the muzzle against my temple. "I don't want to talk about it anymore."

*No problem,* I thought.

## Chapter 27

By the time I took the exit for Ladera Bonita, the clock on the Boxster's dash read eight twenty p.m. Mikki kept the gun aimed at my rib cage as we traveled through town and out Ladera Canyon Road to the Vista Village construction site. The crew was gone for the day, leaving behind the shadowy carcasses of gigantic cranes and earthmoving equipment that were beginning to remind me of childhood nightmares about monsters under the bed. In the distance were acres of wooden skeletons that would soon be trendy shops and condos. Beyond that, there was nothing. No mini malls. No gas stations. Not even a Starbucks. That would come later.

At the edge of the construction site was a mobile trailer much like the one I'd seen at Nathan Boles's building site in West

Los Angeles, but from the logo on the door I saw that Wildwood Properties owned this one. Mikki directed me to park in front of the trailer and turn off the ignition.

"Give me your keys," she said.

I handed them to her.

"Get out of the car."

The temperature outside was still warm. The wind had picked up and was churning my hair around my face. The soil beneath my feet felt loose and powdery as I walked toward the trailer. At the top of the stairs I turned the knob and heard the hollow sucking sound of the door separating from the weather stripping.

Inside I saw a couple of file cabinets, a watercooler, a desk, and several metal chairs. Austen Kistler occupied one of them. He had on that same dirty ball cap and olive shirt and trouser outfit that he had worn to the town hall meeting. A thin gray jacket had been added to the ensemble.

Kistler's eyes opened wide. His gaze traveled from Mikki to the gun to me. "Is she the one you just called me about?"

"Yeah. Why?" Mikki said.

Kistler shook his head. "She's not who you think. She's a reporter for the *New York Times*."

Mikki glanced at me and laughed. "Where'd you get that idea? She's no reporter. She works for a private detective who works for Wildwood Properties. Remember them? They're the enemy. Like I told you before, they hired her to make sure Eve sold her house to them, not you."

Kistler frowned, as if he was processing the information and figuring out where it fit in the big picture.

"You said if I blew up the trailer it would stop the building until I got the house," he said. "What good does it do to kill her?"

"Are you kidding? She dies and construction stops for sure." Mikki lowered the gun to her side and walked over to Kistler, embracing him with her free arm. "Look, Austen." Her voice was soft and soothing. "You want to stop the development and save Ladera Bonita. So do I. All those lawsuits of yours were a waste of time and money. That's why we had to change the plan. This one will work but not if we let her go. She'll tell them everything. They'll take Eve's land and build multimillion-dollar houses on it. More of your friends and neighbors will have to leave. They'll take the horses, too, and there goes your feed store. Do you understand?"

Kistler seemed to be warring with the concept. He stared at the floor for a long time. Finally, he nodded.

"Good," she said. "Did you bring the package?"

He pointed toward the desk. Sitting on top of it was a ten-inch cube wrapped in brown paper and crisscrossed with packing tape. It had an oily stain on the side and was hand addressed in blocky letters to WILDWOOD PROPERTIES, c/o VISTA VILLAGE, LADERA BONITA, CA. There was no return address. One end of the package had been left open and several wires were sticking out. Call me crazy but it looked very much like a bomb.

From all appearances, Kistler may have been planning to mail the package, or at least that was what he wanted people to believe, but I couldn't imagine a bomb getting through the U.S. Postal Service's security these days.

*How perfect*, I thought. The Vista Village development was

controversial. People were protesting. Somebody sets a bomb to make a statement. Meanwhile, good old Tucker comes snooping around the construction site and gets herself blown to bits. I wondered where Kistler had learned about explosives. Vietnam? He had served there. At least that's what he'd told Eugene. How naive of Kistler to think that destroying the trailer or me would stop anything.

"Tie her hands, Austen," Mikki said. "We don't want her in the way while we work."

Kistler took a couple of plastic ties from a black bag filled with tools and electrical tape on the floor near his feet. He bound my hands behind my back. I felt searing pain as the ties went to work. Mikki shoved me toward a nearby chair. It seemed as if my arms wrenched out of the sockets as I fell.

Mikki put the gun in her purse and pulled my cell phone from the pocket of her denim jacket.

"Don't use that thing in here!" Kistler shouted.

"Chill out," she said. "I turned it off in the car."

Kistler's outburst triggered his phlegmy cough. It took him a while to regain control.

Mikki laid my cell phone and car keys on the desk. "I need to borrow your truck, Austen. I don't know how to drive a stick."

He seemed conflicted but handed her his keys.

"I'll meet you back at the store," she said. "You be careful now."

Mikki left the trailer, and a moment later, I heard an engine being gunned. Kistler looked toward the sound and winced. He picked up the tool bag and set it on the table near the package. His back was toward me so I couldn't see what he was doing, but he was close enough for me to catch a whiff of his scent. It was the sweet smell of hay mingled with the acrid odor of nervous sweat. He took something white and malleable from the bag. It looked like bread dough. He fiddled with it for a while. I heard the crinkle of paper as he closed the wrapping around the box.

I worked the ersatz handcuffs, trying to wriggle out of them. They were thin like the ties used to wrap computer cords into a neat bundle in order to keep them out of the way. The plastic cut deeper into my wrists but it wouldn't give.

"Don't go moving around," Kistler said. "Static can set this thing off. Blow us both to kingdom come."

"Mr. Kistler, what you're doing is murder. You'll get caught. You'll die in prison."

He stopped what he was doing, as if he was thinking about what that might be like. "Doesn't matter. I got nothing to lose."

I needed to keep talking. Maybe I could touch some emotion that would persuade him to unhook those wires.

"Mikki was lying to you," I said. "I don't work for Wildwood Properties. I'm a business consultant. You're going to kill an innocent person. It's not too late. We could just get up and walk out of this trailer. Both of us. We could forget the whole thing."

He turned toward me. His face was contorted with anger. "Forget? Frank Lawson stole everything I ever loved. He got away with it before. I won't let him get away with it again."

"Frank Lawson is ill. He's not responsible for Vista Village. His stepson put the project together."

"He stole Dorothy from me. Then he killed her to get her money. Now he wants to destroy this town and everybody in it."

I couldn't figure out what he was talking about until I remembered my conversation with Nathan Boles in Sonoma. He told me that Dorothy was the name of Frank Lawson's first wife. Frank created Wildwood Properties after her death by selling some land that she owned.

"How did he kill her?" I said.

"He gave her pills he got from his pharmacy. Then he pushed her head under the water until she was dead."

"How do you know that?"

"She told me."

"Who told you?"

His voice became low and conspiratorial. "Dorothy. She tells me everything."

The fervor on Kistler's weather-beaten face seemed genuine. He had quoted Balzac at the town hall meeting. "Behind every great fortune is a crime." He must have thought that Frank Lawson built a financial empire from the profits of murder. I wondered if Kistler had gone over the edge of sanity or if there was any truth to his allegations.

I lowered my voice to match his own. "Did Dorothy tell you that Mikki Sloan has already killed at least one person, and that she'll probably kill you, too?"

Kistler's eyes narrowed. "You think I'm crazy, don't you? Well, I'm not. You'll see."

He pulled a pair of pliers from the black tool bag and walked over to one of the windows. It was the sliding kind that appeared to have some type of screw-down lock on it. Kistler used the pliers to tighten the lock, twisting it until his arm trembled from the force of his effort. He moved to each of the locks on all of the windows and tightened them, too.

"How did you hook up with Mikki?" I said.

"I saw her snooping around Frank Lawson's house. At first I thought she worked for Wildwood. Then I found out she was trying to stop the development, too."

Just Sue had warned me that Mikki was a user and a master manipulator, especially where men were concerned. She must have found out that Kistler knew the Lawson family when they lived in Ladera Bonita and that he also knew what Eve Lawson looked like, or at least what she didn't look like. Mikki had to keep him from screwing up her real estate scam by exposing her as an impostor or by trying to buy Lot 84 on his own. Maybe she'd even decided to string him along in case she needed extra muscle. Like now.

"You seem to be doing all the work," I said. "What's Mikki contributing to this partnership?"

His face looked pinched and unyielding. He slipped the pliers back into the tool bag.

"She's a friend of Eve Lawson's," he said. "She found out Eve wants to sell the land to me, but she's afraid Kip Moreland will kill her if she does. She's ready to sign the papers. All we need is a little more time to convince her that it's safe to come back to town."

"Mr. Kistler, Mikki's conning you. She told you she wanted to save Ladera Bonita from developers, but that's not true. She doesn't care about you or your town. In fact, she stole Eve Lawson's identity and used it to sell her property for a lot of money.

If the sale goes through and nobody finds out about the scam, the buyer will sell it to the development partners for even more money. If Mikki's scheme is discovered, the property will probably be returned to Frank Lawson, which means Kip Moreland and Wildwood Properties. So regardless of what you do, Vista Village will move forward."

He pulled a knife from his pocket and started toward me. "You're lying."

My heart was pounding. I thought he was going to kill me with the knife before he even set off the bomb. Instead, he cut the plastic bindings from my wrists and stuffed them into his pocket. Maybe he didn't want the authorities to see that my hands had been tied. Bound hands wouldn't fit the tragic accident story that he and Mikki were likely envisioning. I wondered if he would leave the door unlocked for the same reason.

I rubbed my wrists to ease the pain. Kistler picked up my car keys and slipped them into his jacket pocket. He got my cell phone from the desk, hit some buttons, and waited for the signal. When the screen displayed my number, he jotted it on a piece of paper, as if he planned to call me. Then he set the telephone back on the desk near the bomb. I wondered if he was going to leave it there. If so, he had to know that as soon as he left the trailer I'd use it to call for help.

I remembered how Kistler panicked when he thought Mikki had left my phone on. Now he was turning it on himself. Why? A moment later I answered my own question—because that's how he was going to trigger the bomb. He was going to call my cell phone. That was why he'd written down my number.

Kistler turned toward the door. As if reading my mind, he grabbed the cell phone. Then he picked up his tool bag, pulled the key out of the dead bolt, and left the trailer. I saw the door jiggle and assumed that it was Kistler locking it from the outside. I wondered how he'd gotten the key. I heard a scraping sound at the base of the door, probably Kistler setting the phone down. A moment later I heard the Boxster drive away.

Charley's admonition thundered in my head: *If you can see the bomb, the bomb can see you.* I had to get out of the trailer. I crept toward the door, careful not to create static electricity from the friction of my clothes rubbing together as I walked. I tried the door, but it was locked.

My watch read nine fifteen p.m. I wondered how long I had before Kistler called my cell phone. He'd have to go a safe distance away before activating the bomb but not too far. How long would that take? Five minutes? Ten? Two? He couldn't risk leaving me alone for too long for fear I'd find some way to escape. I figured I had no more than five minutes.

There was no hardwired telephone in the trailer. That made sense. Everybody used mobile phones these days. Calling for help would be futile in any case. No one would arrive in time to save me. I was on my own. Anybody could set off the bomb by calling me—one of my friends, even Charley. He said he would check in as soon as he finished talking to the Lawsons.

I walked to the window closest to me. My hands fumbled with the lock, but Kistler had screwed it down too tight. The other windows were in the same condition. There were no tools in sight that could undo the damage. I considered breaking the glass, but the motion might set off the bomb.

My pulse thundered in my ears. I counted to keep track of the time. Four minutes forty-five seconds . . . forty-four . . . forty-three.

The dead bolt was keyed from both sides. It looked sturdy. Charley could probably defeat it with a bobby pin. I went to my purse and pulled the Visa card from my wallet, not worried about damaging it now. The flashlight I'd bought at Kistler's feed store was at the bottom of my purse. I put it in my pants pocket in case I needed a light source. My hands trembled as I tried to shove the card between the door and the jamb just below the lock. The seal was too tight. I probed higher on the door and found a gap. I used the card as a shim. Slid it down the crease. The gap narrowed. I applied force. Bent the card. Failure. I probed to find the gap again. The air in the trailer was hot and still. My body felt clammy with sweat and ice-cold fear. I continued counting. Three minutes twenty-seven seconds, twenty-six.

Charley made lock picking look effortless. That was far from the reality. His voice buzzed in my head. *Be patient. Feel the resistance.* Two minutes fifty-nine seconds left. I tried not to panic. I rubbed my hands against my thighs to warm them and attacked the lock again. Calmer now. Confident. Taking my time. Two minutes thirty-two seconds. The lock remained impenetrable. Austen Kistler told me that static could set off the bomb, but that was the least of my worries now. My time was running out. I was going to die either way.

Charley had said, *Choose the smart way. Take the easiest path. Believe in yourself.* He was right. If I wanted something bad enough, I didn't need anybody else to believe in me. And what I wanted was to live. I closed my eyes and took a deep breath, searching for courage. Finding it. Fear was replaced by eerie calm and absolute certainty that somehow I was going to get out of this frigging trailer alive.

I made a decision. Knew it was right. I picked up one of the metal chairs and carried it to the window farthest from the package. I swung with all my strength. The automotive glass shattered around me in a shower of green crystals. My gaze darted toward the bomb. It was still sitting placidly on the desk. I enlarged the hole with the flashlight and climbed onto the chair. I teetered in a squatting position on the windowsill. Then I jumped, dropping to the ground with a thud. The shock of the landing reverberated all the way up my spine. I picked myself up and bolted across the field, running until my lungs hurt. The sound of my breath pounded in my ears. I spotted a large earthmoving machine just ahead. Cover. I ran toward it, just as I heard the faint sound of my cell phone chiming *La Traviata*.

A powerful wind swept me off my feet. My head felt as if it was ripping apart. Time passed. How much, I'm not sure. I slammed to the ground. Debris rained down from the sky. Whole things. Pieces of things. Paper. Something metal. A chair. I saw it fall through the air, but I didn't hear it land. I couldn't hear anything.

I lay facedown in the loose soil for what seemed like hours. Finally I staggered to my feet, and with the flashlight illuminating the way, I began stumbling toward the main road, unaware that my shoes were missing. I moved through a silent world past a town in flux. Wooden skeletons of future houses loomed against hills that wore the brown mantel of summer. I wondered if anybody would ever live in those places and if they would ever learn that a bomb planted in a mobile construction trailer had nearly killed a woman named Tucker Sinclair. It didn't matter. There was no time for reflection now. If Kistler came back to survey his handiwork, I had to be far away from here. I had to find help.

## Chapter 28

My salvation came not from a passing motorist but from a horse named May. Lea Brown had been out for an evening ride when she heard the explosion and came to investigate. I think I asked for her help, but I can't be sure. I couldn't hear the words coming out of my own mouth. May bore our weight over the rough terrain until we reached Lea's house, where she called Charley Tate and the police.

It took several days for my hearing to return. While I was recuperating, I read in the newspaper that Austen Kistler had been found shot to death in the back room of his feed store and that Mikki Sloan had been arrested as she drove his truck toward the Mexico border town of Tijuana. The sheriff's department found my Boxster parked near Kistler's horse trailer. A couple of days later, Venus picked it up from impound.

The newspaper reporter assigned to the story gave Tate Investigations credit for uncovering the real estate scam. The fraudulent sale of Eve's property would undoubtedly delay the progress of Vista Village, but Boles would likely get his escrow funds back and the development would move forward. There was too much money at stake to stop now, and as Kip Moreland had said in our first interview, "Money is always the issue."

As a result of the newspaper coverage, Charley had been fielding so many calls from reporters and prospective clients that he had persuaded Eugene to leave Aames & Associates a few days early to book appointments. The two of them now clashed only a couple of times a day and usually over something minor, like Charley's failure to empty the wood chipper on his sci-fi pencil sharpener.

About a week after the trailer explosion, Charley came to the house to see me. The lines in his face seemed to have deepened since I'd last seen him and that mischievous expression of his was missing in action. Muldoon had never met him before, so the pup indulged himself in a few barks and a lot of sniffing.

Charley and I walked onto the deck outside my house. I sat in the chair that rocked. Charley sat in the chair that didn't. After we were settled, he reached into his pocket and pulled out a slim package that was covered in plain blue paper and tied with a ratty white bow that looked as if it had been recycled once too often. It was obvious that he had wrapped the gift himself.

"What is it?" I said. "A peace offering from Lorna?"

"In your dreams," he said. "Open it."

I took the package out of his hand and shook it. "At least it isn't ticking."

That didn't set well with him. He put his elbows on his knees and hung his head, staring at the deck as I imagined Fergie might do as she watched fish swimming in a pond.

"I screwed up, Sinclair. I should never have gotten you involved in one of my cases. When I think about what could have happened . . ." He blew out a gust of air in lieu of words that he couldn't express.

I remembered that old case of his, the young woman and her daughter who'd been killed in a car bombing. Charley had never talked about it except in general terms, but I sensed that those deaths had been devastating for him. I wondered if he was thinking about them now.

I kept my voice soft. "Charley, it's not your fault. I got myself involved. I take full responsibility for what happened. Besides, I'm okay and I want to open my present."

He nodded but didn't look up. I peeled the tape off of the ends of the package and laid back the wrapping. Inside was something that was about the size of a business-card case.

"Uh . . . thanks, Charley. What is it?"

He looked up in mock exasperation. He took the thing out of my hand and opened it up. There were four small metal objects inside. They looked like tools from Barbie and Ken's dental office.

"Okay," I said, dragging out the word to indicate that I was still clueless.

He rolled his eyes. "It's a lock-picking set. There's a tension wrench, two diamond picks, and a hook pick. It's small enough so it can fit in your pocket."

I laughed. "I'm touched."

"Yeah. Whatever. What does the doc say about your ears?"

"He doesn't think there'll be any permanent damage, but no guarantees. Any word on Eve Lawson?"

"I got a fax from the Todos Santos Police Department this morning. They found the remains of a white female in a landfill just outside of town. She had a thirty-eight caliber bullet in her head. The body was pretty decomposed, but they think it's Eve's."

I was already prepared for the worst but hearing the news didn't make it easier to take. Mikki had denied harming Eve, but her history with the truth was spotty at best.

"Mikki's still claiming Rocky Kincaid's death was self-defense," he said. "If she doesn't plead guilty to popping Kistler, the DA's threatening to send her to Mexico to face charges for Eve Lawson's murder."

"How is Meredith Lawson taking the news?"

He shrugged. "She didn't say much when I told her. Just asked me to send her a bill for my expenses. She claims she's going to pay me the hundred grand, too, because I found Eve, even if she wasn't alive. I didn't argue with her. When I get the check, that will be the end of our client relationship."

"Poor Eve," I said.

"Yeah."

We were both quiet for a while, consumed by our thoughts. I felt sorry that Eve Lawson's life had been so troubled. It was hard not to judge her father for banishing her from the house at such a young age, forcing her to live like an emotional vagabond, constantly moving because she had no home or family to come home to. No wonder she spent all those years in therapy.

"Sinclair?" I looked up. Charley's brow was furrowed. He seemed worried about how I was taking the news of Eve Lawson's death. "I got a proposition for you."

I smiled. "Thanks, Charley, but I'm already on Lorna's shit list."

He rolled his eyes. "Don't flatter yourself. I talked to Reygozo. The tenants next door to me just gave notice. The office is small but the rent is reasonable. Manny says he can knock a hole in the wall and make a door."

"You think it's wise to expand so soon?" I said. "The interest from this publicity could just be a temporary blip. I'd wait for a while. See what happens."

He rubbed his hand over his crew cut. "I was thinking the office could be for you. You keep telling me you want a place of your own. We're already sharing Eugene. Might as well share space, too. Reygozo wants a six-month lease. Can you handle that?"

I was taken aback by Charley's offer. There were risks involved, both financial and strategic. I wasn't sure I could afford the expense of an office. Plus, the address wasn't Beverly Hills or Century City. My clients might think I wasn't successful enough to have a posh address or that I wasn't worth the fees I charged. I wasn't even sure I wanted to move out. My house was comfortable. Moving meant I'd be away from Muldoon all day every day. On the other hand, six months wasn't forever. My computer could print temporary letterhead, and I might be able to take Muldoon to work with me.

I looked at Charley and smiled. "Yeah. I think I can handle it."

In the days that followed Charley's visit, I received a call from

Sheldon Greenblatt. Aunt Sylvia's lawyers had advised him that she no longer wished to challenge my status as a Sinclair. I had won the war but at what cost?

I wondered if I should call my aunt and thank her, but doubted that she would welcome the gesture. Leo Tolstoy once said, "All happy families resemble one another, but each unhappy family is unhappy in its own way." The Sinclair family unhappiness dynamic was still unclear to me, so I decided to let the wounds fester while I figured it out.

While I'd been dealing with Mikki Sloan, Eugene had been searching the Internet for dirt on Tracy Fields. He had failed to find anything but didn't want to disappoint. So without telling me, he'd gone undercover at the Sports Club/LA posing as Bix Waverly, investigative reporter for the *New York Times*. He haunted the locker room, telling anyone who would listen that he was writing an op-ed piece on "Love Gone Bad." Before long his notebook was filled with stories from men who were eager to dish dirt about their breakups. Each tale he added was more salacious than the previous one.

The coup de grâce was locating two of Tracy's ex-lovers. The first guy admitted that after he broke up with her, she'd made an anonymous call to his boss claiming that he was on drugs. Luckily, the boss was his mother, who knew the accusation was false. The second guy told Eugene that in a fit of pique Tracy had smashed a window on his Maserati. He was married at the time, so he never reported the incident to the police. He was now divorced. In the name of justice, Eugene persuaded both of them to alert Tracy's employer about the incidents. Then Eugene alerted Joe Deegan.

Venus and Max had booked their tickets for that bicycling vacation in France. Venus continued to encourage me to tag along, claiming that Europe would mend my broken heart. That was a tall order. The trip sounded romantic, but I'd be a third wheel. I kept telling her no, and I kept meaning it. That is, until she and Max staged an intervention. They stood over me until I called the travel agent and confirmed the reservations using my new Visa card, which had replaced the one that blew up in the trailer. Pookie and Bruce agreed to look after Muldoon while I was away.

I had a lot to do in the days before the trip. I took clothes to the cleaners. Found my long abandoned passport. Packed. Made arrangements for a taxi to drive me to the airport. As I ticked each item off my things-to-do list, I waited for Deegan's telephone call begging me not to go, telling me he still cared about me and that all was forgiven. I'd left several messages on his machine but he hadn't called back, and I was too proud to keep pestering him. I had to admit the relationship was over.

Just before I left for the airport, Eugene telephoned to wish me a bon voyage.

"Have you heard what's happening with Tracy's complaint against Deegan?" I said.

"No, but now at least everybody knows she's a loose cannon. Hopefully they'll realize that her claims against Deegan are nothing more than a pity party gone bad."

"Have I told you lately that you're the greatest?" I said.

Eugene clicked his tongue on his palette in one dismissive tsk. "No, and don't tell me now. I'll get emotional."

"Okay, but you *are* the greatest. I just want you to know."

There was an uncomfortable silence that often occurs when two friends drop a warm-and-fuzzy bomb in the middle of a conversation. The moment passed, and I went over some things about Charley's billing system that Eugene needed to know.

"Tucker, you already told me. I haven't forgotten since yesterday."

"Sorry. I just want to make sure everything goes smoothly."

"He hasn't called?"

I glanced at Anne Sinclair's steamer trunk, where the Frisbee that Deegan had bought for Muldoon lay. I remembered teasing Venus that breaking up with a dog was easier than breaking up with a man because you got to keep the Frisbee. That seemed less funny these days.

"He's not going to call, Eugene."

"Does he know you're leaving town?"

"Probably not."

"What if he calls tomorrow and you're gone?"

"I'll call him when I get back."

"What if that's too late?"

"Then it's too late."

Eugene sighed. "I'm sorry it turned out this way."

"Don't be sorry. I'll survive."

"I know you will," he said. "Just try to have fun on your trip. Okay?"

"Will do."

After we hung up, I set my suitcase near the side door. The house was quiet without Muldoon. I walked onto the deck, inhaling the sea air and watching the waves pound against the shore.

For about the millionth time I felt grateful that this little brown shoebox on the sand was still mine.

I was watching a jogger running on the hard sand near the shoreline when I heard the telephone ring. My heart caught in my throat. I told myself that it wasn't Joe Deegan. That sort of thing only happens in sappy movies. Even so, I ran to pick up the receiver. I said hello in a tone that sounded breathless even to me.

A computerized voice responded.

*Your taxi has arrived.*